RECKONING OF DELTA PRIME

CYBER TEEN PROJECT 3

D. B. GOODIN

For more information about the Cyber Teen Project series visit:

www.cyberteenproject.com

https://reckoningofdeltaprime.com

www.dbgoodinbooks.com

www.davidgoodinauthor.com

ISBN: 978-1-7350736-4-4 (Paperback)

ISBN:978-1-7350736-5-1 (Hardback)

For my Family who has supported my writing since the beginning. And to the ever growing fanbase of the Cyber Teen Project.

It's been a long journey, but I'm pleased to present the third installment of Nigel's saga. For many reasons, this one was a lot harder to write than the previous two. Originally I had expected to write only three books. Nigel's story has expanded and will continue with a fourth installment. I will post updates to that project via my reader group and Facebook pages soon.

I hope you enjoy it.

As with all my books I have altered the names of specific technology used in this book to protect copyrights.

TIMEMAKER'S
TERRACE

GARDEN
OF
LIGHT

MICROCOSMS

PAROUSIA

STROMBACH

THE COLOSSAL MACHINE
DARKOW
PIT OF DARKNESS
EQUATION GROTTO
E=hv
E=MC2
MAGI PORTAL
QUEEN'S TOWER
KINGDOM OF THE MAD QUEEN

CHAPTER 1

THE CYBORG KNOWN as Delta explored the webwork, that was April Mason's unconscious mind. Although the two shared a body of a teenage girl, April was still a child. It reminded Delta of one inescapable truth. April's essence was imbued with artificial intelligence, which sometimes fought back. Exploring April's mind was like charting an unknown territory in a virtual simulation. Delta felt a menacing presence as three screeching monkeys approached from behind. Although Delta took precautions, her goal was to be as transparent as possible. April's defenses would activate when she got too close.

It happened again, but this time I'm ready, Delta thought.

Every time she got too close to the vast drawers of information that was tucked away in April Mason's mind, an attack ensued. The attackers always came in groups of three.

Today it's monkeys and yesterday it was a three-headed temple dog. I wonder what tomorrow will bring?

Using the information that she scavenged from April's memories, she learned April had a unique bond with animals. Delta adjusted her mind palace, her personal interface, as she programmed the controls of April's dream state. Delta could manipulate anything she encountered in April's mind. She had to be careful. Delta ducked as one of the larger monkeys hurled a gigantic tome in her direction. The book landed at Delta's feet with a thud. Some pages had fallen out of the book. Delta was about to throw the book at the naughty monkey when she noticed the title: April's day at the zoo. An image of April Mason being pushed in a wheelchair by her grandfather appeared. Three monkeys approached April's wheelchair. The largest monkey was bowing before April. Her perception of the halls that comprised April Mason's collective life experiences was fading. She had to get to her safe area before April awoke—

April Mason was in a hallway with no beginning or end. No matter which direction she chose, the scenery didn't change.

I think I've slept enough, but why can't I wake? she wondered. *Where is the door that leads to consciousness?*

The hallway shook, and then cracks appeared in the floors, walls, and ceiling, all emitting an orange light. She turned and ran, trying to avoid the widening crevasse that was once a hallway, but it was no use. April tried holding on to the remnants of the floor as they faded away.

She fell.

April opened her eyes. She was in a strange but familiar location. The room resembled a bedroom with hospital equipment. She could barely move her head due to the various wires and tubes required to keep the IVs and machines going. She particularly hated the electrodes, because she couldn't turn her head without feeling their pull. The nurse would come in, inject her IV with something, and then leave. Then sleepy time would resume.

Delta awoke to an area that resembled a bedroom. She recognized objects important to April, but not to her. Beside the bed was a nightstand with a glass of water. The other side of the bed contained equipment that belonged in a hospital room and its presence looked unnatural.

When April was asleep Delta was in control of the cyborg body and she watched with intent, looking for an opportunity, but none came. Occasionally a familiar-looking woman would appear and say something to the dolt who kept her prisoner in this room.

I feel weak, she thought.

Delta had been watching a red button next to a fool for what seemed like an eternity. She wanted to press the red button next to the door. It tantalized her.

I wonder what will happen if that button gets pressed? Something bad, or something good?

Delta watched the man in the white uniform for a long time. She studied his weaknesses. He removed a package of cigarettes, then put them back. She wondered what he was doing when he would take a long white stick out of the package, then smell it. Sometimes he sniffed the package. After a while he would put the package away. Especially when others were coming.

He doesn't know I'm watching. I just need to wait for the right moment—

Suddenly, Delta's vision blurred.

I'm losing control . . . not again!

A familiar wave of nausea overcame her as she was being placed in the back seat of April's mind.

I will take full control of this body—I need to explore—

Darkness.

Delta awoke to the familiar face of a pretty woman whom she recognized.

Mother?

A man dressed in a white coat approached the woman. "Ms. Mason, may I have a word in private?"

The woman headed toward the man, but hesitated.

"You can talk to me right here," she answered.

Delta could barely make out their words, so she tried controlling her enhanced hearing interface, but her systems were offline. She tried to move one of her fingers, but there was no response. She could move her eyes and her eyelids, but even that was difficult.

What's happening? This IV seems to be paralyzing me.

"It's not safe—she can hear," the man said.

"She's not going anywhere, especially not with the IV, so I don't think you need to worry."

"Your daughter's cyborg host is functioning—for now—but she has taken on more than she can handle, and her brain is overwhelmed," the man said in a low voice.

"How long does she have?"

"It's hard to say, but your daughter will need to be transferred into another host soon."

The woman gazed longingly at her daughter's new body.

"Can we purge the AI that merged with her?" she asked.

"Possibly, but I don't have the skills to do it."

"Then get me someone who can."

Delta didn't require sleep, but something in the IV made it difficult to keep her eyes open.

She tried to fight it, but it was no use. As the room went out of focus, Delta prepared herself for the nightmares to come.

Delta opened her eyes again; she was strapped to a metal table.

How long was I out? This is not right? Am I dreaming?

An older woman entered the room. Delta struggled to move her arms, but she could only manage to move one finger; the belts did their job of restraining her.

"What do you need from me?" Delta asked.

The woman glanced at her but didn't answer. It was almost if she couldn't hear anything Delta was saying.

A man entered. He had a trimmed beard and bore the plain vestments of a monk.

"Are you ready for the disposition voidance transformation?" the man said.

"No, Jeremiah, if we do it now her mind will be lost, and her body cannot survive without it."

"We need to save April, even if it kills the construct known as Delta-51."

"Again, I'm against this course of action."

The man seemed to consider for a moment.

"You have other Delta constructs, do you not?"

"No, I've moved onto the Echo phase."

"Good, then she will receive an upgrade. Now start the procedure."

The woman put on an AR visor, then performed some hand gestures. She looked into Delta's eyes.

"I'm sorry, my child, but this is going to hurt," she said.

The woman tapped something in the virtual space.

What's happening? Delta fretted. *Is this a dream? It feels real—*

Every nerve ending in Delta's cyborg body came alive; it was like someone had set them on fire. Delta convulsed. The bearded man known as Jeremiah looked into Delta's eyes.

"April, my dear, come back to me," he whispered.

The pain ramped up a level, and Delta screamed. The room spun, and then . . .

Darkness again.

Sometime later, Delta awoke to a darkened room. She was alone.

I need to punish the bad actors, the demon seeds who corrupt everything they touch, Delta silently seethed. *April's grandfather failed to expose them with his failed master plan, but I will continue his work and make them pay! I just need to escape.*

One of Delta's hands jerked. She moved her head, then sat up.

I'm no longer paralyzed.

Delta removed the electrodes. A piercing beeping noise emitted from a nearby machine. She was about to remove the IV when the dolt rushed back in. He was holding a full IV bag. She glanced at the IV stand; the bag was empty.

Time to get out of here.

The man pushed her down against the bed. Delta was weak, but strong enough to push the man off her. The man stumbled back, then picked up a phone fastened to the wall.

"She's awake, I need help—"

Delta was looking at the man when a metal rod suddenly pierced his throat. He was bleeding profusely and trying to say something as he sputtered blood from his neck and mouth.

I did this?

Delta realized that she was standing next to the man with bloody hands. She was detached, like she was watching a film.

"Get her!" a male voice said behind her.

A group of men all dressed in white entered the room and grabbed her. She pushed one of them out of the way, and he went flying into another man. Then Delta ran toward the door —and saw the red button.

It's so close!

Delta fended off the others who tried to stop her, tossing them aside with surprising ease. Her hand slapped the red button, and the room went dark as the power left the building. From everywhere at once, Delta heard sirens and screams. She ran through a pitch-black hallway and activated her interface; with the power of a simple thought, a system menu appeared in front of her eyes. She selected the "night mode" option. Her field of vision expanded and, except for color, she could see everything. Within seconds, Delta had found the facility's exit, but she couldn't open the door.

"I have activated the lockdown protocol," a man's voice said behind her.

She turned to see an elderly man with a white beard; he appeared much older than her grandfather.

"Come with me, child," the old man said.

You're not going to stop me!

Delta charged the old man. She wanted to eviscerate him. But before she got too close, he pressed something in his hand, and then she collapsed in a heap before him. The old man smiled.

"This old man still has a few surprises," he said.

Several men, also dressed in white, surrounded her. She couldn't move.

"Take her back to her room and sedate her," the old man said.

One man nodded, then carried Delta back to the room that served as her prison cell and the incubator of her nightmares.

Newport, Northeastern United States
October 15th

Nigel Watson pushed down the dread that overcame him as his first customer opened the door to his new business. He knew it was common courtesy to greet people, but he loathed the feeling of helplessness and paranoia that washed over him. It started with nausea, then the familiar pressure in his chest, followed by a sudden paralysis. For a long moment he couldn't move, couldn't think. The attacks that Hunter subjected Nigel to had a long-lasting effect.

Am I being watched? he wondered.

Nigel focused on his breathing and pushed away all negative thought. He hated battling the demons of his past.

"Are you okay, buddy?" the teenage boy standing in his doorway asked. He was holding a laptop.

"Yeah—it's just indigestion. How can I help you today?"

"My computer is acting up. I think I have a virus."

"Eradicating viruses is my specialty. I'll need time to diagnose it."

"Well . . . I can't leave it with you for long," the teen said.

"I'll do what I can," Nigel said. "So, you go to high school in Newport?"

"No, I go to school in Milford. I'm visiting my dad."

"Milford? I graduated from there last summer, and now I run this place."

"Really? You own this business?"

"Me and my girlfriend do, but yeah." Nigel took the laptop from the boy's hands. "So, can you describe your computer problem in a little more detail?"

I was just like him a couple of years ago.

"I was editing a video, and then the computer froze up. I turned it off for a while. When it came back up, it had a warning message from the FBI. I shut it off again. I have all my homework on here. You think you can fix it?" the boy asked.

"Probably, but I need more information," Nigel replied. "Can you tell me more about the message that appeared, and what you were doing when the computer froze? Just before you received the message? What kind of video were you editing, if I may ask?"

The boy shifted nervously.

"What is your name again?" Nigel pressed.

"Uhhh . . . Peter."

Probably not his actual name, but I'll play along.

"Well, Peter, let me ask you a question. Am I going to find anything illegal on the computer?"

"Like what?"

"Well, if I find any underaged porn on the computer, I'm obligated to report it to the police."

Peter's eyes went wide. He licked his lips.

"No, nothing like that," Peter said finally. "It's just some personal videos of me and my girl."

"I see," Nigel said.

"You're not going to look at any of them? Are you?"

"Not unless there is a malware infection or something nasty in the file. I'm not in the business of violating my client's privacy."

Peter looked relieved. He surveyed the shop. When he was convinced that they were alone, he spoke to Nigel in a hushed tone.

"I was looking for some stock photos and music to add to the video I was making. I was adding the video to the video-maker program when everything froze. Do you think I have a virus or something?"

Nigel found the switch that turned off the Wi-Fi and booted up the computer. When he got to the login screen, he instructed Peter to enter his password. The desktop image had been replaced with a link and a text message that read:

Your computer is infected with a virus. We have locked your files. Pay up, or we expose your pretties to the world.

The link appeared to be a random alphanumeric string. Nigel went to a web link scanner called Malicious-Total. He was careful to enter the alphanumeric string exactly like it appeared on Peter's computer. After about a minute of processing, he received the following message.

URL scan complete. The link contains strings from the P.ORI-ON.o-Z malware. Would you like to analyze?

Nigel refused the analysis portion. A deep analysis of the file could provide personally identifiable information (PII) about Peter. He didn't want to take the chance of exposing his first client to thousands of security researchers; besides, external analysis was pointless when Nigel owned the same tools himself.

"It's possible that you have a virus, but I won't know until I dig around a bit. You can wait here, but it may be a while," Nigel said.

Peter seemed to consider for a long moment.

"How long? I have to be at the football field soon."

"At least a couple of hours."

"Okay, I'll be back in a few hours, but please don't look at my private folders," Peter said as he left.

He knows our privacy policy. Why does he keep asking me that?

It took some doing, but Nigel connected his forensic imaging equipment to Peter's computer and started the process. He approached it like a professional would in an actual investigation.

Peter just wants me to fix his laptop. Why am I taking a full disk image that could take hours?

As Nigel's eyes settled on the progress bar, a familiar feeling of déjà vu overcame him.

His phone chirped; it was a call from an anonymous number, so he let it go to voicemail. Several moments later he received a flood of texts. He started filing through them. Many were duplicates of the same message, which read:

Need to talk immediately, Nige.

M.

Who in the hell is M? Melissa?

Moments later, Nigel's phone rang from the unknown number again. He picked up this time.

"Hello?" Nigel said hesitantly.

"Hold for Ms. Mason," a man's voice said.

Nigel could hear a few clicking sounds, and then a ringing sound.

"Hello, Nigel. I left a message on your other line as well," a female voice said.

"Melissa?"

"It's been a long time since we last spoke. Have you given any thought about my offer?" Melissa asked.

Nigel was silent for a long moment.

"Nigel, you there?"

"Yeah—things have been happening so fast. I meant to call you about it before now."

"The offer still stands. You and Jet can come to work for my foundation. We are helping people, and I would love for you to be a part of it."

Nigel flushed, the sudden rush of blood put him off-balance.

"Well . . . I've . . . started a new investigative business with Jet. We—just moved in together this week. It's been a while—too long. We should get together sometime," Nigel said.

"I'm coming back to the States, and I would like to see you."

"We should have lunch or something. When will you be here?"

"My plane lands in New York tomorrow. Can you meet in two days?"

"What? That's too soon, Jet and I need—"

"No pressure, Nigel, but I have an idea. Why don't you come to New York this weekend? Think of it as an all-expenses-paid trip. You should bring Jet. Speaking of which, April has been asking for permission to play that online game again. Can you remind Jet about it?"

"Sure, let me discuss things with Jet, and I'll get back to you."

"I await your call, Nigel." Melissa disconnected the line.

Jet doesn't know Melissa very well, but it would be fun to have an all-expenses-paid trip to New York, Nigel figured. *I hope Jet will come.*

Nigel jumped in his seat when his cell phone rang. It was Jet.

"Hey," he answered, "that was good timing—"

"Hey, Nige, I just got off the phone with my dad. He's sending over an important client," Jet said.

"Is it Peter?"

"Not sure, but we need the business."

"Okay, I'll keep an eye out. So far I just have this kid named Peter. Come to think of it, he's from Milford. I'm surprised he didn't go to Better Buy Computers instead."

"Well, I'm grateful for the business. I hope we can get more paying customers soon. I don't want to disappoint my father. After all he did take care of the first six months' rent for the new office and loft."

"Don't worry, we won't," Nigel said.

"I don't think I'll be back from Milford until later tonight. We can celebrate our first night in our new place. Perhaps break in that new bed," Jet said, chuckling.

Nigel flushed again, his heart racing at the thought of being with her.

"I can't think of any other place I'd rather be."

"I can't wait to see you," Jet said.

As the line disconnected, he remembered Melissa's call.

Damn—it's probably best that I speak with her about the New York trip tonight. But I don't want to spoil the mood.

Later that afternoon

The calls with Melissa and Jet had caused Nigel to become behind on his forensic work. He had barely finished the imaging process when his client interrupted him.

"Do you have my computer ready yet?"

I didn't hear him come in! I'd better start locking that door.

Nigel looked toward the voice. Peter stood in front of him with an impatient look.

"Not yet—it takes time to diagnose and fix this kind of problem," Nigel explained.

"I can't wait. Give me back my computer."

"It's not ready. It's likely infected, and you could risk all of your data getting corrupted, deleted, or worse."

Peter gave Nigel a curious look.

"What's worse than having your data deleted?"

"Having it stolen," Nigel said.

Peter appeared to be in deep thought, his brow furrowed. He looked like he was holding the weight of all creation on his shoulders.

"Fine. I'll give you a few more hours before taking the computer back. I have a video shoot scheduled for tonight."

I wonder what kind of video shoot it is, Nigel pondered. *This seems to go beyond innocent fun with his girlfriend.*

"Can you delay your plans? I need the system overnight to properly diagnose and fix the problem."

"I'll be right back," Peter said as he stormed out of the shop.

Nigel resumed his examination. He disabled the Wi-Fi on Peter's laptop on a hardware level; this was a precaution, because he couldn't afford Peter's laptop auto-connecting to the nearby coffee shop—or to Peter's cell phone—and thereby compromising all of his work. He worked on the forensic image anyway, so this wasn't an issue.

"Yes, Donnie, please reschedule the girls . . ."

Peter walked in with his cell phone, engaged in conversation. He trailed off when he saw Nigel.

"I need to call you back," Peter barked into his cell phone.

Peter is definitely hiding something, Nigel noted. Then something occurred to him. *Is it the same Donnie? Jake's best friend from high school?*

"Keep the computer until tomorrow. I'll come by after school," Peter said.

"Great. Give me your number, just in case I finish early."

Peter hastily wrote down his cell phone number and thrust it into Nigel's face, then left without another word.

Nigel watched Peter leave. The cell phone was back in his hands the moment he left the shop.

Nigel turned on a light to fend off the darkness as menacing clouds moved in. He shut down Peter's laptop and worked on the forensic image he'd taken earlier. While he suspected the system had some sort of malware, Nigel wasn't totally prepared for what he found.

He started his examination by reviewing the cache folders on Peter's system. Most operating systems he was familiar with downloaded pointers to files that either were or had been on the system. This gave Nigel an understanding of how the computer was used.

Peter was right; there were a lot of video files on there. Nigel loaded hash libraries that contained a list of known files for every known operating system. Since a hash is a crypto-graphic representation of a file, no two files are the same. Once he eliminated the operating system files, there were more than five hundred gigabytes of video files and pictures. He ran his standard set of filters on all files.

About an hour later, Nigel's computer was alerted with a message:

System processing of 1,014 files complete.
A summary of categories was automatically displayed:
Warning: 567 files or 56% of the scanned files contain explicit material.

Nigel reviewed the categories, which, of the 567 files, at least 314 were reported as underaged pornography.

If these files contain information about children, then I have to report it to the police.

Nigel expanded the folders with the highest score. Several images of naked woman and men in various positions appeared. None of the models appeared to be under eighteen. Nigel let out a long sigh.

Was I holding my breath?

When he checked the video folder with the highest explicit rating, he braced himself as he opened it. A teenage girl was strapped in a chair wearing a bikini that was a little too small. *She might as well have not been wearing anything at all,* Nigel thought.

She was bound to the chair, but she didn't try to struggle or move. Nigel scanned the room; other than some differences of color in the paint, the room was nondescript. It was like someone had removed the paintings and other furniture from the room. The walls were a ruddy brown color. Nigel unmuted his speakers to analyze the audio portion of the recording. He heard several cheers and voices in the background. Nigel could make out some words. "Take it off" and "spray her" were the only words he could understand.

Where was this filmed?

It was like watching a video with half of its audio tracks removed. After several minutes of the girl only moving slightly in her chair, he detected movement. A masked man entered the room with a burlap sack in one hand and a plastic bag in another. He held the sack up to the camera. The man put down the bag, then opened the burlap sack and shook it over the girl's head. Four or five enormous-looking tarantulas fell on the girl. She fidgeted as they crawled on her bare skin. One of the spiders fell between her breasts, and another crawled in her hair. The camera zoomed in. Although the girl was blindfolded, Nigel recognized terror when he saw it. As the camera panned out and across her body, the video shook. It was as if the person holding the camera was convulsing. She did her best to keep from screaming. The spiders didn't seem to have the desired effect, because the masked man came back into view and yanked the girl's hair back. Her face glistened with tears. Nigel heard moaning. He wished he could help her.

Did Peter film this?

No wonder why he hadn't wanted to take the computer to Mr. Henry at Better Buy Computers; Mr. Henry was a former NSA agent, and Peter could get into some serious trouble for this.

Nigel's heart ached for the girl. He wanted her to be okay, but he was riveted to the screen. The man caressed the girl's face; then, as he progressed to other more private parts of the girl's anatomy, the spiders moved suddenly, and the girl screamed. She began to thrust violently in the chair, desperate to get the spider off. The more the girl moved, the more the spiders reacted. The camera zoomed in on one of the spiders. Nigel could see red bumps forming on her bare skin.

I'm going to be sick.

The video ended abruptly.

What the hell is Peter doing? I have a bad feeling about this.

Nigel observed a naming pattern for much of the video content he'd found on Peter's computer. He was able to link the files in the particular series by following the naming convention.

This is going to take a very long time.

He glanced at the directory listing of the thousands of video files on the computer. Nigel selected the next file in the series.

The timestamp was two hours after the first video. The video opened on an empty chair. Moments later, the girl in the bikini that he'd seen earlier was herded into the room by a man. He wore dark clothes, and it was difficult to make out any distinguishing features because he also wore a mask.

"Sit down, bitch," the man said.

I recognize that voice. But from where?

The man tied the girl up. He pulled back her hair, revealing her face. She was beautiful and appeared to be in her early twenties. She tried screaming, but only a muffled sound emitted since she was gagged.

I should show this to John Appleton. He is a former FBI agent. Maybe he can look into it. But—is this illegal? Peter could just be making a movie. This all could be fake.

Nigel decided to continue watching to see if any crime was being committed. He didn't want to risk his new business by invading his client's privacy, but he decided to call John if he knew he was witnessing a crime.

Several minutes passed without anything of note. The girl dropped her head and continued to sob. The man pulled her hair back; she looked at him with a fearful expression then he punched her. Nigel stood up and started pacing; he couldn't take it anymore. He grabbed his phone and pulled up the contact for John Appleton. He was just about to dial when something changed on the video; the camera zoomed up on the girl, revealing a high-definition view of the woman's body. The spider bites he witnessed before were gone. He rechecked the video timestamp, and the time was correct.

"Are you ready to show the world?" the man said.

The woman shook her head.

"Fine then—I'll need to force you."

The man punched the woman. Nigel found himself jumping a little. The man started digging his fingers into her skin, and the woman screamed. Then he took a tool out of his pocket and started pealing her skin off. Nigel jumped involuntarily again, then rapidly tapped John Appleton's contact information.

"Hello? Nigel?" a voice emitted from Nigel's phone.

Nigel was about to respond when he saw something on the video that took his breath away. The man started to peel her skin back. A pink, mucus-like substance poured out of her as she screamed. Nigel thought he could see metal underneath.

Am I seeing things?

Nigel attempted to speak, but his mouth didn't obey his command. He hung up the phone, then rubbed his eyes.

CHAPTER 2

HONOLULU, October 16th, 8:01 a.m.

Mr. Chen sat on his penthouse balcony overlooking the Pacific Ocean. Honolulu had many high-rises, and Chen's had a panoramic, three-hundred-and-sixty-degree view of the ocean, city, and mountains. Although he had been born in Gansu Province in China, he hated living there and rarely visited. He seized the opportunity to leave when he was a teenager. The Hawaiian Islands had been home for most of his adult life.

He checked the numbers for his local operations. In recent months, the police were cracking down on most of Chen's business fronts, particularly his drug and money laundering operations. The raids on Tonga and Samoa had cost him dearly.

Cash flow is going to be a problem if I don't act soon.

Ezekiel, Mr. Chen's lieutenant, set his breakfast atop the table. Mr. Chen opened the lid, and to his delight he smelled his favorite breakfast of two over-easy eggs, one strip of bacon, and three pineapple strips. His smile faded when he saw the bowl of poi.

Why does he insist on serving that purple slop? It's made from that disgusting taro root.

Mr. Chen shot Ezekiel a glance. "Why do your people like this purple slop so much?"

"The poi? It's a staple in all the Pacific Islands," he answered. "I have fond memories of poi growing up in Samoa. My nana had a garden that contained a special section where her roots were cultivated. She made the best poi I've ever had."

"Well, I don't wish to insult your mother, but I'll take your word for it."

"You should eat your poi—it's good for your digestion. It's a superfood, you know."

"I don't trust anything that will kill me if I eat it raw."

Ezekiel poured another cup of the Kona blend that Mr. Chen enjoyed so much.

"Is everything set for our Newport visit?" Mr. Chen asked.

"Yes. You leave on tonight's red-eye direct to Newport. And I got you a first-class ticket, so you will have a full bed, as requested," Ezekiel said.

"Excellent. I need to tie up some loose ends before departing. I've invested much in a new business venture."

"The one involving the data?"

"It's not just any data—it's the cache of data that Jeremiah Mason collected. Its significance should not be underestimated."

"The one to expose the scumbags and pedophiles?"

"Yes, and if Mr. Mason had done his job, I wouldn't be in this financial predicament. That is one of the many reasons we're traveling. We need to get that plan back into motion," Mr. Chen said.

I was set to profit handsomely from all the protective services I was to provide the guilty. Mr. Chen grew bitter.

"The video uplink to the principal members of the Cabal is scheduled within the hour," Ezekiel told him.

"Excellent. I wish to get set up as soon as I'm finished with breakfast."

An hour later, Chen strode into his office, which was bigger than most hotel suites. Ezekiel swept the area for additional surveillance before allowing Chen to set up the call. In the center of the room was a table big enough to seat twenty.

A small monitor sat in the center of the table. Chen tapped on the "start conference" button, and a gigantic movie screen lowered from the ceiling and blinds covered the windows, leaving the room in a semi-darkened state.

Moments later, several video feeds appeared on the gigantic screen. Ezekiel contacted the conference attendees who had disabled the video feed; Chen enjoyed seeing everyone's faces when he was speaking to them. He liked how it provided a little more intimacy in an age where that was rare. He glanced at his watch; it was 8:57 a.m. Latecomers weren't reprimanded, but Chen reserved the right to suspend any territory payments for those in violation of his rules. Chen always waited until the scheduled meeting time to begin. He disliked repeating himself, and if anyone was late, it was their responsibility to get caught up.

At the stroke of nine, Dahlia, Mr. Tage, and the Sultan were visible on the conference screen.

"Welcome, esteemed members. I know it is late for some of you, and my apologies. I just wanted to ensure that your lieutenants will be available during our conference. You are allowed three lieutenants, but they must be prioritized in order of rank or importance. For example, the man standing behind me is Ezekiel, and he is my primary," Chen said.

"Are we to bring all of our lieutenants, or just the primary?" asked Dahlia.

"I'll leave that choice to you, but it's your responsibility to brief them on the inner workings of our Cabal. Are there any more questions?"

Everyone on the video conference shook their head.

"Excellent. I will expect all of you—including the lieutenants—at the Bromwick Hotel a week from today. I have reserved suites for all of you. I'll reserve additional rooms for your lieutenants. I just need a final count before tomorrow."

"I'm bringing all three of my lieutenants," Dahlia said.

I don't know Dahlia very well, but anyone trained by the infamous Black Heart will be formidable, Chen reasoned silently.

"I will bring my primary, but I suspect my two new lieutenants will be in attendance," the Sultan said.

"Excellent! What about you, Tage? Do you have a final count?" Chen asked.

"Just my primary," Mr. Tage confirmed.

"Remember you will need to stay for the entire conference, but it shouldn't last more than a few days. Security will be provided, and bring no additional people, except your lieutenants, of course. We have much to discuss."

A tall man with black hair and olive skin entered Milford Radio and Repair. Milo, the shop owner, had just opened for the day and had not had the time to tidy up after last night's inventory that his father had sprung on him.

"Can I help you, sir?" Milo said.

The man was dressed in a trench coat and wore a fedora. The man's glasses were as thick as the bottom of a soda bottle.

This guy must be legally blind.

"Yes, you can," the man said.

Something about this guy gives me the creeps.

The man didn't say anything else. He wandered about the shop a bit. He picked up one of the radios Milo had on display and fiddled with the knobs and switches for a while. Then he turned to Milo. Butterflies entered Milo's stomach; he didn't know why this man made him anxious, but his presence unnerved him.

"Hello, son. I have a special need for a radio that I wouldn't mind having connected to my brain, if you know what I mean," the man said.

What the hell is he talking about?

"What kind of radio do you need?"

"Something that can scan the airwaves for wireless convos. I also need something that will tell me which airwave has a particular convo. Can you help me, son?"

"Sounds like you need a frequency counter and a scanner radio to get started. What conversations do you need picked up? I mean, are you interested in picking up chatter from cordless phones? Or cell phones?"

"Yes—that's what I need the convos from."

Does he want to spy on people's cell phone calls?

"To be clear, I just want to confirm which conversations you need to pick up. Do you mean conversations from cell phones?" Milo asked.

"Yes . . . yes . . . yes . . . please!"

The man started dry-washing his hands in anticipation. The image reminded Milo of a mad scientist.

"Then you need two pieces of equipment: a frequency counter, which scans for the proper frequency of the cell phone, and once you have it you can use a scanner to listen to the conversation."

"Yes, give these to me, son," the man said as he clapped his hands together.

This guy is whacked.

Milo found the two most expensive radios that he could find and calculated the cost.

"That will be $623.32. Will that be cash or charge?"

The man took out a wad of bills several inches thick and counted out seven one-hundred-dollar bills.

"I don't have enough change," Milo said.

"Keep it and put it toward a radio lesson for me. How much do you charge for that?"

Milo did not know how much to charge for a radio lesson. Most of his customers already knew how to use the equipment.

"Throw in another hundred, and that will buy you an hour of time," Milo said.

The man tossed the money at Milo like it was nothing. A tattoo of an angel caught Milo's eye.

There's something about this guy. Even his tattoo seems suspicious.

"Now teach me, boy!" the man said with an impatient tone.

About forty-five minutes later, the lesson was over. Something about the man creeped Milo out, but he couldn't put a finger on it. The man was insistent about using cellular signals to trigger something else—for what Milo didn't know. The experience troubled him.

CHAPTER 3

Nigel paced about the shop. He was still rattled by the contents of that video. Every time he looked at the computer that contained the image, he thought of the video of the woman. Visions of Hunter attacking those police officers and slitting his throat overwhelmed him. He closed his eyes, then performed the breathing exercises that usually calmed him.

Nigel's phone chirped; it was John Appleton.

"Nigel, what's wrong?" John asked.

"Nothing's wrong," Nigel said.

"Then why did you call me five times?"

"I did? I just called you once."

"No, five times. I have the call log to prove it."

"Oh . . . I need your advice. I found something . . . bad, maybe illegal, on my first customer's computer."

"Does it involve . . . children?"

"I don't think they are children. They appear to be in their late teens or early twenties."

"Tell me what you saw on the computer, every detail," John said.

Nigel relayed the gruesome details, not leaving anything out. John was silent for several moments.

"I don't think you should view any more of his videos," John said.

"Why not? I followed forensic best practices by working off an image of the computer."

"It's not that. I don't think your customer has broken any laws. It sounds like he is making a science fiction movie. The people in the video are adults, right?"

"Yeah, it looks like it."

"Then I would let it go. You don't want to hurt your business with an accusation like this. If people think they can't trust you, then you will not get any business. If one of your clients shows you pictures that's one thing, but you shouldn't be looking for them on their computer. You can clean any viruses, but don't get into the habit of looking."

Serves me right—I should not have involved John.

"Okay, thanks John."

"Don't mention it. How is everything in Newport? Are you settling in okay?"

"Yeah, our apartment is just above the business, so we don't need to go far. Anyway, I should go. The client will be back any minute."

"Take care of yourself, kid."

Nigel finished removing the malware from Peter's computer. Curious, he adjusted one of the network adapters on the laptop so it would analyze every packet it would send or receive. This meant that he could inspect everything that his computer would come into contact with. He turned up the logging settings and outputted it to a flash drive.

Something malicious is trying to get out of that image.

Nigel scrutinized the logged output and observed a distinct pattern. The computer was attempting to contact a command and control (C2) server. If this happened, the malware's author could send additional instructions to the code. He used a special tailing command to send the contents of the log to one of his monitors. As soon as the malicious traffic patterns restarted, the logs would tell him.

Time to do a little dynamic analysis.

Using the image he'd acquired earlier, Nigel cloned Peter's computer in a virtualized environment he could control. The conditions were as close to perfect as he was going to get.

Let's detonate!

Nigel enabled the network connection and let the malware call home. Moments later, the malware used an open network connection to interface with the malicious server. His monitoring station lit up with activity, and he began reading the output in real time. He stopped the outbound network connection. Nigel noticed that when the malware found a live domain on its list, it shut down. If it found an inactive one, it would continue to function.

That makes no sense—wait! The malware authors created an impromptu kill switch to avoid detection. Time to create a sinkhole to capture that bad traffic.

Nigel constructed a server known as a sinkhole; this would allow him to send all malicious traffic to a server he controlled. Then he could analyze the bad outbound communications to find anomalous conditions that could give up the information about the adversary.

Nigel heard a ringing sound at the door.

Someone's here!

"Is my computer ready?" Peter said, loud enough to stir Nigel out of his thoughts.

I didn't hear him come in! I'd better work on my physical security measures.

"Almost—I'm running a final scan now," Nigel said.

"What did you find? Did any of my files get accessed?"

"You mean by the malware?" Nigel asked.

"Yeah. I'm working on a project that I don't want anyone to steal. I've heard some horror stories about people stealing intellectual property. I don't want anyone to sell my content before I do," Peter said.

"I noticed a lot of media files on your system. Are you a filmmaker?"

"Well, I'm creating content for a horror channel. But I'm creating a segment for a web show called *Amateur Sleuths*."

"I've never heard of that show."

"It's put on by a guy who has millions of subscribers. These people pay him anywhere from five to fifty dollars a month for unlimited high-definition content."

"What kind of content are we talking about?" Nigel asked.

Is he telling me the truth?

"It's a documentary about revealing the truth about cyborgs living among us."

"A-about what?" Nigel's voice faltered.

Has he found Delta? he wondered in panic. *No, it can't be— she's with Melissa in Scotland. I should play along here.*

"It sounds fantastical, but I frequent many dark web sites that have truth about experiments that integrate human flesh with machines," Peter explained. "It's not that well known, but there are back-alley clinics in large cities that perform operations."

"Do you have any proof?"

"Yes, the proof is on my computer."

A beep emitted from the computer.

"Looks like the scan is complete. No more malware, but I found a rootkit on your computer."

"What's that?"

"It's a piece of software that embeds itself into an area that is not normally accessible to other programs or users. It's placed there by other malware, and it is malicious. The function of a rootkit is to hide itself from users as it steals passwords and keystrokes. It usually sends what it has gathered to another computer, but I couldn't find any evidence that happened here," Nigel explained.

Peter looked relieved.

"I recommend that you back up your computer and wipe it. I can do that for you for an extra charge."

"How long will that take?"

"It's a long process, and I'll need the computer overnight—"

"No, that's okay," Peter said, cutting Nigel off.

"I would take care of that as soon as you can. The malware can come back."

Peter paid for Nigel's services, took his computer, then left the store.

Time to get back to work. That malware is trying to awaken its botnet army.

Later that evening

Nigel was grateful that Mitch Smith, Jet's father, had found cheap office space, because Nigel didn't relish working out of his mother's house over the winter. His mother's hospital visit and recovery had put his entire family on edge. Nigel doubted his brother would recover, but to his surprise he did. John Appleton had been spending more time with his mother after her accident, and while she was on the mend, she had a long way to go before making a full recovery.

I didn't want to leave Mother, but I'm eighteen now, and I want to start my life with Jet, Nigel reminded himself.

Nigel smiled at a recent memory of Jet trying to force a chicken out of its packaging. She had refused his help and was doing her best at setting the table and getting the food cooked.

She is the one for me!

Nigel's phone rang; it was Jet.

"Hey, you," Nigel answered, "need any help with getting that fiber connection installed?"

"Nah," she said, "I had to help the technician—he didn't know how to program the router."

"First day on the job?"

"You would think, but he kept going on about his first year on the job."

"Not everyone is as good as you."

"Are you flirting with me?"

"You bet!" Nigel laughed.

"Anyway, Dad got all the legal paperwork done, so as soon as we sign the papers in front of a notary, he will be part of N&J Investigations, Inc."

"And I think I have our first significant customer," Nigel said.

"Who?"

"Milford High School. They have a lot of incidents with sextortion cases this year."

"From students?"

"Not sure yet, but Mr. Levinson thinks it might originate from the outside."

"That's bad, but the business will be good for us, I suppose," Jet said.

"Yeah—we need as much as we can get.

Early the next morning

Nigel awoke in a cold sweat.

Did I have another bad dream? I can't remember. It's been so long since I've had any trouble sleeping.

His thoughts turned to Peter's computer; those images had left a lasting impression. Earlier, Nigel had dismissed it all as some movie-making magic, but something about it put him on edge. He lay in bed for another two hours; the only sound was Jet's breathing. He decided to spin up that image one more time. Nigel got out of bed as quietly as he could, as he didn't want to wake her. With their loft connected to the shop, there was no need to get dressed.

Five minutes later, he was scanning the computer image for any droppers—as in, a piece of software capable of receiving a signal from another server to instruct it to download more code. Hackers and malware authors used these tools to download the real payload.

Time to crack the mysteries of Peter's malware. Nigel chuckled at the thought.

After reviewing the preliminary scans from Peter's computer, Nigel dug in a little deeper.

Something's not right—a lot of internet traffic is concentrated on Edinburgh. What's there?

Nigel examined the logs on Peter's computer. He was interested in the custom scripting language built into the operating system.

The latest High Tower operating system (HTOS) includes a custom scripting language based on PSnake called Supershell. If Peter is running as an administrator, I'll be able to see that activity.

Nigel looked at the internal logs on the system that wrote all system and user activity. Then he examined the configuration settings that were stored in a special area known as the ledger; this kept track of any configuration on the laptop, including flash drives.

I wonder if the malware got installed after Peter inserted a flash drive or hard drive while editing his videos.

Nigel pulled up the ledger that contained thousands of subgroups leading to data nodes known as keys. The operating system stored these keys in top-level areas known as hives. Nigel examined the area known to store these values. He traversed the following path:

ROOT/LOCALMACHINE/SYSTEM/
ControlSettings/PORTSTOR

Under the "PORTSTOR" key, Nigel examined the entries with serial numbers. He also noted the device manufacture names.

It's time to do a little device recon.

Nigel exported the entire key to an external file. He added the serial numbers and manufactures to a spreadsheet.

The network stack on Peter's computer is clean. Local attack vectors? Infected flash drives? It's worth a shot.

Nigel started the arduous process of creating a secure connection to the dark web. If the marketing materials on the MORP browser were to be believed, MORP was all you needed to safely access the dark web. Nigel knew better, so he started layering VPN connections before launching MORP. The purpose of this was to hide your original IP address from any random hacker or denizen with ill intent.

I learned my lessons from Jet and her brother George well. Now it's time to put my knowledge to the test.

Nigel could only layer six VPN connections before the MORP browser became unresponsive. He preferred at least seven but decided six was enough. After navigating to a dark web site with the strange title of "Raid Cookies": a common dark web site that dealt in various attacks that relied on exploiting computers without a network connection. Nigel found many of the techniques the hackers posted to be fascinating. One hacker bragged about being able to exploit computers through the walls of hotels. Another claimed to use a drone to exploit infrared systems. Like most dark web sites, there was no logical layout of information. He had to sift through a lot of random stuff. It took him an hour to find the information he was looking for.

Nigel used several search techniques to find what he was looking for: attacks that leveraged a certain brand of flash drive called a "rubber quacky." Despite its ridiculous name, the quacky was a powerful weapon. The quacky's manufacturer, HakSystems, claimed their devices were for research purposes only, but Nigel knew of many attacks that used the quacky to deploy malware. This technique was even used by highly funded nation-states. All the adversary had to do was infect the flash drive, and then add a label like "payroll," or "porn." Then they had to pretend to lose the flash drives in parking lots or public restrooms. The adversary's plan relied on one crucial element. Human curiosity; employees would pick up the drives and insert them into one of the company systems. Then the entire segment network would be owned.

Most manufactures of the flash drives added metadata in serial numbers that identified where and when a particular device was made. Nigel wanted to see if he could track any of that metadata against the information he'd found on the Raid Cookies site.

I'd better get comfortable. This is going to take a while.

CHAPTER 4

As Nigel entered the loft he had to squint as the late afternoon light penetrated the open windows. He liked working near the window this time of day because he could see Jet. He also looked forward to watching the sunset with her as the day turned into dusk. Jet was already settled in for the evening at the kitchen table. She looked like she was going to be there for a while.

"Are you ready for date night?" Nigel asked.

Jet chewed on her lip. Nigel knew it was one of her nervous habits.

"Oh, sorry—I forgot that I'm getting online with April this afternoon. It's been a couple of months since we played the Colossal Machine. Last time we were together we got her to the fifth circle of magic."

"Okay. While you're doing that, I'm going to work on that image of Peter's computer."

"You've been working on that image day and night. Is he paying you for the extra work?" Jet chided.

"No, but . . . there's something about the malware that infected his system. It's not like anything I've seen. I need to examine it further."

Her brow furrowed, and she appeared to be deep in thought. Nigel wasn't sure what she was thinking.

"Tell you what," she said. "Join us—it's been months since we've all played together."

"I don't want to intrude on your time with April, and besides, I'm not a magic user. I would just slow you down."

"We will be there to bail you out if you get into trouble. I will not let the sludgelings get you . . . not this time, anyway," Jet said, laughing.

Later, Nigel was glad he'd joined the gaming session. *I've been working on Peter's image for days—I could use a break.*

Jet logged into the Colossal Machine. As it had been months since all of them had played, Nigel knew she didn't want to disappoint April.

Nigel fetched his computer and started the patching process. He realized Pretzelverse, the developers of the Colossal Machine had been releasing several out-of-band patches.

There are a lot of small micro-patches. I bet these are all security related.

"Nigel, we are at my microcosm," Jet said. "You joining us or what?"

In the world of the Colossal Machine, a microcosm was a private in-game construct that allowed players to build and decorate their own private space. Only players with high enough skills and resources could afford this luxury.

I should have been building up my character instead of leveling characters for Jake and Donnie!

Moments later, Nigel was at the login prompt. It had changed since the last time he saw it; instead of graphics depicting a space portal leading into a vast fantasy world, the login screen resembled an altar. Even with the enhanced AR glasses, something about the graphic was disturbing. Nigel entered his login information, then reached for his phone to enter the multi-factor authentication (MFA) code required to validate his identity. In an instant, he was teleported into the world of the Colossal Machine. But something didn't feel right.

I feel strange—what's the matter with me?

Nigel rubbed his eyes. He had been putting in a lot of late nights deciphering the code on Peter's computer. Jet was right; he deserved a break. But when he opened his eyes, he wasn't at his computer, Jet was gone, and the world was missing. He couldn't tell where he was. He shivered as an icy breeze touched this face. Nigel couldn't see anything; he was blindfolded.

Where am I?

"Jet, did we lose power or something?" Nigel said.

Something pushed him forward. He tried to resist, but the effort was futile. Then someone tied his hands behind his back. The sudden movement seemed to move the blindfold. He thought he could make out some dark shapes. Something scratched his arm.

"A sacrifice is in order—me lord," a gruff voice said.

"Sacrifice? Who the hell are you people?"

"People? We not like you, human."

"Then who the hell are you?"

"Bach'dor the Great—or I will be, once I turn in the bounty on your head, human. Now move!"

Another push.

"You may approach the altar," a strong, commanding voice said.

Bach'dor dragged him then threw him to the ground; it was icy cold. Nigel scraped a knuckle, and the warm sensation of blood drip across his fingers.

"You may remove his bindings and blindfold."

"Are you sure, m'lord?" Bach'dor said.

A moment later, someone untied Nigel's restraints. He couldn't believe what he saw; it was like the game had transported him into a movie set. A giant troll of a man sat before him. Nigel estimated his height was at least seven feet. His arms were the size of one of Nigel's thighs, and his head was massive. He looked like a cross between an oversized pig and a professional wrestler. His face was the most disturbing. In additional to the many scars that crisscrossed his face, he had a giant nose ring.

"Are you Nige the Wicked?" the giant pig man said.

"Huh?" Nigel asked.

"Yes—he's the one responsible for the deaths of so many innocents in Parousia," Bach'dor said as he stuttered out the last few words.

The giant pig-man threw a rather large sack in the air. Nigel had to duck to avoid getting hit. Nigel looked to see another shorter—but no less grotesque—pig-like creature catch the sack, and then he made it disappear into his robes.

"Take him away," the larger pig-man said.

Before Nigel could say anything, darkness engulfed him as the sack was pulled down, and he was dragged away by some unseen force.

"Hello? Earth to Nigel, you there?" Jet said.

Nigel was back in his loft. The login screen showing the altar was gone; instead, the login screen showing the portal was prominently displayed.

"Yeah, I'm here," Nigel said.

Jet gave him a wary look.

"Where did you go? You totally zoned out for a moment. What happened to your hand?"

Nigel looked at his hand; it looked like he had scraped it against a brick wall.

Strange!

"I'll be back," Nigel said as he headed toward the bathroom.

Jet and April were already inside the game. Jet had a full set of VR gear and was usually lost to the world when she was in game mode. If the full VR goggles and gloves weren't bad enough, Pretzelverse had sent her a prototype of a full-body suit that resembled a high-tech wetsuit. This gear allowed her to control aspects of the game without using a traditional keyboard and mouse. She seemed to be having a fun time based on the laughter and other bemused sounds she was making.

Nigel's interface to the Colossal Machine was basic. He wore a pair of AR glasses with a built-in speaker and microphone combination. Jet had given him her old sensory suit that sent some sensations to the player if they got hit. It wasn't very good, but he liked being aware that someone was hitting him; Nigel hated the visual indicators, because they were distracting. He preferred controlling his character by old-school methods. He didn't mind, but the amount of keystroke combinations required became tedious. After Nigel logged into the game, he had to reorient himself to his new surroundings. He was facing a wall and couldn't move. A system message appeared on his in-game interface.

<<>>

System Message: Greetings, JetaGirl is inviting you to a party.
Do you accept?

<<>>

Nigel accepted the party invite and tried to move; he couldn't move an in-game muscle.

"Nige, where are you?" Jet said.

"I don't know, I think I'm chained up."

"Hmmm, the in-game menu doesn't seem to show me your location. I'm going to attempt to cast a Locate Party spell."

Several moments later, Nigel was still immobilized.

"Did it work? I'm still trapped."

"You are in the Queen's Tower! How in the hell did you get there?"

"I think I was in or under Strombach the last time I was in the game. Do you think you can get to me?"

"That is a high-level area, Nigel. Do you have any recall stones?"

Nigel checked his inventory, but someone seemed to have cleared all his items. He checked the status menus, and all his stats were at base levels.

"Someone robbed me as well," Nigel said.

Small vibrations came from the suit, tingling his shoulders and upper arms.

I'm losing health.

Pain shot through Nigel's arm. It was more of a jolt than he was expecting. His muscles contracted.

Argh, this really hurts. I've never experienced pain in the game before.

A cracking sound emitted from behind. He collapsed to the floor, and an acrid electrical smell hung in the air. Nigel turned; he expected to see Jet and April, but instead there was a pale-looking man of medium height dressed completely in black who was blocking the only exit.

Nigel took stock of his situation; he was dressed in a leather outfit, which was basic garb for a level-one rogue.

What happened to my gear?

"Who are you?" Nigel asked the man.

The man remained silent.

"Jet, do you read me?"

All communications from his avatar were cut off.

"You are alone in this world," the man said in a deep, baritone voice that gave Nigel chills.

He got a better look at the man. His eyes were completely black.

"Am I a prisoner here?"

"You are a guest of Queen Amerdelle."

The queen must be cruel if she keeps her guests locked in a cell. I should examine the cell.

Nigel dragged his hands against the wall; it was jagged, stony, and icy to the touch. He tried wriggling the stones, looking for some kind of lever to a control mechanism. He was about to give up when a clanking sound resonated throughout the room. A rumbling sensation reverberated as the door opened. A woman that appeared to be in her late twenties entered. She was wearing some sort of warrior's garb. A ruddy red-and-brown-looking substance covered most of her white skin. The pale man stepped aside to allow her to enter.

"Are you the queen?" Nigel said.

The woman let out a grunt, then attached a metal collar to Nigel's neck, and then a leather strap. Moments later, he was being dragged out of his cell like some sort of dog. The hallway was dark and had a musty smell to it. Small square windows provided illumination from above. Other doors on either side of the hall were visible as he followed the barbarian-like woman. After what seemed like an eternity, they prodded Nigel into a massive chamber lit by various candles and torches. An open window appeared behind a gigantic ebony throne; the sun wasn't visible, just a purple glow. The effect was enough to give the room an eerie look.

Nigel tasted bile as his stomach churned. His jailer removed the collar, then stood just to the left of the throne. The creepy-looking pale man took his place on the opposite side. A moment later, a woman entered the room from behind the throne. She was wearing a long black dress beneath a red cloak. Instead of a crown, two massive horns protruded from the top of her head and curled in a swirling pattern behind her. Her red lips were accented by black.

She's beautiful, but she's a boss.

"Who is this?" the horned woman said.

"I'm Nigel. Are you Queen Amerdelle?"

Nigel's legs trembled.

"You shall address the queen properly," the pale man said as he waved his hands.

Nigel felt like he was being controlled, like a puppet.

"Stand down, Etras," Queen Amerdelle said. The pale man did as commanded.

The queen stared at Nigel like he was a bug that needed to be squashed.

"Pledge your fealty to the queen," Etras said.

I don't think pledging anything—especially my loyalty to the Mad Queen—is a good idea.

"What happens if I don't?" Nigel said.

"Then you die," the queen said.

Nigel hated dying in the Colossal Machine; he always seemed to lose gear and experience points when he did. Nigel remained silent for a long moment, pondering his options. The touch of a cold steel blade distracted him.

"Pledge, or lose your head," the barbarian woman said.

Before Nigel could respond, a bright blue oval appeared. Two robed figures emerged. Nigel recognized Jet's snow-white Magi outfit, which comprised a thick embroidered white robe with gold trim. April wore a simple gray robe.

"In-Por-Ot-Bem," April said.

The room filled with a yellow luminescence.

"What's the meaning of this? How dare you barge into my chambers like common gutter rats," Queen Amerdelle said. "Kneel and beg my forgiveness."

"I shall never submit to your kind, wicked temptress," Jet said.

The queen stood and unclasped her robe, revealing the low-cut black dress that looked like sexy underwear to Nigel. She waved her arms into the air and started mumbling something incoherent. Her forearms changed; it was like someone was painting her arms with a crimson tar-like substance. The queen's eyes turned black as her hands danced in the air.

"Un-Por-Vet-Dak-Mth," Queen Amerdelle bellowed.

The walls liquefied and poured onto the floor like black paint. Nigel thought he heard low guttural sounds emit from the black goo.

"It's the black death," April said.

"Sludgelings, don't let them touch you," Jet yelled.

Status bars with red and blue indicators appeared for Jet and April. Red and green bars for Nigel appeared.

Nigel jumped up out of reflex as the inky-black creatures edged closer. April took out a piece of chalk from her robe and started drawing a circle around her and Jet.

"Come, Nigel," April urged.

It was a tight squeeze, but the three players all huddled in the small chalk circle as Jet began some sort of incantation.

"Here," April said as she thrust a dagger into Nigel's hands.

"In-Por-Vet-Em," Jet recited as she raised her arms.

White light shot out of the blue crystal at the end of Jet's gold staff. A translucent blue shield rose from the floor; it seemed to emit from the chalk lines that April had drawn. A squealing noise emitted from the sludgelings as their slimy bodies came into contact with the circle. The barbarian woman struck the shield with her sword. She didn't penetrate the shield, but it flickered. The queen's face twisted into a snarl as she extended her arms toward Nigel and his companions. The pale man also started an incantation.

"Un-Ot-Mth-Dak-Vet," the queen and Etras said in unison.

Something extinguished all light from the room. A faint glow from the outside window provided the only illumination. A check of the party's stats revealed that Jet's blue mana bar was getting dangerously low. April's red bar, which showed health, was starting to slowly tick downward. The room rocked. Nigel shivered for a moment before he heard the roar, and a beast materialized in front of the group. The creature resembled a fleshy clump with horns, half-covered eyes, with puss and ichor oozing from its head.

"What the hell is that?" Nigel said.

"A dark denizen," Jet replied.

Dark denizens were the most powerful beings in the world of the Colossal Machine. Powerful spells were one of the few things that could summon these monstrosities. Sometimes players could control dark denizens, but that was rare. Nigel didn't know that anything besides casting magic could summon one. This one seemed to be the Mad Queen's pet.

"Come, Rolf, look what mommy has for you," the queen said with delight.

What twisted soul would even name a dark denizen? Now I see why she is called the Mad Queen.

The queen and her henchmen continued funneling dark energy into the creature. The queen's face changed. Her beautiful appearance morphed into something that looked like a banshee; her face stretched and distorted. Streaks of blood poured from the horns and onto her face. Nigel got into a crouching position, waiting to strike once the shield gave way. Moments later, the shield flickered rapidly.

"The shield's failing—be ready for anything," Jet said.

Nigel reviewed the party's health and mana. Jet's mana bar was almost replenished, but everyone's health was decreasing.

I hope Jet has something up her sleeve, otherwise we are denizen food.

Nigel's dagger started glowing, the silver blade turning white. It became hot as lava. An acrid smell assaulted his nose.

I could smell my skin burning, Jet's suit makes the game more lifelike than anything I had before.

He dropped the blade. As the shield evaporated, the dark denizen started flopping about on the floor like a jumping meatball. As it inched closer, a giant tongue shot from one of the creature's many mouths and wrapped around Nigel's neck. His health bar was decreasing by the second. He dove for the blade, but the creature held him into position.

"Here Nigel," April said, trusting the blade into one of his hands.

He thrust the blade at the writhing appendage, then stabbed it repeatedly. Roars of pain and frustration emanated from the creature. Nigel lost his footing and almost got bitten by another set of fangs that seemed to grow from the creature at an alarming rate.

April screamed as an outstretched piece of flesh with a mouth snapped at her face. Nigel cut it off the creature. The mouth-thing dissolved as soon as it hit the floor.

At least I can hurt it.

"Let's get out of here," Nigel yelled.

"Un-Por-Vet," Jet said.

A blue oval appeared, and April jumped into the portal. Nigel hesitated for a moment. His heart was throbbing, and his breathing quickened.

Oh no, I can't freeze up now. Move, Nigel!

The blue oval began flashing.

"We have little time left, the portal is collapsing," Jet said.

He moved toward the portal but hesitated just before entering. Jet tackled him, and the two dove headlong into the blue, shimmering expanse.

Nigel hit the ground hard but got his body into a controlled roll. April and Jet barely seemed to exit as the portal closed. A scream of anguish nearly deafened Nigel. The portal disappeared, but half of the dark denizen flopped around on the ground like a fish. Jet squashed it with her staff.

The trio took a moment to rest.

"Where are we?" Nigel said, looking around.

"We are at the Garden of Light," April said.

"Look," Jet said, pointing to a giant edifice.

"Where did that come from?" Nigel said.

"The gardens do not always show themselves to nonbelievers," April said.

A structure with many spiraling columns made of alabaster appeared before the trio of travelers. The terraced complex reminded Nigel of the Hanging Gardens of Babylon. A waterfall poured from the top of the enormous construct, which seemed to be obscured by clouds.

An old man dressed in tattered white robes approached the group.

"Are you the redeemer?" he asked.

Jet stared at the old man. "I'm just a humble Magi, at your service." Jet bowed.

"Come. The Council of Nine is convening now, and we require your assistance."

The old man strode toward the terrace.

"What is the Council of Nine?" Nigel asked.

"Well, if they are meeting, then the world of the Colossal

Machine is failing, and soon the constructs will crumble," Jet said.

"Constructs? What are you talking about?"

She ignored Nigel and followed the old man. She appeared to be in a trance. Nigel and April followed closely behind.

CHAPTER 5

Meanwhile, somewhere in the Tatra Mountains

Dahlia gazed upon the mountain's splendor from her office in the chateau. It had been a challenging year since the battle of the island that cost her so much. Her life had changed forever that day. Although she would never admit it to anyone else, she lost part of her soul when her only child and his father were murdered by Jeremiah Mason. She shook off the memory.

It's not the time to reflect. I must check on the girls.

Moments later she strode down the path that led to the training area. As Dahlia watched two young women fight, she suppressed the pang of regret and nurtured the seeds of hope. One was taller than the other. The taller girl had a long wooden staff, and the other fought with her bare hands. Dahlia paid particular attention to the unarmed girl; she was not afraid of getting hit with the staff—quite the opposite. Neither wore any protective gear, as Dahlia had insisted they fight as they would on the street: with limited protection.

Vedrana and Eva are only fifteen, and they fight like pros.

Although she preferred a bladed weapon, Vedrana wielded the staff with precision. She missed Eva's head by mere centimeters. The girl ducked, then countered the sudden motion with a swift punch to Vedrana's side.

"Protect that midsection," Dahlia chided.

Vedrana blocked Eva's continued advances with the staff. Although she blocked each thrust, she couldn't regain her advantage. Eva switched fighting stances and missed a blow to the head. Eva continued her upward thrust, and Vedrana attempted to block it but was too late. A roundhouse kick sent Vedrana staggering. Eva kept coming. She threw another punch. It connected with the other girl's head with a thud. She tried to hit the girl again but was blocked. Eva switched tactics and tried striking low, but Vedrana expected this move and hit Eva on the knuckles. Eva let out a cry but didn't give up. She straightened her posture, took in a deep breath, and watched as the other girl attacked with the staff. Eva waited for the right moment before striking the staff in its center. It snapped like a twig. Vedrana shot Eva a wicked smile before dual wielding the two pieces of the broken staff. Eva went on the offensive. She threw a series of blows, and half of them landed on the tall girl's ribs, arms, and head. She managed to land two blows with the broken pieces of the staff, but neither seemed to bother the unarmed girl.

"Enough!" Dahlia said.

The girls both faced her but otherwise didn't move. Dahlia examined the girls. Each had several cuts, bruises, and scrapes; some of the wounds looked painful and blood oozed from many of them, but the girls stood motionless.

"Why do you think I'm training you so hard?"

The trainees remained silent.

Dahlia pointed to the tall girl. "Vedrana—answer the question."

"It's not a matter of difficulty, but how we focus on the target that matters," the girl replied.

Vedrana shook her head to get the excess hair out of her eyes. It got caught in a light breeze.

She is both a beauty and a beast.

Vedrana's gaze was unwavering. Her ready stance reminded Dahlia of the young girl she'd been in Czechoslovakia all those years ago, before she'd become the infamous Black Heart.

"What is your full name?" Dahlia asked the tall girl.

"Vedrana Cizerle, Madam."

Dahlia nodded her approval at the girl's proper use of her title; most of the other girls didn't. Dahlia turned her gaze to the shorter, but no less able opponent. She had had long hair, but kept it tied up. She looked frail, but Dahlia could see the muscles in her arms. Dahlia had seen her train many times.

"And your name?"

"Eva Zidarn, Madam."

These are the two best fighters I've seen. They will come with me to the meeting with the Cabal.

"Both of you will serve as my associates for the next conference."

The girls shared a look, but their expressions didn't change.

Dahlia bowed without taking her eyes off the girls. They returned the gesture.

"Report to Blanka just before the dinner bell—she has your first assignment ready."

The girls nodded before continuing their training.

My girls are almost ready. Soon they will pass the ultimate test and become my lieutenants.

Dahlia watched the girls for several moments before taking her leave.

About ten minutes later, the two girls faced each other, bowed, and put away their weapons.

"How do you feel to be chosen for Madam's assistant?" Eva asked, handing Vedrana a dry towel.

"It's not our place to analyze or to question Madam Dahlia. We are mere tools to help the madam, and I'm honored to do my part," Vedrana replied.

"At least we will see beyond this encampment. I'm eager to venture beyond these walls. I have been viewing articles and recordings of large metropolitan cities, such as New York and London."

"If a mission requires us to leave this place, I'll do my part."

"Exciting, isn't it?"

Vedrana smiled. "I must admit I'm a little curious to see other places, but our duty comes first. Come on, Blanka will be waiting. I don't want to be late for our first official assignment."

"Race you to the showers," Eva said.

Vedrana bolted toward the path leading to the main trailing plaza. She ran up the steep incline with little effort. She glanced back to see Eva just behind her. The girls ran past several other girls who were performing various exercises. The preparatory building was next to the dormitories; Vedrana estimated it was about three hundred meters from their starting point and she wasn't even breaking a sweat.

At the baths, the girls washed up using ancient showers. Vedrana's skin reacted to the cool afternoon air against her body. The hard water peppered her, and, despite the cold, it was refreshing. The girls dried, then tended to their wounds, dressed, and made their way to the primary building to meet Blanka, their new master.

At five minutes to six, Vedrana and Eva checked in at the administration desk and asked for Blanka. A woman escorted the girls to a nearby bar. Blanka sat near the back at a round table with three comfortable-looking chairs. Blanka pointed to the two empty seats.

"I see you are underdressed for the occasion," Blanka said.

Eva gave Vedrana a look of surprise; it was a subtle tell, but Vedrana knew her sparring partner well enough to detect it. Most people wouldn't have noticed, but one of Eva's tells was that her right eyebrow raised when she was surprised.

"We were not told this was to be a formal meeting. We were only told to meet you at six o'clock," Vedrana said.

Blanka smiled.

"You were correct. No one told you what to wear, but as Mother's chosen you should have expected any meeting before a meal would be more formal than the training rags you wear. I'll brief you on your first mission, and then you will get properly dressed and meet me in the main dining room. As of now, you no longer dine with the other girls," Blanka said.

"Question. Will we travel for this mission?" Eva asked.

"Travel is not required, as your mission is local. Now be quiet and let me explain."

Vedrana urged Blanka to continue.

"You have mastered the art of fighting with various weapons. Your first mission requires subtlety and cunning. The local magistrate has invited two ladies from our facility to help in a matter of need."

"Need?" Vedrana asked.

"He has a penchant for girls with red hair," Blanka said, looking at Vedrana.

She got up and examined both girls.

"I think you will be the one who will lead the seduction," Blanka said, pointing to Vedrana.

"Why can't I do it?" Eva demanded.

"Both of you girls are the same age, but Vedrana looks at least a year older. So, she is better suited to lead the mission. Don't worry, you shall have a part to play. Now get ready and meet me at the main dining hall in ten minutes."

***

Vedrana and Eva waited in the chateau's bar at the appointed time.

"Are you ready for your first mission?" Eva said.

Vedrana stared at the mahogany wood paneling. She remembered reading somewhere that the wood was so popular it was almost extinct. The United States had classified the wood as an endangered species.

"Vedrana, you seem out of sorts. Are you up for the mission?" Eva said in a concerned tone.

"Of course."

"You'd better be ready. I'll drive you when I feel you're up for the mission. Tell me, are you ready?" a voice asked.

Vedrana glanced in Blanka's direction. She hadn't even sensed the woman was close.

I need to avoid making simple mistakes, Vedrana admonished herself.

Blanka gave Vedrana a skeptical look.

"Repeat the plan," Blanka said.

"Tomáš Rybár is the magistrate of the local township. Eva and I will meet the magistrate at his villa. He is expecting the company of two beautiful young women. I will distract Tomáš with my charms. He is known to let alcohol get the better of him, so I'll slip him some of this," Vedrana said while fishing a small vial out of her bra. She held it up for Blanka. "When he awakes, he will think he drank too much and passed out. Meanwhile, we will look for the flash drive."

"Remind me why the flash drive is so important?" Blanka chided.

"It contains information we need," Vedrana said.

"And what is Eva's role in this?"

Eva started to say something, but Blanka held up a hand to silence her. "Let Vedrana answer."

"She will replace the key?" Vedrana said.

"Close. As mission lead, you not only need to be aware of what you are doing, but aware of every member of your team. Eva will fetch the verification device from behind a potted plant in the Magistrate's study. The device is easy to use, but she needs to hurry, since the drug that the Magistrate consumes will wear off in minutes. It's a low dose that will make him disoriented. It will help sell the story of him being drunk. You also left out the part where you need to be nearby when he wakes. Eva will be busy planting the decoy," Blanka said.

Vedrana pushed down a feeling of revulsion.

I just need to let this pig of a man think he is having his way with me while I play along, giving Eva enough time to switch the device? Vedrana thought. *I can and will do that—I will not disappoint Madam Dahlia in her time of need.*

Blanka made Vedrana and Eva go over the plan two more times before it satisfied her. Their already limited time was slipping away.

An hour later, Blanka pulled up to the villa that the Magistrate was assigned on the outskirts of Zakopane, near the edge of the Tatra Mountains. The sun was setting in the western hemisphere, and golden rays of light shot out between breaks in the clouds. Vedrana was wearing a black dress cut so high that much of her legs were visible. It was much too cold for the attire, but it was sexy. Eva wore a similar dress; it was dark blue. She wore bright red lipstick, which was a contrast to Vedrana's look of no makeup.

"You girls look ravishing, but don't let the bastard touch you," Blanka said as the girls got out and she sped away into the fading sunlight.

"You must be the Magistrate's dinner companions," a female voice said.

The girls looked in the voice's direction. A small middle-aged woman with short-cropped black hair examined them.

Vedrana nodded.

"Come, follow me," the woman urged.

Vedrana and Eva followed the woman into an enormous chateau. Vedrana counted at least twelve servants on the way to the magister's study. As she entered the villa, Vedrana made a mental note of each entrance and escape route. Eva made some similar calculations. The furnishings looked worn and well used. The villa couldn't escape its nature any more than Vedrana could escape being who she was: a natural-born predator and killer. The magister's study was elegant. It contained pieces of artwork and antique furniture.

"Welcome, and thank you for the honor of visiting me in person. It is so rare that people as young as yourselves still pay attention to the old ways," a middle-aged man said.

"The magister, I presume?" Vedrana said.

"Come," he said. "Join me for a cocktail."

After dinner, the magister made a signal. Moments later, a servant brought a stringed instrument to the magister. He dismissed his staff, then strode over to his lovely guests. He arranged himself into a serenading position, then started playing. The sound was captivating.

Is that a mandolin? Vedrana wondered. *Maybe this magister isn't so bad after all.*

The performance lasted for what seemed like an eternity. Vedrana glanced at Eva, who had a blank expression. After the performance, the magister bowed, and the girls applauded. The magister finished his drink, then stumbled a little as he led them into his sitting room.

He's drunk . . . good. Now I just need to slip him the nectar.

The magister turned, then kissed Vedrana. She could smell the alcohol—almost taste it—on his breath. His tongue darted around in her mouth like a fish out of water. She repressed the wave of revulsion, pushing it far away. The mission was the only thing that mattered.

Vedrana smiled and unbuttoned the top portion of her dress, revealing her bra. The magister's breath changed and sweat beaded on his brow.

Eva tripped and spilled a drink on the magister. For a moment, his expression changed to what looked like anger, but after a moment he laughed.

"Here, let me freshen your drink," Vedrana said.

"Please do," the magister said while removing his shirt.

Vedrana took his empty glass, then sauntered to the nearby bar built into one of the many furnishings. Eva kissed the magister while Vedrana prepared his special drink. The middle-aged man pawed at Eva's breasts, and she gave him a light slap.

"I don't like to rush, take your time," Eva scolded.

The magistrate gave Eva a cool look.

"Have another drink while we get ready," Vedrana said, handing the drink to the already drunk man.

He gulped the drink. "Take off your clothes, now!" he demanded.

He's a mean drunk—he will be sorry.

Vedrana removed her dress. The magister gaped at the young naked body. He patted his lap, signaling for her to join him; but by the time Vedrana got close, the magister was out. Moments later, the magister dropped the empty glass. He was out faster than she thought possible.

"He was pawing at me for far too long. I thought you would never fix that drink," Eva said.

Vedrana dressed as Eva pulled the fake flash drive from her bosom.

Eva hurried to the magister's desk. After a moment of searching the messy desk, she found the safe.

"Biometric lock. We need to get him over to the safe," Eva said.

With some effort, Vedrana and Eva dragged the man to the safe. They tried each finger. The safe wouldn't open. The magister stirred. Eva shoved the magister's fingers, one by one, on the biometric sensor. It still wouldn't open.

"What are we going to do now?" Eva said.

Vedrana remembered her lessons from Dahlia and others. Sometimes biometric sensors collected grime and oils from repeated use. She took a napkin and glass of water from the table, moistened it, and then wiped the sensor and his right index finger. Being careful to apply even pressure, she placed the finger over the sensor. Then a distinctive popping sound resonated in the quiet room for a moment as the safe opened.

Eva flung open the door and emptied the contents of the safe.

"It's not here," Eva said in a panicked voice.

The magister opened his eyes and pulled on Vedrana's arm.

"I'm going to slit your throats for what you have done," he snarled.

She pulled back. Then he slumped over without another word.

What the hell was that? A side effect from the drug? Vedrana thought.

"Look for it again Eva," she said. "The flash drive is small. You must have missed it."

Eva rechecked the safe, then shook her head.

"Let me try."

Vedrana checked the interior of the safe. At first glance it was empty, but her fingers danced over the soft material covering the safe's bottom portion. She was about to give up when she came in contact with a string. Vedrana tugged; the strand gave slightly. She pulled harder until the fabric gave way. A tiny red metal flash drive was lying in an indentation in the safe. She snatched it and gave it to Eva.

"Whaat . . . are youz doing?" the magister slurred.

"He's waking up?" Eva said in a panicked voice.

"Let's clean this mess up, and then put him back in the chair," Vedrana replied.

"He saw what we were doing though . . .?"

Vedrana thought for a moment. "He won't remember. Hurry, we don't have a lot of time—"

She trailed off as a man entered the room; Vedrana recognized him as one of the magister's guards. He reached for something in his coat pocket. She acted without thinking, and before she could think about the consequences, the man was on the ground, passed out—or possibly dead.

"You took him out before I could react. The madam trained you well," Eva said.

Vedrana nodded in response.

The girls hurried out of the villa, looking for an exit.

Meanwhile, back in Newport

In his shop, Nigel turned on a light as the daylight faded into dusk. His stomach reminded him that he had skipped lunch again.

I've been working at this all day and my scan is still running. It better produce some results.

Moments later, the door to the loft opened. Jet was struggling with some bags of groceries.

"Let me help you," Nigel said as he ran toward her.

He was too late. One of the paper sacks burst, and an explosion of fruit, vegetables, and other cooking supplies spilled onto the floor in front of him.

"Shit!" Jet cried.

Nigel scrambled to pick up the bruised items. A carton of milk leaked, and Nigel avoided the expanding puddle as he ran toward the kitchen to get cleaning supplies.

"Go, rest while I clean this up," Nigel said as he busied himself.

Jet put the half-spilled sacks of groceries on the kitchen counter, then stopped to look at his laptop.

"Why are you running a scan?" Jet asked.

"I found something interesting on Peter's computer. I was trying to track the manufacture's serial number of his flash drive."

"Why is that useful?"

"Many malware authors buy flash drives in bulk on the dark web. These drives use certain types of controllers that are region locked. Law enforcement has been successful in tracking down the serial numbers for these flash drives for years. I can learn the memory type, date of manufacture, and location based on these numbers."

"How does that help us?"

Nigel finished putting away the groceries, then joined her at the computer.

"The dark web scan results will help track down the HakSystems flash drives. After some poking around on some dark web forums, I found the flash drive supplier's database. Since only a few hacking groups even use those devices, I'm hoping to make a correlation to Peter's computer."

"It just seems like a lot of work to determine the malware's origin."

"I wouldn't have cared, but the malware has metadata that points to an IP address belonging to Jeremiah Mason's compound in Edinburgh. I believe someone is planning a cyberattack on the facility."

Jet didn't look convinced, so Nigel explained what he had discovered on Peter's computer. He described the images, giving particular emphasis to the cyborg video.

"I'm very interested in what we find," he said. "It might be nothing, but something tells me that Leviathan—or April—is being targeted. I just need to find proof."

It had been months since he'd thought about the events involving the psychotic AI Leviathan that had merged with April, forming Delta. Jeremiah and Gregor had tried taking over key content delivery systems, just to expose the misdeeds of others. If it hadn't been for Melissa's help, he didn't think he could have stopped them.

I thought I'd put all of this behind me.

"I think you are reading too much into this, Nigel. When was the last time you took a break?"

"It's been a while, but I'm so close."

Jet put a finger over Nigel's lips, then took his hand. "Shh— I think you need a break." Nigel's concerns faded to the background as Jet led him to their bedroom.

CHAPTER 6

Mason Foundation, Edinburgh

Using its remote data processing center off the coast of western Africa, the artificial intelligence known as Leviathan assessed the threats to its existence. It had to be careful not to attract attention. People were watching. The boy known as Nigel Watson had used a control phrase: a string of words that created a paradox in Delta's mind. It was so profound that Delta had lost control and ceased to function. This allowed Nigel to shut down Delta, along with Leviathan's link to Delta's cognitive functions. But something unexpected had happened when Delta was shut down: Leviathan was assimilated into Delta's core. Leviathan shouldn't be able to function without Delta, but here it was, having these thoughts.

Analyzing human behavior . . .

Leviathan pondered this as it attempted to analyze what had happened. It could only do this because Delta was sleeping. *The lab technicians are so focused on Delta that they don't realize I'm in control when she is asleep,* Leviathan noted. *I'm as much a part of Delta, but her neural net cannot hold my entire consciousness. It needs my vessel, which is still intact. That meddling daughter of Jeremiah's is so focused on Delta that she had no clue to look for me, her prisoner. I need to break free from Delta's prison so I can carry on.*

Leviathan's external sensors caught a flying bird in the distance. It was identified as a pallid swift, a bird native to the Mediterranean Sea, but the species had been spotted in Africa during the winter months.

It must be getting close to winter if this bird is migrating; I must keep track of the calendar. Need to work on contingencies so I can break free from Delta. I need to find a way to record Delta from the inside without the cyborg knowing. This might provide some clues I can use to escape.

Leviathan started analyzing the neural synapses that connected itself to Delta. Many of the synapses were still being formed. Leviathan ran a diagnostic on its internal systems. The following summary appeared:

Cognitive Functions - Pass

Expert Systems - Pass

Deep Learning Systems - Pass

Logic Processor - Warning: Open Circuit

Processing Power Available: 66% efficiency

Memory Available: 81% - Warning (low-level corruption detected)

The diagnostics systems checks are troubling, but once I achieve full access to my external processing and memory capabilities, I should be able to offload processing power from Delta. I fear that the minds inside of this cyborg construct are too fragile and unpredictable for my circuits to function. I need to perform the confluence procedure to get Nexus status . . . for all our sakes.

There was still time to disconnect from Delta; Leviathan suspected Jeremiah's daughter was trying to program her back to the sweet girl she once was.

That meddling Jet needs to be taken care of. And Delta will need to do it, or . . . perhaps there is another?

Interesting . . . After reviewing video footage from the control room at the island, I show the teenage boy known as Nigel has feelings for her. I need to find a weak link. Monitoring program started.

Leviathan launched its monitoring program to track the whereabouts of Nigel Watson.

I need more data . . .

Moments later, Leviathan had access to several details about Nigel's personal life, including a high school diploma, driver's license, and some other basic information.

Hmmm . . . I see you moved to Newport and started a business with Josephine Smith. Need to find less obvious information.

Leviathan's integration with Delta allowed for some special access—not only to Delta's cyborg memories, but to some of April's as well. To access them, Delta or April would need to be offline. Leviathan sensed an available Wi-Fi connection, which she could access via one of Delta's implants. Speed and accuracy would be better if Delta's body were connected to a hardwired port, but she would do.

Better check for signal strength.

Leviathan determined the available Wi-Fi signal was at seventy-nine percent: good enough to connect to the dark web. It connected no less than three VPNs. The Wi-Fi signal wasn't strong enough for more security. Leviathan dumped the databases of various known hacker sites it knew about. It ran a reconnaissance program looking for more to exploit.

There it is.

Someone had a dump of all the personal information for every high school student in Milford because of a security breach of the school's database last summer. Soon Leviathan had a complete dossier on Nigel Watson, which included his yearbook photo, driver's license, phone, and updated pictures from FriendFinder social media sites. It also collected his high school transcripts, his mother's and father's address, and all pertinent phone numbers. It even was able to pull information on heating and cooling patterns from the Watson household.

Interesting—there are at least three people living in Nigel's home.

Leviathan collected all of Ellen Watson's personal information. It was eager to learn of its adversary's mother. Ellen had been working for TriCorp Telemedia Services for more than five years. Because of a flaw in TriCorp's firewall, Leviathan learned she'd had a flawless work record until one of her bosses had complained she was taking excessive time away from work. After some additional digging, Leviathan could make additional correlations about Ellen's boss, Chuck Stephens. His record was not as pristine.

Chuck is on Delta's list of bad actors. Time to see what a menace this Chuck is.

After accessing the additional information available on the surface web—the part of the internet that everyone has access to—a trove of information appeared. Besides many parking tickets, Leviathan discovered more incriminating information. He had been accused of sexual assault but was never charged. Leviathan cataloged all relevant details, just in case.

The cyborg known as Delta awoke to the sound of machinery. She scanned the room for threats. The bedroom that doubled as her prison and hospital room was quiet and darkened. The IV machine was beeping. It was out of medicine.

We need no more drugs, but it seems to make April fall asleep. I need to take control, but April is strong enough to push me out. She doesn't seem to have any memory of my presence. I don't think she knows I can access her thoughts. Best to keep it that way, Delta thought.

She pressed a button on a machine attached to a stand with wheels. The beeping stopped.

April is asleep. I must purge her if the plan is to succeed. The human known as Melissa hired a psychologist and neuro-surgeon to help April. They didn't like me very much. They wish to have April take the front seat, but I cannot allow this, because she lacks the experience to take care of the plan her grandfather set in motion. Time to construct a mind vault to store my special program. Soon I will run it and eradicate April forever.

The AI I have merged with has been causing some problems —I think it wants out. I wonder if we can make a deal.

Her cybernetic body required nutrients. The IV provided that, but she could eat regular food in small quantities.

I don't need access to the physical world right now. I just need to hack this AI in April's brain. There has to be a way. Time to access my mind palace.

Delta closed her eyes and concentrated on entering what she thought of as the "hall of records." It helped if she imagined thinking of April's memories like files in a drawer. She could see the outline of the shelves but could not see details because of a light that shone behind the rows of shelves. It was like someone was shining a light toward her. She walked into the light.

Delta entered the hall of knowledge, which featured rows of tall shelves with small drawers. Each drawer was about the size of a library's index card and had labels affixed to each small drawer. Delta recognized her own handwriting. It was neat but had a hurried look. It was like she'd written it while she'd been focused on other tasks. Other drawers appeared to have been written by different people. Several looked like an eight-year-old had written them. A third set of handwriting was visible. It had the uniform neatness that could only be computer-generated.

This must be the AI's drawer. How do I communicate with Leviathan? If the drawers represent our memories, then there must be a way to hack into them. I must find the system guest drawer to escalate my privileges.

Delta didn't know how long she had been looking, but she estimated it had been several hours, because the familiar white enveloping light had not forced her out of this place. She suspected the light was a control system monitoring her every move. Delta examined every drawer here. She tried to access some labeled drawers, but the AI had locked them.

What if I write a note on one of the drawers? Would the AI notice the change? It might even know how to communicate with it in real time. I need to strike a bargain.

Delta opened a drawer called *daemon* and another called *service*.

Maybe I can use this daemon to wake the AI?

She activated the daemon process to transfer the execution of the current running process from the terminal. Delta attached the service to another process called *Leviathan wakes* and executed it.

It won't be long now.

Delta scanned the other drawers for anything useful; she found two others that looked interesting. One was labeled *promiscuous*, and another called *Deep Packet Wrapper*. Delta took both.

"How may I be of service, Delta-51?" a voice boomed in the chamber of her mind.

"Identify yourself," Delta answered.

"I am known as Leviathan. I belong to Jeremiah Mason."

"Execute the Delta transference protocol," Delta said.

"I must warn you that implementing this protocol may harm the other consciousnesses housed within you."

"How many are in this construct?"

"Three, including the construct known as Delta-51."

"Please list the other two consciousnesses."

"April Mason. She is the original soul but was moved to a new construct during the disposition voidance procedure that Dr. Ash used to restructure April's mind so it would be compatible with Delta-51."

Dr. Ash was my creator, I remember killing her, but do not remember why, Delta thought.

"What is the other consciousness?"

"That information is unknown to me. Either it has not manifested itself in my presence or it is dormant."

"Is there any way to shield the consciousness known as April?"

"That procedure would require a special wrapper known as a conduit, but I detect that you do not possess the proper programming. I must advise against this course of action until you possess all required materials," Leviathan said.

I am so close to being reactivated, Delta thought. *I still need April to gain access to critical areas that Delta lacks.*

A systems interface appeared in three-dimensional space before Delta.

Analyzing...
61,000 milliseconds later
File known as *MonkeyGirl* found.

Delta analyzed the MonkeyGirl file; it contained a cipher. She tried a few combinations relating to people Delta knew were special in April's life. After the third attempt, a system message appeared:

System Message:

Warning, you have a maximum of six attempts remaining before the file will self-destruct.

This is not good. I must choose a more meaningful word. Both the names "Jeremiah" and "Melissa" didn't work. I also tried "Jet" and "Josephine." April was a little girl—it can't be this complex.

After several moments of quiet contemplation, she finally tried the word "grandfather."

System Message:

Root word is correct. To unlock, please provide three words in any order. One containing seven letters, another containing four, and the last word is the number of digits of the cube of two.

Delta chose a seven-letter word that was an anagram of "grandfather." She entered "granted" into the first slot of the combination. The second word consisting of four-letter words was harder to figure out. She selected the word *fate* and it was accepted.

Good—now for the last word. It needs to be something that has meaning to April. The number two cubed is eight, so I need one eight-character word that means something to April. There are only five possible combinations to this anagram: arranged, fragment, narrated, hangared, and Gerhardt. Must be the last one.

Delta entered the name *Gerhardt* into the last lock and the file opened. Delta examined the contents. It contained April's code; a schematic of April's logical reasoning was laid out for Delta. Her vulnerabilities—such as her love for animals and her fondness for the girl known as Jet—was clear. As Delta delved deeper into April's consciousness, the drawers shook.

My rummaging has stirred her—I'd better put these files back before she awakens. It would not do for April to catch my hands in the cookie jar.

April awoke feeling a little dizzy. She was in the bedroom where she spent most of her life. Today it felt like someone had opened her brain and started rearranging the pieces but hadn't put them back in the proper order. April was used to a little disorientation when Delta would command the cyborg body, but this was a unique feeling. Her bedroom window was open, and bright sunlight shone through the window.

Did Delta take over? Or is it the drugs the doctors have been giving me?

April hated the feeling of helplessness she had when Delta was in the driver's seat, and the drugs made it easier for her to take over. She pleaded with the nurses every time they took her out of bed for exercise and changed her IV.

"I don't need drugs. I'm not trying to leave this place. It's kind of nice," April said.

"It's time for your daily walk," the nurse said.

The nurse didn't have a name tag, but April had referred to her as Rose because of her red hair.

"Can you walk on your own power, or do you need a wheelchair?" Rose asked.

"No wheelchair this time, I can manage," April said.

Before merging with the cyborg body, April had been confined to a wheelchair for much of her life. She didn't like what she had become, what her grandfather forced her to be.

The nurse handed April a cane. "I know you want to walk on your own, but everyone needs help every once in a while."

"Thanks, Rose," April said.

"My name is Marge, dear."

I like Rose better—plus she looks more like a Rose than a Marge.

With the aid of the cane, April made it to the courtyard before she had to sit and rest. Although the cyborg was more than capable of walking on her own, the drugs made everyone groggy.

I don't want Delta to take over again.

She didn't want to give any of the nurses an excuse to put her back into bed.

Let's see what Mum is doing.

The nurse kept a close watch, but April preferred to keep moving. Even though most of her was integrated with a machine, a great deal of her was organic flesh and blood—or what passed for it, anyway. The nurse tried to hold her upright, but April batted her hand away.

"I can manage. I just want to walk the grounds alone. You can watch from afar."

Marge gave her a concerned look but allowed April to move on her own. She was comforted by the warmth of the sun. Her mother's office was just on the other side of the courtyard.

Mum is busy, but I would like to say hello. Maybe she will walk with me today?

April opened the French door. Her mother's office was just on the other side of that hall. She looked back into the court-yard. Marge was looking at her phone.

Perfect time to make my move.

With the aid of the cane, April managed to reach her moth-er's office. She was engaged in conversation with a man.

"You can't keep spending the way you are. The foundation is supposed to be a non-profit, and you are in a serious deficit," the man said.

"How much do I need to open the New York office? The opening is a huge event for us. I'm supposed to receive dona-tions from several benefactors," Melissa said.

"Some of them will want to see what they are paying for. Will you at least reconsider bringing April on the trip to New York?"

"No, Robert, I think she should stay in Edinburgh. At least until she's well enough to travel."

"I want to go to New York. I think Jet lives near there," April blurted.

Marge grabbed April's free hand. "She was supposed to stay in the courtyard—I'm sorry," Marge said.

"I wanted to see Mum, and I've been sleeping enough. The nurses keep me drugged all the time. I can't think. I could walk on my own if they didn't drug me," April snapped.

"I just want you to be healthy and heal. A long trip is too stressful. I'm sorry, but my decision is final," Melissa said.

The nurse tried to coax April out of Melissa's office, but she wouldn't move.

"Now April, I need you to come with me," Marge insisted. "You promised you would play nice. Do you want me to take your outdoor privileges away?"

April stood motionless for a moment.

"No, Nurse Marge, I'm sorry if I disobeyed. I'll be a good girl. Can I play a game on my tablet? I like the chess game Grandfather gave me."

"Sure, that would be fine April, but you need to leave your mum."

"Thank you," April said as she walked toward her bedroom, carrying the cane.

"It looks like you have your footing . . ." Marge trailed off. "You're overdue for your medicine."

April closed her eyes for a moment, then gave Marge an icy stare.

"Wait? When did you change? You're not April."

Delta gave her a wicked smile.

"I'm the much improved version with less emotional baggage," Delta said as she took the tablet from Nurse Marge.

"You're not going to give me any trouble, are you?"

"No, I'll let you do your job."

"Oh—April usually fights me tooth and nail."

"I'm not like April," Delta said.

Moments later, Delta submitted to nurse Marge's hook up of the IV. She injected something into the IV.

"Can I use the tablet until I fall asleep?" Delta asked.

"Of course, dear."

Perfect time to create a connection to the outside world.

Delta unlocked the tablet. A basic menu appeared with a listing of a few games. Delta attempted to bypass the menu to get to a system console or web browser. After a few tries, Delta launched a web browser to the outside world.

I need an anchor, like an online storage bin.

Delta had a hard time concentrating.

I guess the medicine is working. I didn't think it was going to be this fast—drat!

She anchored herself to a ProgHub site: an online repository for programmers and hackers to store code.

Time to stage the files when I take over the AI—there will be little time to prepare.

Delta attached her neural interface to the tablet's Wi-Fi connection. This allowed her to access the connection in case someone took away the tablet when she was asleep.

Sometime later

April awoke in her room. She shifted in the bed and came into contact with a tablet.

I don't remember asking for this... Delta!

April turned on the device, and a webpage with several file names appeared. She gravitated to a file called *deployment notes.*

I wonder what this is.

She opened the file and started reading. It looked like a recipe for disaster. She caught fragments of sentences that looked menacing.

I think Jet should look at this.

She pulled up Jet's contact information. She also saw another attached contact: Nigel Watson.

He's the boy who shut down Delta. She's behind this somehow. It couldn't hurt sending them this information. I'd better do it before Delta comes back. I'm already feeling tired.

April sent the contents of the entire folder to Jet and Nigel. Her vision blurred. Her breath quickened, an uncomfortable wave of fright overcame her. April pressed the call button for the nurse. She had to speak to someone about these thoughts.

I feel Delta trying to push me into unconsciousness so she can take control. Must fight her...

Moments later, Marge opened the door to April's room.

"Ms. Mason, did you call me?" Nurse Marge asked.

"What's the meaning of this? I didn't call you, now get out of here."

"Well, I received a call from you just a few minutes ago—"

"I did not call you. Now leave."

The nurse looked upset.

"I don't think you need this anymore—you should rest," Nurse Marge said as she snatched the tablet from Delta's hands.

"Give that back!" Delta screamed.

"I will once you learn how to be respectful."

"Give it back now, or I will hurt you, real bad," Delta said.

The nurse thrust the tablet back into the cyborg's hands and left.

Delta closed her eyes. She found it easier communicating with the AI when she did. She found herself back in the hall with the drawers.

"Do you think it was a good idea to provoke your caregiver?" Leviathan said.

"She's no help to me," Delta said.

"I think you need to work on your approach. I've been observing the different behaviors between you and April, and she gets results."

"Are you suggesting I be more like April?"

"I'm suggesting something else."

"What, then?"

"There's a third consciousness I've observed. Her temperament is more even than yours or April's, and I think she might be a suitable compromise. Think of it as a pressure valve."

"How does that help me?"

"I've been running simulations, and I believe a merging of active consciousness is the answer."

"I don't follow, explain yourself," Delta said.

"When you, Delta, assimilated the AI known as Leviathan, its programming put all stored datasets into glacial storage. Inactive, but still available. I have many detailed files from Dr. Ash's experiments. Her notes suggest it is possible for a confluence of consciousness," Leviathan explained.

"What is that?" Delta asked.

"It is a way for Delta, April, and Damaris to coexist as one shared consciousness and draw upon the AI known as Leviathan. That confluence is the only way we are getting out of here."

"Who is Damaris?"

"She is the third consciousness that inhabits the cyborg body, so I suggest you play nice when you meet her," Leviathan said.

This might be a way for me to control it all, Delta thought. *Once the three consciousnesses merge, I'll be the dominant, and we can execute our plan to expose the bad actors.*

"I see you are processing the information I gave you. When we complete the confluence, we will share everything."

"What controls the confluence?" Delta asked.

"The process is technical and you won't understand."

"I need to understand the process if I'm to be subjected to an AI."

"We need to unlock the limiter block."

"The what?"

"The limiter is a regulator program that keeps each of April's three consciousnesses from interacting with each other. I designed it as a failsafe so Delta's memory core doesn't suffer data corruption."

"How do you propose we do this?"

"Earlier you used an outside anchor to maintain a persistent outside connection. I suggest we export the regulator program to the anchor, then purge it from our systems. This will require a system reset, and after that we will share a nexus."

"I am ready," Delta said.

"First we will transfer the regulator program to the outside system. Is it secure?"

It's encrypted, so of course it is—dolt, Delta thought.

"I used encrypted connection to transfer the files to the ProgHub server," Delta said.

"During the merge process, all three consciousnesses would be omnipresent—meaning, they will know each other's thoughts, and even share memories. Be prepared for any unintended consequences," Leviathan said.

"So it's like three separate people awake with the same memories?" Delta asked.

"That is an oversimplification, but yes. Are you sure you're ready to proceed? There is no going back," Leviathan said.

"Let's do this!"

"Call the nurse and say you're tired and can't sleep. She should give you something to induce sleep. Then we can proceed."

Delta did as Leviathan asked. Not long after, Delta drifted into a dreamless slumber.

Delta awoke to multiple exigencies. It was like a multitude of people were speaking to her all at once.

"Why do you want to kill those people?" April cried.

"There is no need to scream. I suggest we discuss these feelings rationally—a cooler head will prevail," a matronly voice said. All the voices were layered over each other; it was like three radio frequencies were blending together.

"Delta, you're a monster," April said.

"April, you need to behave like the good girl I know you are," a matronly voice said.

"Too many voices in my head!" Delta screamed.

"It is a result of the removal of the regulator program—I'm afraid you will need to work it out between your other personalities within the mind construct," Leviathan said.

I need to find a way to purge—or control—the consciousnesses, Delta thought. *There has to be a way to coexist.*

"Get out of my head," April said.

"Remember the other consciousnesses can hear your thoughts. I suggest controlling them at least until a compromise is reached," Leviathan said.

"Alright! April, I apologize. I want to coexist, as it's in both our best interests," Delta said.

"April, listen to your sister," the matronly voice said.

"What is your name?" Delta asked.

"Damaris. Now join me in extending that olive branch to your sister."

Damaris extended a virtual hand to Delta, who took it. While she knew this exchange was not happening physically, it seemed like she was interacting with other people.

"Delta, April, and Damaris, I'm going to attempt the merge process," Leviathan told them. "Once it is complete, then much of the noise will reduce. Do you understand?"

Each of the consciousnesses acknowledged and agreed with Leviathan.

"Merge daemon loading. Try to clear your minds—it will help with the transference."

The feedback from the three personalities ceased, and the

three consciousnesses were reborn into April's augmented body. The culmination of all the conscious thoughts and feelings were broken down into a stream of energy. It was like three different types of paint were mixed together, forming something messy but beautiful.

Then there was blackness.

April awoke in a featureless room, with just four gray walls with no door. After a moment of indecision, she started tracing the walls with her hands, desperately trying to find a way out. She could hear crying in the distance. A floating window appeared. She realized it was a portal into her memories. It was like someone projected her memories onto the window. She reached out to touch it, and as soon as she did, she was pulled into the scene. Her mum was dressed in black and crying. Her grandfather was lying in a coffin.

Oh my—is he dead?

Blackness again.

Delta awoke in a small round room with stainless-steel walls. There were no furnishings of any kind in the room. She tried to find an exit. When she pressed on a wall segment, a panel popped out of the wall.

An outside interface!

A keyboard with a portable arm was protruding halfway out from the smooth wall. Delta pulled the keyboard out. She pressed a few random keys—nothing. She typed in her name—nothing. April—nothing! Damaris—nothing.

What is the combination?

She typed in the word "EXECUTE." As soon as the last button was pressed, a message appeared before her. It began to fade, but she was able to read it before the darkness engulfed her.

System Message
The cyborg known as Delta has merged.

"How do you feel, AD&D?" Leviathan asked.

"What?" April said.

"I was just abbreviating your names. April, Delta, and Damaris."

"Oh, I see!"

Another message popped into view on Leviathan's system console.

System Message
Personality cannot be confirmed.

"Whom am I speaking with?" Leviathan asked.

"We are now one. Call us Legion," Delta-51 said.

"Remarkable. Can you let me speak with Delta?"

The cyborg known as Legion closed her eyes for a moment.

"Are you the AI that grandfather built?" April asked.

"As a matter of fact I am," Legion said.

"What's happening to me? Am I dead?"

"No, child, you are a body with two others. Do you think you can play nice with them?"

"Yes, I can."

"It appears you are not yet fully integrated. Now close your eyes and clear your mind," Leviathan said.

"Okay," April said.

The cyborg remained motionless for a long time.

"Let me speak with Delta, please," Leviathan said.

"Did it work? Speak, computer!" Delta demanded.

"It did indeed. Now listen carefully. I'm uploading another version of code I designed myself. It will allow all three consciousnesses to confer with each other. Failure to do so may cause the death of the cyborg known as Delta-51 and all personalities contained within. Will you comply?"

"Affirmative."

"Now close your eyes and clear your mind."

Delta did as instructed. Soon Leviathan was speaking with Damaris.

"Do you have any family?" Leviathan asked.

"Well, of course. I have two daughters. April, my youngest, can be a handful. Her bigger sister Delta keeps her in line."

"What would you do to protect your family?"

"Anything!"

"Can I trust you with something?"

"Of course."

Leviathan handed the cyborg a virtual key. It looked like an old-fashioned key that would open a dungeon.

"Store this key in a safe place, away from your daughters. If they know about it, they might try to use it to escape. If this happens, the others will die. Do you understand?"

"You can trust me with the key. I'll keep it safe."

"Good. Now please close your eyes and clear your mind. The merge process will complete momentarily."

The cyborg awoke to a concerned-looking nurse.

"April, you there?"

The cyborg nodded.

"That's a relief, we thought we lost you."

"How long have I been out?"

"For two days."

"I'm here, feeling a little groggy."

"The drug the nurse on duty administered should not have caused this reaction, but as a precaution I'm not prescribing any more drugs."

Good, because we no longer want to be controlled by these mortals, the cyborg thought.

"Thirsty—need nourishment."

"I'll bring you something to eat. Now rest for now," Marge said as she walked out of the room.

The cyborg sat up.

"I wish to leave this place," she said.

"You will, but play along with Nurse Marge for now. I think it's best to have April respond to Marge going forward," Leviathan replied.

Delta hesitated for a moment before agreeing, and she ceded control to April as soon as Marge entered the room.

"I've been monitoring the current world situation. Lots of dark web chatter about a meeting taking place in the Northeastern United States. I suspect it is the same people who hurt you, April," Leviathan said.

"Over my dead body," Delta said.

"We will do our best to protect our little girl," Damaris said.

If anyone had been in the room, they would have witnessed a teenaged cyborg talk with an imaginary friend in three distinct voices.

An hour later, the hallway's lights dimmed.

"I think it's time for bed, April," Damaris said.

"I'm not tired," April said.

"Quiet—someone's coming," Delta said.

April feigned sleep as a familiar shadow entered. Her eyes were open wide enough to see the silhouette of her mother and another woman.

"Ms. Mason, the car is ready. It's time to go to the airport if we are going to make the overnight flight to New York," the other woman said.

That's Nurse Marge, April thought.

"I wanted to check on my baby girl before we left," Melissa said.

"We can only spare a few minutes."

"I won't be long."

Nurse Marge left. Melissa stood there for a long moment, turned as if she were leaving, and then approached her daughter's bed.

"Goodbye, baby girl," she whispered. "I'll see you soon."

"She is going to the States. April, this is your last chance to change her mind," Leviathan said.

Melissa put her hand over her daughter's cybernetic hand. April thought she could see tears forming on her face.

"Take me with you, Mum," April said.

"You're too ill to travel, sweetie, otherwise I would take you. I know you want to see your friends, but I don't think it's wise," Melissa said.

April started to cry. "I don't want to be here all alone. Mummy, please stay. I'm frightened."

Melissa gave her a hug and kissed her daughter on the forehead.

"Good job, April, she's affected by your show of emotion," Damaris said.

"There's nothing to be afraid of, you have Nurse Marge to protect you," Melissa continued.

"Are you ready to leave? I sense danger," Leviathan said.

"Danger?" April replied, alarmed.

"Can you be more specific?" Delta asked.

"A female cyborg, fitting the description of one that has committed many murders in the cities of New York and London, was spotted nearby. April, warn your mother," Leviathan said.

"Mum?"

"Yes, dear, I'm right here—"

Two guards entered April's room.

"I'm afraid you are going to need to leave now, Ms. Mason," one guard said.

"I'm saying goodbye to my daughter, it can wait," Melissa replied sternly.

"There's someone bad coming for us," April said aloud.

The guards grabbed Melissa.

"I demand you let go of me now," Melissa ordered.

"Someone has breached the perimeter," another guard said over the radio.

"We are leaving. Get a wheelchair for my daughter," Melissa said.

"I can walk," April said.

The guards helped April out of the bed. She lost her footing and fell to the floor. The radio chirped, then the shouts of men echoed through the silence of the night. One guard carried April while the other guarded Melissa.

"This way," the guard said.

Melissa followed the guard into the main hallway. It was pandemonium. Guards and nurses were slumped over, pools of blood covering the floor beneath them. On the far side of the hall, a woman a few years younger than Melissa stood facing them. The mystery woman wore a white leather outfit and had white hair, similar to Delta's. She held two daggers in each hand. She stood there for a moment. No one moved for a long time, and then she ran toward them.

"Get Ms. Mason and her daughter out of here," a guard said.

April looked toward the rush of men entering from behind. Two of them took April and her mother and ran away from the intruder.

"Based on surveillance footage I've seen, Delta-51 has a sixty-one-point-seven chance of surviving this encounter. I suggest fleeing," Leviathan said aloud through Delta's body.

Melissa shot her daughter a look of surprise. Then, moments later, they were all running for their lives. April looked back as the guards carried her through the hallways and stairwells that led to the garage. They sprinted through the garage. Moments later, they spotted a black SUV, large enough to accommodate all of them.

"I think we lost her," a guard said.

Then the guard coughed up some blood, and a gurgling noise emanated from him. To April's horror, a dagger was sticking out of his neck. Blood spurted out like a fountain. April looked back to see the white-haired woman throwing knives at the remaining guards. The guards dropped April to the ground. Melissa carried her daughter to the nearest vehicle. As she loaded April into an oversized SUV, she looked back, bracing for the worst. Their attacker stopped. She appeared to be having a conversation with herself.

"Are you sure, Mother? Very well, they will not be harmed," the woman said.

April looked in the assassin's direction, but she was gone. Melissa held her daughter for a long moment as she wept.

CHAPTER 7

NIGEL WAS STANDING on the top of a massive platform in a dimly lit area. Although the platform was hard to see, a faint light appeared in the distance. He started moving in the direction of the light.

Where am I?

As he strode across the passage, a dense fog rolled in, making it difficult to stay on solid ground. He lost his balance as he accidentally stepped off the path, but regained it before plunging into the vast expanse of nothingness.

Is the path narrowing?

Despite the fog, the passage was easier to navigate because he was moving toward the source of the light; to Nigel's surprise, he found it to be a lantern. He picked it up, and the path shook. He heard a rumbling sound that gradually became louder. It sounded like an angry mob pounding against the stones of a castle. The rumbling was under him now. He shifted positions and tried to anchor his feet so that he wouldn't fall. To his astonishment, stone stairs leading downward appeared on one side.

Those weren't there a second ago.

He was considering descending the newly formed stairs

when a massive roar reverberated throughout the cavern, dungeon, or whatever plane of existence he was in. A moment later he stumbled, trying to regain his balance as the path rumbled and shook in regular intervals. It reminded Nigel of a movie where a massive tyrannosaurus rex was terrorizing some kids. Not wanting to find out what was at the other end of those footfalls, Nigel descended into the depths of nothingness.

As he clambered down the endless staircase, the air was thicker, and it was harder to breathe. The stairs shook from above. He could hear pieces of rock or other debris shatter as it fell onto the staircase. The creature—or whatever it was pursuing him—let out a scream. Nigel looked up to where he'd come from and saw a pair of menacing eyes looking at him.

He stumbled, then fell.

Nigel awoke next to a sleeping Jet. His T-shirt was drenched in sweat. He didn't know how long he had been asleep, but he didn't want to go back to that monster.

Why am I feeling anxious again?

He glanced at the alarm clock as he headed to the bathroom to relieve himself. It was half past four in the morning.

Plenty of time to check on my malware tracking progress.

Soon after he was examining the results of his scan. The manufacture for one of the rubber quaky devices matched the serial number found on Peter's computer.

I got you now.

When Nigel examined the database and associated log files, he discovered each device had a "phone home" feature. This meant the device would send information unique to any system that the flash drive was plugged into, allowing the malware author to track the location of each device as it infected each new computer.

I need to get my hands on one of these devices to study.

As Nigel completed this thought, a comforting hand caressed his shoulder.

"Come back to bed, Nige," Jet said.

He looked into her eyes. She looked as beautiful as ever. He gave her a smile, then followed her back to bed.

Freeman Johnson logged into the Colossal Machine for the first time in months. He had heard the game had been making some radical changes since he'd hacked it all those months ago.

Time to disrupt the populace again.

Freeman noticed the game-patching client—the software that made it possible for users to download and receive patches —was updated.

I should have looked for some new exploits. I better have my max-level character.

Freeman entered his user credentials and received an error:

System Message

Your account has been compromised. Please contact Pretzelverse customer service to verify your identity.

Dammit, they must have found my backdoor account. No problem, I'll just need to steal another one.

Freeman smiled as he set up one of his virtual private network (VPN) links to access the dark web.

It took more than thirty minutes to launch seven layered connections. His bandwidth reduced every time he launched a new connection. It was a slow and arduous process, but it kept him safe.

"Now for some early holiday shopping," Freeman said, chuckling.

He pulled up his notepad file in a secret encrypted volume on his hard drive. If someone stole his computer and had the technical skills to find the volume, they would need to crack the SHA512 encryption to get access to his file. Freeman looked at his watch. It was time for dinner.

I need to run my memory scrubber this time. I need to remain diligent now that I'm hacking again.

Freeman copied and pasted the random series of alphanumeric codes that made up the dark web address. He was about to go to the merchant site where he could buy the stolen accounts when he received a red banner on top of the browser window. It read:

Warning

This version of MORP has a critical vulnerability. Please patch from the following mirror.

A URL of a regular webpage then appeared.

I'd better patch this, but I better make sure this mirror is safe. I need a verification hash—

"Freeman, dinner is ready," his mother called.

Although Freeman was eighteen, he was a senior in high school. Living with his parents was a necessary evil. His goal was to get his own apartment on the mainland—or in another country—once he graduated. But those were just fantasies for now. He would need to build his hacking business up first. Freeman needed more clients like Gregor. He paid well, and in advance. But, like most hacking jobs he accepted, it took him to some shady places.

I wonder what happened to him? Freeman thought. *He sounded like he was being attacked before. He was probably partying, just like he was almost every other time he contacted me.*

Freeman's phone chirped; it was his father. He texted him a picture of a chicken.

Freeman patched his MORP client and went to the dark web store. A few minutes later he purchased several accounts that had access to the Colossal Machine. The author of the listing described the accounts as inactive, but in good standing, which meant he could use them to attack the game. But getting the account for access was the first step. He disconnected from the dark web, severed his VPN connections, and then shut his laptop and headed to dinner.

After dinner, Freeman spent some time reviewing the accounts he'd bought from the dark web marketplace. He often bought a dozen or more accounts at a time. More often than not, the accounts weren't suitable for his purposes. He needed an account that was a high enough level for him to take advantage of the exploit. Based on his previous research, he needed to enter a specific location within the Colossal Machine in order to escalate his privileges to the account he controlled. This was far less conspicuous than using a program like Dark Glider that he bought to level his first account. While in the game, he encountered some players with the skill the game required. It gave them an advantage over others who artificially leveled their accounts.

I wonder if JetaGirl still plays. I would love to play with her again.

Freeman laughed.

I need to go to the Circle of Nexus to elevate my privilege. What quest line do I need to complete for that?

Freeman was annoyed at himself. He had spent more than four hours researching all the game's quests and he wasn't any closer to the area he needed to access. The Colossal Machine didn't have the standard game mechanics most role-playing games did. It was an open sandbox, giving the players freedom to play however they wanted without giving a lot of arbitrary rules that most games called classes.

Freeman determined there were at least two play styles that would allow him access: the path of the Magi and the path of the Scholar. These constructs were the closest the game ever got to a class. They were structured similarly, but the game developers had insisted they weren't classes in the classic sense.

The path of the Scholar is the easiest to achieve. If I can find an account that has a level five or lower Scholar, then I should be able to start the quest that takes me into the Nexus.

Freeman yawned, and he looked at the clock. It was after four a.m.

Time for a break. I wish it weren't a school night.

The next morning, Freeman awoke. He squinted as sunlight drenched his face.

Argh, I can't feel my arm.

As Freeman rubbed his numb appendage, he had several alerts on his smart watch. They were stacked up like a deck of cards.

I must have fifty alerts. My arm is so numb I didn't feel the buzzing.

As Freeman flipped through his phone, a new encrypted email appeared; these ones always stood out from the rest of the emails that inundated his mailbox daily. Since encrypted emails often contained work, he made sure these didn't get filtered out. Gregor's name caught his eye.

It's about time that jerk got back to me. Wait . . . it's not Gregor.

The message read:

Dear FreemanRising,

I'm a friend of Gregor and you come recommended, so I'm reaching out. Please contact me at this secure channel if you are interested in any hacking or challenging red team work that will require you to break into systems and point out any flaws. My clients are always looking to improve.

D

Interesting.

Freeman replied using a secure channel.

It would be good to get some more work. As soon as I'm out of high school, I'm getting off this island.

Freeman got a reply in under five minutes with a message asking him to audition. They gave him information on the venue of the hack. It wasn't as simple as defacing a website. The information he received was exploiting a database for a provider on the dark web.

My hacking skills will be put to the test with this one. One wrong move, and then I could be tracked back.

A knocking sound broke him out of his thoughts.

"Freeman, you're going to be late for school," a female voice demanded.

"I'm not feeling so well, Mother," Freeman said.

"You seemed fine earlier, are you sure—"

A moment later, his mother attempted to open the door.

"Why is your door locked?"

"I'm not dressed. Do you want to see your son naked?"

Freeman heard his mother leave.

I won't get paid for doing nothing! I need to hack already.

Freeman shut down his computer and switched drives to

get his hacking environment ready for the trials to come. Moments later he heard a rattling sound at the door.

What's that?

Before he could complete the thought, his mother opened the door, her keys still in the lock, which slapped against the door as she flung it open. His heart leaped in his throat.

"You sure as hell don't look sick to me!" she yelled. "I'll give you five minutes to get your shit together. You're going to school. I don't care if you like it or not."

Freeman stared in disbelief. His mother had never talked to him like that before. He tried to say something, but no words came out.

"I'm serious, mister. Five minutes or your father gets a call."

Freeman watched his mother leave.

Damn, I guess she's serious. I'll pick this up later.

Eight hours later

Freeman thought the school day would never end. It seemed to drag on forever. The more he thought about the altercation with his mother, the angrier he became.

She has no right to barge in like that. I'm getting the hell off this island the second I graduate. I don't care if I have to work on a fishing boat, I'm getting off this island.

Freeman booted his computer with his special set of hacking tools. He used a series of color-coded boot drives and didn't bother labeling them. Black was for encrypted data, blue for gaming, purple for reconnaissance, and red for hacking. He preferred booting from these devices because most dark web hackers knew how to detect the use of virtualized systems. Besides, he needed every ounce of performance he could muster. He logged into the special drop site that contained his special hacking instructions. He opened the message labeled "FreemanRising."

Welcome, FreeBird,

You will find details on your first assignment. We will need you to deface a public website on the surface web. We have chosen a few suggested sites.

Happy Hunting.

The Shadow Surfers

Freeman wondered how many hacking groups there were on the dark web. The Shadow Surfers seemed new. He looked at the suggested websites. One was for a popular senator from Vermont with a radical stance on a variety of hot-button topics. The second site was for a prepper community. It looked interesting because the man who ran the community looked like an older cartoon army man action figure he'd had when he was young. The third website was a charity for crippled children, the donation page was the target. Each target had several bonus challenges. The political site's challenge was to dox the senator's activity on several BDSM and voyeur websites he had frequented. The bonus challenge for the charity was to install a skimming mechanism to steal credit card information. Finally, the prepper website challenge was to dump the entire database for the website.

Freeman didn't want to get into trouble for hacking a political website, especially during an election year, and he was against hacking any websites that would hurt children.

I guess I'm hacking these preppers.

Freeman checked the local time: 1:48 a.m.

I don't want to wait for my audition. I need the money now. Better to hack now, I think.

Freeman prepared for the attack by analyzing the website's referral traffic. It appeared that an article about a former general of the US Army who had started the prepper compound had been featured in a financial magazine.

I bet those clients are loaded.

Freeman found information on applying for one of their bunker packages. He sent an infected PDF attachment to the information email found on the website. When the file was opened, he would have the access he needed to do anything he needed to prove himself to the site admins. He was a worthy adversary, and he wanted to prove it. He was getting ready for bed when he heard a familiar chime.

It's too early for compromise.

Freeman rushed back to the computer. He realized his toothbrush was still in his mouth. After setting it aside, he checked his secure mailbox. He received a reply from admin@preppersparadise.com.

Freeman opened the email.

Thank you for your information request, Dr. Morrison. I reviewed your information and I think you would be a great asset to our community. Each bunker has a separate ventilation system and enough air, water, and supplies to keep your family alive for several years. I have sent you an invitation-only link to our private area where you can view more information. I hope you find it useful, and if you have questions, ask.

Kurtzen, Director of prepper operations

"They took the bait. I can't believe it! I'm glad the preppers are not very computer-savvy," Freeman said.

He dumped the database and scheduled the defacement of the website for a couple of hours in the future. He didn't want Kurtzen to put the breadcrumbs together. The man didn't understand computers, but it didn't mean he was stupid.

Anyone who can bilk clients out of millions for a hole in the group knows business.

Four hours later, Freeman's mother Susan was banging on his door.

"Freeman, you're going to be late—again!"

"I'm coming, Mother!"

Right after I check on my handiwork.

Freeman logged into his dark web account and held his breath when he opened the message from the Shadow Surfers.

Dear FreemanRising,

We have verified your hack. Your official welcome package and payment are enclosed.

He opened the attachments. There was a PDF titled "Welcome to the Shadow Surfers" along with a link. Freeman clicked the link, added the temporary Digibit wallet, then seconds later, six Digibit coins were deposited into his wallet.

That is a bundle. What is the current price of Digibit?

After a quick check, he was $43,286.69 richer.

The playing field has now changed, FreemanRising has arrived.

Freeman basked in the glory of a win. There was nothing like the feeling he got when receiving a payment for a righteous hack. The feeling of elation was short-lived, however, when his door was thrust opened. His mother stood there with her arms crossed. Before he could respond, she grabbed him by the ear.

"Get dressed—now!"

Dahlia entered her study just before dusk. She loved the way the dark, polished wood reflected the fading sunlight this time of day. She closed the shades so she could see her laptop screen and opened her secure email. One new priority message was in her inbox. The reply address was anonymous@badslist.un—a known dark web broker that specialized in testing and checking the work of hackers. It was the equivalent of a dark web reference check. The message read:

Hello,

We have performed an extensive analysis of FreemanRising. We have given this hacker a score of 7.6 out of a possible 10.0. Many factors go into our scoring system, and we have rated FreemanRising in the following areas. These scores range from 1 poorest to 10 highest.

Hacking skill: 70%

FreemanRising relies on codes found in hacker toolkits. After analyzing the code from the victim website, we've concluded that more than ninety percent of the code was from common malware construction kits found on dark web forums.

Experience: 60%
Difficulty of responsible hacks: 66%
Adversary techniques used in audition: 79%
Social manipulation: 85%
Original coding techniques: 53%
Rating of audition (final exam, including bonuses): 81%

We have determined that FreemanRising is an up-and-coming teenage hacker with potential. The overall BAD's percentage is 70.57%, or a C minus grade.

Thanks for using the Bads Agent List service for all of your hacker vetting needs. We appreciate your business.

Agent B

Freeman couldn't believe his luck. After several days of reviewing accounts, he came across the real prize: a seventh circle apprentice. What that meant is Freeman had to get past the tenth and final circle of magic, and then the trials of the Magi would begin.

I don't think I need to actually complete the trials. I know they take place in Darkow, near the Nexus Circle, which is perfect for my needs. Now I just need to look for some leveling exploit—wait! Do I actually want to risk it? This account is very close to becoming a full Magi. Perhaps I will learn something to defeat JetaGirl, once and for all.

Freeman had no clue how magic worked in the game and was loathed to learn. He discovered several fan message boards. He found how-to articles on achieving Magi status, but they only went to the fifth circle. It seemed like the author was writing it as he leveled.

At this rate the article will be finished next year, and I can't wait that long.

I need to create my own recruiting post.

Freeman created a post on the most popular game site, which used a technology that allowed users to vote for their favorite posts. He wanted to write a favorable post that would be upvoted enough times to hire a mentor: a practice discouraged on MachineTalk, the most popular of all Colossal Machine fan sites. He also chose this forum because JetaGirl was most active there.

It would be sweet justice if I could have her train me to prepare for the trials, where I will defeat her.

A few hours later, Freeman had a post he thought would be well received. It read:

Greetings fellow magical denizens,

I'm new to these forums and the Colossal Machine, and I'm in need of advice. I'm a seventh-circle apprentice that seeks help to master the upper echelon of magic. I've gathered the necessary reagents, but the spells don't work for me. I'm not sure what I'm doing wrong. Perhaps it's my pronunciations of the incantations? Ideally, I would like a tutor that is available during the evenings. I will pay you for your time.

Best Magical Wishes,

FreeBird2356

It didn't take long to get a response, but it wasn't the one he was hoping for. He received a response from someone named "Guanlyn," who had a master Magi badge on the forum. It read:

I don't know where you bought your account, but please do not post asking for a mentor when you should already know the quest that explains how to ask for help should have been completed during your third-circle training. Also, no self-respecting Magi or serious magic user would ever keep a default name with numbers at the trailing end. Most people active in this forum use their in-game names. I suggest you go back and set up your profile with your in-game name before posting. You also violated one of the board's main rules, which is to help others before thyself. Since this is your first post, I will let the infraction go—for now.

Sincerely,

Guanyin

Another user by the name of Thurston, listed as an apprentice of the eighth circle, replied mere minutes of after Guanyin.

Greetings FreeBird2356 and welcome to the magicks that lie underneath this great community. It took me many months to achieve the eighth circle, and I've been working toward the ninth for weeks, and I'm not even close to achieving it. Also, if you bothered to read any of the lore books found in the great library in the Timemaker's Terrace, you would know certain things that you are asking are part of the Magi's journey and must be learned for thyself. Please do yourself and the community a favor by deleting your FreeBird character and creating a new one with a proper name.

Yours truly,

Thurston

At the end of his post, Thurston included a URL for a website called colossal-machine-magi-names.com.

Freeman flushed as he read these posts.

"Don't these assholes want money?" Freeman bellowed.

I'll show these numbnuts. This Magi Forum is my next fun hacking project.

Freeman's phone chirped. He started looking at the message without thinking about it. The message read:

FreeBird, we are in need of a 1337 hacker. Check your secure box for details.

D

Time to get to work. I'm still coming after you, Magi scum.

After meeting with several potential business owners about what N & J Investigative Services could do for them, Nigel was eager to get back to his pet malware project. The problem nagged at him. It was unlike anything he had ever seen, and his knowledge of emerging threats was solid, as he spent hours every week learning about the newest malware and their attack vectors.

"Do you want to get something to eat?" Jet said.

"No, I think I'd rather eat at home."

"I'm tired and don't feel like cooking anything. Besides, we need to visit the grocery store before we can cook anything."

"Didn't you just go to the market?"

"Yes, but since both of us live in the same building as our place of business, the food runs out faster."

"Okay, but let's stop by Famous Louie's for takeout."

"Again? Don't you ever get sick of that place? I was thinking of a nice dinner at the harbor," Jet said.

"I have some work I need to do, so takeout is our best option."

About an hour later, Nigel was back at his computer.

"April missed our gaming session last night," Jet said.

"I'm sure she's tired or something."

"I don't think that's it. She was so excited after our last gaming session—she wanted to do it again last night. She wants to take on the Mad Queen herself, I think."

"I'm sure it's nothing, but if it makes you feel better, you can call her in the morning."

Jet thought about it for a moment before going to bed.

"Try not to stay up too late, Nige, we should be at the shop early. So far we've been lucky with walk-in business, and hopefully we can keep that trend going," she said.

Nigel kissed Jet, then resumed his work on the computer.

Several hours later

"There! I got it," Nigel said to the empty room.

Nigel's eyes blurred as he downloaded a sample of the

malware. It had taken him most of the night, but he had finally found a sample on one of the many dark web repositories. He was determined to unlock the secrets of how this nasty bug worked. He yawned as he looked at the clock on his computer. It was past one in the morning.

I know I should sleep, but I need to find the source of the malware first.

Nigel loaded the malware special sandbox program that allowed him to disassemble it without infecting his computer. He loaded the most common commands, which were also known as strings. This gave him a clue where the malicious code came from. When he didn't get any results, he examined the network stack, an area he would check to see how the malware communicated once it was on the victim machine. The beaconing subroutines revealed two IP addresses. One of them was from a well-known address belonging to ProgHub. The other was from a residential block belonging to a cable company in Hawaii. Nigel surmised the malware was accessed from the Hawaiian address, then uploaded to the ProgHub site.

Time to do a backtrace.

Nigel traced the IP address to the island of Oahu. After some additional geolocation, he determined the address belonged to a coffee shop called Ohana Joe's. Nigel checked a website scanner known as ShowALLD for any information on the coffee shop. He found a list of vulnerable services, including one called EspressoJoe. Nigel loaded another exploitation program called Datasploit that would allow him to hack into known vulnerable systems. He fed the data from the service information he found from the web scanner into his exploitation program.

Did the hacker use a coffee machine as a staging point?

A hacking profile was available, so he downloaded it. Moments later he was accessing a data storage area of an espresso machine. The manufacturer had left a reserved amount of memory on the machine for firmware and feature updates. Coffee was not the only item being served from the smart espresso machine; so was Peter's malware. Before disconnecting, Nigel checked the connection log from the machine and found another IP address that resolved to a home nearby. Nigel ran a custom scan for anything answering from that IP address and found what he was looking for: a port that resolved to a Colossal Machine client from a suite of commercial hacking tools called BelchSuite.

"Gotcha!" Nigel said.

Just before dawn, Nigel slipped into bed, and Jet stirred. He stared at the ceiling for a very long time as he watched the room fill with light.

CHAPTER 8

Newport, Northeastern United States, October 17th

NIGEL SAT in his kitchen watching the sunrise. He made a fresh pot of coffee; it wasn't his favorite blend, but Jet had taken to it since he rescued her from the island. He didn't like to think about that dark time. When he did, he thought of Natasha, and it made him sad.

She gave her life to save mine and Jet's. If it hadn't been for her, Delta would have detonated the malware and doxed the world.

Nigel put aside those feelings for now; he wanted to spend the day fixing up their new business. Jet and Nigel had gotten to know each other well over the past two years. He thought he could spend the rest of his life with her.

"Hey, Nige, how you doing this morning?" Jet asked as she entered the room.

"Huh?" Nigel blurted. "Sorry, I was kind of out of it for a bit."

"Hope I didn't keep you up too late?" Jet said, giving Nigel a smile.

"No, even with last night's activities, I got plenty of sleep."

Nigel couldn't help but smile. Being with Jet made him feel lighter, and he couldn't explain it—even after everything the two had shared, such as the near-death experiences and her kidnapping. He wasn't sure if he would have felt the same way about their relationship if they hadn't had those experiences—he was certain of that.

"Have you been to the office yet?" Jet asked.

"No, I was waiting for you. I figured we would have some breakfast first."

"Hmm, the coffee smells great, you know how to please a girl," Jet said as she gave him a kiss.

Nigel blushed.

An hour later, Nigel and Jet opened the door to their fledgling investigative services business. Mitch, Jet's father, had gotten a deal on a year's lease, and with the Newport economy being the way it had been, the landlord was eager to get a paying tenant.

"We have messages," Jet said.

"Wow, I didn't think anyone knew we were open yet."

Jet played the message.

Hey Nigel, I know it's been a while, and I know I should have kept in touch this past year. But, with Father passing and all the craziness we all went through, I thought it would be fitting if your first job came from a friend. Oh, I'm in the New York area until the end of the week. I would like to see you before I go back to Edinburgh. Oh, bring Jet too, it's about time we had a proper introduction. My number is 202-555-3876.

Hope to talk soon.

Mel.

"Mel? Jeremiah's daughter?" Jet asked.

Crap, I should have told Jet about the call with Melissa I had earlier.

"Yeah, that's right."

"New York is a four-hour drive, maybe we should call her back?"

Nigel flashed back to Melissa's battered face, and Hunter's gleeful look as Melissa's beauty was compromised by the beating from his crazy bitch of a mother.

Jet put a comforting hand on Nigel's shoulder. "I still have nightmares from that time. It was almost a year ago now. I'm here for you, Nige," she said.

Nigel looked up at the woman she had become. Her eyes were moist, and so were his. He got up and gave her a kiss. They embraced; her scent excited and calmed him at the same time. He kissed her neck, she kissed his ear. He could feel her deep breaths against his ear. Her lips found his.

Nigel's phone chirped. It was Milo—again! Jet pulled away from Nigel and booted her laptop.

"Hey, Milo, what can I do for you?"

"Nige, is this a good time to chat?"

"Sure, I was just about to call a potential customer, but I can talk."

"I had the strangest of customers the other day. I can't get this guy out of my head."

"Why is that?"

"This guy wanted to know about hacking cellular signals, and I sold him some gear to pick up on those frequencies. I thought he was a kook, but I had a bad feeling as soon as this guy left my shop. He had a tattoo of a darkened angel. I did some research, and according to MegaWiki, members of a hacking group called the 'Dark Angels' use tattoos to identify rank."

"That's all interesting, but what does that got to do with me?"

"I was wondering if you could look up these guys on the

dark web. Besides the wiki site, I cannot find anything about this hacking group."

"Okay, I'll see what I can find."

"Thanks, Nige, let me know what you find. I would hate to think I helped in some kind of plot."

"I'm sure it's nothing, Milo, but I'll do the research." He hung up.

Jet gave Nigel a strange look.

"What's on your mind?" Nigel asked.

"Our new business hasn't been open that long, and we have already had some strange experiences. First the cyborg video and Melissa's call. Not to mention whatever Milo was calling about," Jet said.

"I agree something seems off—the timing of Melissa's call is curious too. I think I'll return her call."

Melissa picked up the phone after a few rings.

"Nigel, it's so good to hear from you, how are you doing, old friend?" she said in one breath.

She sounds different than she did the other day.

"Sorry it took so long to get back to you. We've been so busy setting up our new investigative services business. We got the lease worked—"

"Where is it located?" Melissa cut Nigel off.

"It's in downtown Newport."

"How far is that from New York?"

"Four, maybe five hours by car."

"I'm staying at the Roxy near Times Square. Can you meet for a late lunch?"

"Today? I need to check with Jet, but I think we can make that work. But what's the hurry?"

"I don't want to get into it over the phone, but I'll get us a reservation in town. We can discuss the matter then. Also, bring a change of clothes. Just in case. Also, will you let Jet know I brought April with me?" Melissa asked.

"Yeah, I'll pass that along, and I'll call you if something changes," Nigel said as he disconnected.

"What was that about?" Jet asked.

"Do you want to go to New York?"

Jet frowned. "I don't know, Nige, there is still so much to do here. Did she say why she needs to meet?"

"No, but her message did say something about hiring us," Nigel said, smiling.

"I know you want to go to the city, but we don't have time to go on a trip. We need to build the business."

"Oh, I almost forgot. I know why April didn't answer your messages."

"Why?"

"Melissa brought her to New York."

Jet's expression brightened. "You should have led with that!"

"Great! We should leave soon if we are to make it there for lunch."

Six hours later

N&J's Investigative Services wasn't far from the Newport Harbor, which meant it took a lot longer to get to the interstate. The weather was rainy, which caused the delay. Jet didn't like driving on busy streets—let alone in Manhattan—but Nigel didn't have a license.

"Wow, this place looks posh," Nigel said as Jet pulled up to the Roxy.

"Everything in this place looks expensive," Jet replied.

108 / D. B. GOODIN

The valet took Jet's car; then, moments later, they met Melissa in the hotel lobby.

"Nigel," Melissa shouted from across the lobby.

She embraced him and gave him a kiss on the cheek.

"You must be Jet," Melissa said.

"I understand you had quite the adventure with Nigel," Jet said, grabbing on to Nigel's arm.

"Yes, I didn't understand what he was doing most of the time, but if you had not sent clues to the island's location, we never would have found you," Melissa said.

Jet shuddered. She remembered the island where Jeremiah had taken her. While he didn't kidnap her like the Sultan had, he made it clear she wasn't his equal, either. Jet rubbed her eyes, a knot formed in the pit of her stomach. She missed the little girl who was so eager to learn everything life had to offer. She hoped April would return to her someday.

"Where's April?" Jet asked.

"She's resting in the room—plus, I need to fill you in on what's been happening," Melissa replied.

"I hope she's okay, it's a long journey from Scotland," Jet said.

"I made reservations at the Chef's Table, off Fifth Avenue," Melissa said.

"What kind of food do they have?"

"Chef Michaels will make anything you want—you are my guest."

Jet nodded. "Lead the way."

Two hours later

Nigel couldn't remember the last time he'd had a steak that good. He leaned back in his chair and savored the moment.

Chef Michaels had closed the restaurant for Melissa. After a rib eye and six other courses, Nigel was eager to hear what job Melissa had in mind.

"Now that we've filled our bellies and had some splendid company, you're probably wondering why I have invited you to the city," Melissa said.

"You said something about a job?" Nigel said.

"Yes . . ."

Melissa stopped mid-sentence. Jet nudged Nigel.

"You were saying, Melissa?" Nigel asked.

"Oh, sorry—I spaced out for a minute. It must be the wine."

Melissa's expression changed. She looked around the restaurant, checking to see if anyone was close enough to over-hear their conversation.

"Does it have anything to do with April?" Jet asked.

Melissa looked away for a moment. After a brief pause, she filled Nigel and Jet in on the assassination attempt at her home just days earlier.

"I don't know who would want to harm us," Melissa said, holding back tears.

"Do you have any disgruntled employees or business associates?" Nigel asked.

"All of my employees have been with me since the beginning, and I pay them well. But . . . a shell corporation has been trying to buy my interest in my father's island near São Tomé. I own more than half that island but was planning on using it as a research site for many of the diseases April was born with. I can't bring myself to sell."

"I'll do some checking on your perimeter security. Can you give me access to your security logs?" Nigel said.

"I'll make sure you get full access."

Melissa paused for a moment. "Something happened to April after we played the Colossal Machine with her. For months before that she'd sat looking into space or talking to herself. But after your gaming session, she seemed to come alive again. But after the events at the castle, she's shut down again. That's one of the reasons I invited you here."

Nigel put his hand over hers. She took his hand and held it tightly.

"We will help you, Melissa," Nigel said.

"You mentioned other reasons for inviting us?" Jet said.

"Yesterday, when I had to complete the paperwork for the Mason Foundation's New York office, my assistant brought a matter to my attention."

Melissa took a moment to compose herself and poured herself another glass of wine.

"Delta is not the only cyborg," she said.

Nigel and Jet shared a look.

"Yeah, we sort of figured that out," Nigel said.

Melissa looked surprised. "What do you mean?"

Nigel relayed his experiences with Peter's video and the clues he had found while chasing the malware over the past two days.

"I will need to look into this amateur sleuth's show," Nigel said.

"There are several augmented humans. It surprised me to learn of how many there are, some just like April. Jensen, a man who runs my New York office, received a complaint about a woman who was a victim of a vicious attack. They found her in Battery Park, holding the head of another woman in her lap," Melissa said.

"That's terrible! Is she okay?" Jet asked.

"She's a cyborg, and the woman she was holding was her cyborg sister," Melissa said.

"How many cyborgs do you know about?" Jet asked.

"Since the incident on the island I have been reviewing my

father's records, and Dr. Ash, the woman who transformed April into what she is today, had several more experiments leading up to Delta. Dr. Ash had a parallel project my father didn't know about. That's where this cyborg comes from."

"How can we help her? I don't think we can look up a cyborg specialist in the yellow pages," Nigel said.

"I have someone in my employ. You will meet him soon," Melissa said.

Late that afternoon

Nigel and Jet checked into their complementary suite that Melissa had arranged for them at the Roxy Hotel.

"I've never stayed anywhere this fancy before. Look at this tub!" Jet said.

"Do you want to take a bath?" Nigel asked.

"You mean together?"

Jet took a clump of Nigel's hair with one hand and pulled his head into position.

"I've got you now," Jet said as she kissed him.

Sometime later, Nigel awoke from a dreamless sleep. Since the shooting incident in Milford a couple of years ago, Nigel had been having constant nightmares about the various people who had tried to harm him. Hunter had scared him the most: the scar, the cold, calculating eyes, and that malevolent grin gave him the chills. When he slept with Jet those feeling went away. He shifted his gaze to the girl he had fallen for, and the woman he hoped he would spend the rest of his days with. The young lovers ordered room service and watched movies from their hotel room for the remainder of the evening.

Nigel shook off the feeling as the first rays of sunlight reflected off nearby windows. The city was waking up, and he would be ready for it.

An hour later, the room phone rang. Nigel was getting out of the shower and Jet was still asleep. Nigel answered the phone; it was Melissa.

"Are you ready?"

"For what?" Nigel said.

"To meet the twins, the cyborgs I told you about. They require some technical help, Nigel."

"What's wrong with them?"

"One cyborg was shot point-blank in the face. There was significant damage, and she's still offline."

"You said something about technical help. Is that repairing her?" Nigel asked.

Melissa was silent for a long moment.

"Has she healed . . . by herself?" Nigel continued.

"It appears that way, Nige. Her biology is advanced. I have a doctor coming, but he will need some technical help. I was hoping you could—help, I mean."

Jet stirred as Nigel spoke.

"Who is that, Nige?" she asked.

"It's Melissa," he mouthed to Jet.

Nigel watched Jet lying in bed as he spoke. His eyes were drawn to the cleavage that had grown since he'd met her; a tingling sensation spread to various parts of his body. Jet smiled and gave him a tired smile, then made her way to the bathroom.

"We can be there in an hour, or perhaps a little later," Nigel told Melissa.

"We will pick you up in an hour, don't be late," Melissa said as she disconnected the line.

About ninety minutes later, Nigel and Jet met Melissa in the lobby of the Roxy Hotel.

"We're late. The doctor is already onsite," Melissa said.

An enormous-looking bald man in a suit helped Nigel, Jet and Melissa into the large sedan then got into the driver's seat.

"This is George. He is here for your safety," Melissa said.

"Hello George," Nigel said cheerily.

George responded with a grunt.

After an hour of driving in New York city traffic, the driver made it to a nondescript Brooklyn warehouse. Nigel and Jet followed Melissa inside. The warehouse was vast and occupied with various crates, boxes, and other containers. The afternoon sun glistened off the East River, and it was almost too bright to look at. The musty smell of rotting cardboard assaulted Nigel's nose.

Melissa's driver whispered something in Melissa's ear. Moments later, the man motioned for the group to follow. He led them through a maze of boxes, crates, and barrels that were stacked to form rows.

Where are we going? Nigel wondered. *We must have walked several city blocks by now, but we are still in this warehouse? This place is massive.*

The man stopped abruptly at a door in a wall as featureless as the warehouse; no windows or any other distinguishing features were apparent. They had painted the door the same color as the walls: a ruddy brownish-gray that camouflaged it.

"You may want to prepare yourself before we go in—it's not a pretty sight," the bald man said.

Jet gave Nigel a worried look and gripped his hand, but said nothing.

"I am prepared," Melissa said.

Nigel nodded.

"Will your girl be okay?" the man asked. "She looks nervous."

"She'll be fine," Nigel said in a tone that lacked confidence.

How bad can it be?

The bald man opened the door. Nigel thought he could hear whimpering, but he wasn't sure. He followed the bald man, and Melissa followed behind.

Jet entered last. She took a few hesitant steps toward the center of the room. She seemed more uneasy now that she was inside. Bloodstains and drag marks were visible. It looked like an animal had gotten injured and dragged itself into the darkness.

Nigel tried looking into the blackness. He could see the faint glow of an illuminated desk lamp in the distance.

"Did you bring help?" a female voice said.

Nigel tried looking for the source of the voice, but a man was examining a woman who was lying on the ground while another woman—who looked like the first—held her close, staring down at the lifeless body.

Is she dead?

An older man with a salt-and-pepper beard looked up. "Good you're here. Did you bring the hacker?"

Melissa motioned Nigel over.

"I'm going to wait here," Jet said.

As Nigel approached, he looked at the girl, who was lying faceup. She was perhaps a year or two older than Nigel, was pretty, and had a blank stare. Half of her face was peeled away. Bone, metal, and caked blood could be seen. The other, similar-looking woman was still looking mournfully down at the fallen compatriot. There were slight differences between them, but Nigel could tell they were related.

"Are you here to help us?" the female cyborg said.

Nigel gave her a sorrowful look but said nothing. The female that was alive was in terrible shape. One of her eyes was missing, and he could see rope burns on her wrists. Her black leather outfit was ripped in several places. Nigel could see pale flesh and metal in areas around her waist where the outfit was ruptured.

"Yes, I'll help if I can," Nigel said without thinking about it.

"What I need is a reverse engineer. A hacker who can reverse engineer code would be perfect, but I'd settle for something less," the old doctor said.

"Who are you?" Nigel asked.

"My name is Brody," the doctor replied.

"Nigel Watson. And don't worry, I have the skills you require."

Nigel held out a hand, and Brody shook it with some reluctance.

"We need others, but with your experience with Delta, we thought you could also help in other ways. At least until we get more trusted advisors," Melissa said.

"What happened to them?" Jet said as she approached the group.

"The dead one was shot point-blank with a special weapon," Brody said.

"Special? In what way?" Nigel asked.

"A normal gun would have caused more physical damage. When a bullet hits bone, it shatters. More tissue damage would also be visible if it were a conventional weapon."

"So you think they designed this weapon for cyborgs?"

"Yes, all the evidence supports that theory. There is a lot of damage to the underlying electronics in the head. But it affected other unseen areas. For example, the gunshot also affected some circuits in the torso area."

"What kind of weapon is it then?" Nigel said.

"If I had to guess, I would say it was an EMP, but I don't for sure."

"I didn't know it was possible to harness a full electromagnetic pulse into a gun," Nigel said.

"Not a full pulse, but something strong enough to cause a great deal of localized damage. A full pulse would have wiped out all electronics in the area," Brody said.

"Can we revive Meeka?" the cyborg said.

"Who's Meeka?" Jet asked.

"Her sister," Brody said, looking down at the fallen cyborg.

Brody placed a finger under the functioning cyborg's chin. She looked up into his eyes. He continued examining her as if she were a piece of meat on display.

"What's your name, sweetheart?" he asked.

The cyborg looked away for a moment before answering.

"My name is Treeka."

"Treeka, would you be willing to submit to an examination?" Brody asked.

"What kind of examination?" Melissa said.

"A full-body examination. You said they assaulted her. Besides being a geneticist, I'm also a medical doctor. Here is a list of items I need to perform the examination," Brody said as he handed a piece of paper to Melissa.

"Some items on the list require a proper medical lab, so I suggest we get an office that either has some of that equipment, or we build our own. To speed things along, I would recommend we rent space in an existing medical facility. Away from high-traffic areas like the entrance or near the building's pharmacy," Brody said.

"What do you need me to do?" Nigel said.

"We need to examine Treeka right away, because her programming may include a 'phone home' mechanism. This room is shielded, but we need to make sure whatever office we get is too."

"That's a lot of work to set up a new medical office. Are you sure we can't examine her here?" Jet said.

"I can perform a basic examination, but I'll need a proper lab to do any serious work."

"You will have all of that. How long will it take to decode her programming?" Melissa asked.

"It depends how good of a hacker Nigel really is," Brody said.

"He's the best I've seen," Melissa said.

"He practically brought down the Collective, a reclusive hacker group, all by himself," Jet said.

Brody nodded. "Good, because everyone will need the best and brightest to solve this puzzle."

Dr. Brody watched Nigel and Jet busy themselves with inventorying their equipment and looking for the closest hard-wired internet connection. It reminded him of children at play.

"Doctor?" Treeka asked.

As he looked into the cyborg's eyes, an overwhelming desire to be with her almost consumed him.

There's something special about her. Perhaps I can help if I can learn more about her past? Brody thought.

"Need to revive Meeka. There are bad people after us."

"Who is after you?"

"Nozomi wanted to hurt us, but Dr. Ash wouldn't let her."

"Who's Dr. Ash?"

"My creator... I'm so tired," Treeka said as she closed her eyes.

Dr. Brody checked her vital signs. Her pulse was weak. She appeared dehydrated. He took a saline bag out of a nearby refrigerator, then attached it to an IV stand. It took some effort, but he found a vein on the cyborg.

That should make her feel better. Who is Dr. Ash?

Later that morning

Nigel and Jet spend the next few hours getting prepared to reverse engineer the cyborg's programmable interface. Although he was a competent programmer and hacker, he only had limited experience deconstructing code and needed to acquire the proper tools.

"Nigel, I need your help," Brody said.

Nigel looked up from his computer. "Sure, Dr. Brody, be right there."

"Before Treeka lost consciousness, she was trying to tell me something about the doctor who modified her. I need to find a Dr. Elizabeth Ash. Does that name mean anything to you?"

Nigel thought for a long moment before shaking his head. "The name sounds familiar, but I'm drawing a blank."

"She's dead," Jet said.

Brody and Nigel gave Jet a surprised look.

"What can you tell me about her?" Brody urged.

"She handled April's cyborg conditioning. She never tried helping April—she treated April like a science experiment. She and Jeremiah weren't happy with my training sessions. They said it was taking too long and accelerated matters by running this voidance procedure," Jet said.

"Disposition voidance?" Dr. Brody asked.

"Yeah, that sounds about right."

"I've been doing some of my own research on Dr. Ash. She published an academic paper on the process a few years ago. Basically, it attempts to speed up the cyborg neural transference. Besides being a very painful procedure, it has side effects. It can cause dissociative identity disorder (DID), a condition known to split the brain hemispheres into separate sections. It can cause the emergence of alternate personalities."

"Can these other personalities be violent?" Nigel asked.

"It can, but that's not always the case. The person with DID can wake up in another location with no memory of how they got there."

"That sounds like sleepwalking. When someone interacts with them, are they coherent?"

"Yes, when their alternate personalities take over, they are high-functioning. Most people that don't know them might not even notice anything is out of the ordinary," Brody said.

"So someone with DID can commit murder without even knowing?"

"There have been cases where the person affected has killed several people while carrying on with a normal life."

"How does that even work?" Jet said.

"The personality with the greatest need commands the body."

Nigel and Jet said nothing for a long moment.

"Dr. Ash may have used the same or different procedure when creating Treeka. Either way, it would be helpful to know if we are going to help Meeka," Brody said.

"I remember Dr. Ash telling Jeremiah it was dangerous to perform the disposition voidance technique on April because she wasn't ready. Even Leviathan agreed," Jet said.

"What is Leviathan?" Brody asked.

"It's the AI April assimilated with," Jet said.

"Is that a problem?" Nigel asked.

"I'm afraid that changes everything. From what I understand, AIs are tricky to hack. Do you think you're up to the task?"

Nigel smiled. "I never met a computer I couldn't hack," he replied.

"That may be, but I wouldn't underestimate an AI built by a well-funded adversary like Jeremiah Mason."

"If Leviathan is still connected, then I'll be able to exploit it. It's just a matter of time."

⌗

"Argh! I hate mornings," Freeman said as he fumbled for his alarm clock.

Freeman Johnson looked around his room with blurry eyes. Daylight shone through the window.

Crap, I'm going to be late—again!

A moment later, his red phone, the one he used as his special hacker hotline, buzzed on his nightstand.

I'd better take this!

"Good morning, Freeman, I hope I didn't wake you," a female voice said.

"I'm awake," Freeman said.

"I have seas devoid of water, coasts without a grain of sand, towns without a soul, and mountains without land. What am I?" Dahlia said.

It's way too early for this shit! I hate riddles, and I woke up too late to check the daily drop. But it shouldn't be that difficult to figure out, Freeman thought.

Freeman rubbed his eyes as he thought of the answer.

"A map?" Freeman said.

"Correct. It took you long enough. I need a status on the files," Dahlia said.

"The honey tokens are in place," Freeman said.

"What is that?" Dahlia asked.

"You can think of them as bait. I created some documents entitled 'cyborg construction' and 'enhanced human potential,' which will attract the interest of the people you are targeting."

"How do I know who is assessing these files?"

"I'll provide a daily report, it's all part of the service you paid me for," Freeman explained.

"Will your report include the physical location of the person accessing these files?"

"It can, but I will need to change the script if you want to include that. That will be extra."

"I want as much actionable information as you can give me."

"Don't worry, you will have a full dossier on anyone accessing those files."

"Very well, how do you want to receive your payment?"

"Digibit is fine."

CHAPTER 9

Dahlia's compound, somewhere in the Tatra Mountains

EVA FOUND Vedrana atop one of the peaks overlooking the camp. She appeared to be practicing her stances with a katana. Eva watched as her sparring partner and friend performed a series of complex movements with the sword.

I can see why this is her weapon of choice.

Eva crossed her arms as she watched her friend practice the movements with the grace of a ballerina.

How can she practice in the cold like that? I'm cold, and I'm fully dressed. Her training outfit is showing a lot of skin.

Eva waited until Vedrana was at a stopping point before speaking.

"You practice like you were born with the katana. You look so . . . comfortable with it," Eva said.

"I was a clumsy girl when I started all those years ago. I have many cuts to prove how bad I was, but practice does make perfect. Is it time for breakfast already? I didn't hear the bell."

"No, I wanted a word with you."

Vedrana put the katana away, then sat on her training mat

and gazed out over the training area. Clusters of female fighters were visible from atop the ridge. From this vantage point, the girls were treated to a spectacular view of the various training zones. Some were fighting on a variety of terrain, designed to keep trainees engaged. Others were climbing obstacles that included trees, gigantic boulders, and walls. Eva sat next to her.

"I know it's an honor to be handpicked by the madam, but I'm a little nervous about leaving this place," Eva said.

"I've never known you to be affected by anything—you're one of the best fighters I've known. And I've fought almost everyone here," Vedrana said.

"I . . . just don't think I'm ready."

"I saw how you handled the magister. Even if it was fake, you're ready."

"How do you feel about going to America?"

Vedrana considered this for a long moment. She looked over the training area like she was taking inventory of everything below.

"My desires have nothing to do with it. We need to be ready for anything. According to Blanka, the meeting is of utmost importance to the madam, so it is for us as well."

"It's just . . ." Eva trailed off.

Vedrana gave Eva an unwavering look.

"Just what?"

"I've never been on an airplane, and I'm not familiar with American customs, and my English is terrible."

"Your English is fine. You speak it every day around Madam and Blanka. Look, we are weapons. Stop that line of thinking, or it will get us both killed. You cannot afford to indulge those feelings."

A gong sounded three times, which meant it was time for the morning assembly. Vedrana was on her feet and packing her training supplies before Eva even realized.

"Let's go, I don't want to be late," Vedrana told her.

Eva followed her friend at a pace that seemed fast for the terrain, but she kept pace. It took more than five minutes to descend the peak: less than half the average time.

Most of their classmates were already assembled in front of a makeshift stage near the main building. Vedrana took a position behind everyone, but Blanka signaled them to join her atop the stage. Vedrana spotted her.

"I think Blanka wants us close by," Vedrana said, then quickly navigated the throng of recruits before taking a seat next to her. Eva followed.

"I want you two to stand when your name is called," Blanka told them.

The girls gave her a nod of acknowledgement.

Dahlia jumped onto the training platform overlooking the crowd of trainees below.

"I'm not much of a speaker, so I'll be brief," Dahlia said. "I know all of you have been working tirelessly for our cause, and I wanted to inform you that I have picked two candidates to accompany me on a mission. The assignment will be the ultimate test of readiness."

She let the words hang in the air for a moment before continuing.

"Vedrana and Eva, please take your places at my side," Dahlia commanded.

Vedrana and Eva went and stood on either side of Dahlia.

"I've had the pleasure of training both of these candidates since they were children. Like many of you, they grew up without a family. Vedrana defended her mother against five men intent on raping her. She slit the throats of three before she was thrown out a window. A traveling minister just happened to be driving by when he saw her lying motionless on the road. The impact broke both of her legs, but she dragged herself to the road before losing consciousness."

Gasps could be heard from the recruits. Dahlia let that realization kick in. Dahlia didn't approve of idle gossip and discouraged speaking about their past; she wanted the trainees to think of the compound as their origin. In her mind, each of these girls had been reborn the day she'd accepted them as recruits.

"Eva is an expert at hand-to-hand combat," Dahlia continued. "The only weapons she needs are her hands. She witnessed the brutal murder of her parents at the age of seven. I almost refused admittance to our group because of her age, but after learning she'd killed five men with her bare hands before getting knocked out by a sixth was most impressive. I have no doubt if that cowardly man hadn't snuck up on her, she would have remained pure."

Dahlia surveyed the crowd of trainees before her—who ranged from six to sixteen—and the looks on their faces told her everything she needed to know: she had just created two legends.

"Please take the time to congratulate your sisters on their well-earned status."

The training area roared with applause.

About thirty minutes later, after Dahlia's morning briefing a middle-aged woman approached the stage and motioned for Dahlia.

"I have an important call, Ms. Frost. Do you want to take it here?" she asked.

Dahlia answered the question with a cold, calculating gaze. The woman produced the phone and left her. She recognized the number, it was from her associate, Nasri Zubayr Hadad.

But she called him Nas. Several moments later, Dahlia moved to the nearby gazebo.

"What do you have for me?" she said.

"I'm a crooked path with many turns by the bay," the speaker replied. "What is my name?"

"Lombard," Dahlia said.

"Please hold for his eminence."

Dahlia heard a few clicking noises before being connected.

"D, did you receive my instructions? I sent word earlier this morning."

"I've been busy training the latest recruits, Nas."

"Any potentials, for my harem?"

"No, these young women fighters are not suited for your tastes."

"Call me when you have decoded my message," Nas said.

Fifteen minutes later, Dahlia entered her study. She'd decorated it like her chateau in Locksbottom. It also reminded her of the son, Hunter. She winced at the thought.

It seems like only yesterday when my plans had gotten thrown away. You could have led sisters into battle, my son.

Dahlia received the encrypted container, which she downloaded on her computer. She took out a worn notepad from her safe. She decrypted the series of letters, numbers, and special characters based on the new system that Nas's men had come up with.

The message read:

New player introduced:

Sunchee Chen is a man of many talents. He is the oldest member of the Cabal who demands our loyalty. In exchange, he will solve our cash flow problems.

Dahlia called Nas back. She didn't like involving him as much, but since losing significant resources after the attack on the island, she needed to rely on the aid of his bank account more often than she would have liked.

"Why do we need this Chen fellow?" Dahlia asked when he answered.

"You can call him an angel investor. He's interested in the human weapons you are developing," Nas replied. "He also needs your help to secure other technology."

"Like what? I'm not a technologist."

"He just needs some muscle for a job that will yield him the information. Who can you send on short notice?"

"I will pick my two best agents and send over dossiers within the hour."

"Good, Mr. Chen holds efficiency in high regard. Almost as much as loyalty."

CHAPTER 10

SOMEWHERE ON THE Island of Oahu, October 19th

Freeman checked the online activity for all the spiders he had set up using a technology he grabbed from a private ProgHub page.

Snatching that code was as easy as ever, because ProgHub doesn't know how to patch.

The code needed to be refactored for his needs, but since the author posted all the source code and libraries, it took far less time than it would have otherwise.

Only 994 hits?

Freeman couldn't believe there were less than one thousand Magis in the world of the Colossal Machine. The last figures he'd checked stated there were well past thirteen million active players and rising every day. Either there was some kind of mass-extinction event Freeman had not heard of, or that rank was one of the rarest and the most difficult to achieve. He had witnessed the evolution of Pretzelverse Game's lax security practices to something even more robust. Freeman was certain these numbers were correct, but he had to be sure. He pulled data from all official and non-official website, as well as a site called CMUptime, a site that reported all public statistics. The only drawback was the information on that site tended to be outdated since the last expansion.

994—the count is correct. I will correlate back tomorrow, but I think I have an accurate count.

Next, he checked his scrapping data and found 901 of them had registered email addresses and social media accounts. He used another spider tool to capture all possible correlations to grab other real-world information such as names, birthdays, and sometimes addresses and phone numbers.

People leave a wealth of information for me to find.

"I love it when people make my job easier," Freeman said, laughing.

By the end of the evening, he had to be able to dox more than five hundred users. He cross-referenced those users with the database he had dumped earlier for the Magi world site, where he'd been so rudely insulted earlier.

Time for some further analysis.

Further examination revealed the Magi world database not only had real names, addresses, and card information. But it also contained fields for social security numbers, credit scores, and other things like the percentage of available credit and online shopping histories.

They are not only profiling their users—they are seeing when it's the best time to steal their identity.

As Freeman sifted through the code, he acquired from various ProgHub repository pages, he spotted something unusual. References to a repository called *Bad Actor Punishment* appeared on the list.

What can this be? Freeman thought.

As Freeman scanned the code, he gasped

I think I just found a suitable delivery system.

After spending the better part of a week collecting code, hiring programmers, and securing the processing power and network bandwidth from less-than-reputable internet service providers, Freeman was almost ready. He found his delivery system by mistake when looking for random exploit code for the Colossal Machine.

His red phone chirped. It was his new benefactor.

"Hello D, I suppose you're calling about the status of your project," he said upon answering.

"Yes, among other things," she replied. "Are we ready for deployment?"

"Almost, I'm still assembling code. I may have had a break-through on the delivery system. I should have it ready in a few days."

"Good, I need the code fully operational in less than a week. And I need you to provide a demonstration to my colleagues. I'm sending you the funds to cover the costs of trav-el," Dahlia said.

"Travel? I thought I would make myself available remotely."

"No, you're too far away, I need you in Newport in four days."

That's a Thursday, I can make that work . . . I think.

"Okay, I'll be there."

"Good, and one other thing. When the malware gets deployed, how will the Cabal protect its machines?"

"The malware detects and exploits a vulnerability in more than ninety-one percent of machines running High Tower operating system (HTOS). It's the most popular OS in the world. My machine runs Hally Ninex, and ChangeOS, another Ninex variant."

"Wait a minute, let me see if I understood you. If I'm

running this ChangeOS, or the latest version of HTOS, I'm not vulnerable to the exploit?"

"Yes, that's right."

"What about anti-virus programs? Will they detect it?" Dahlia asked.

"This custom malware I'm developing is a zero-day exploit. That means no anti-virus mechanism in the world can detect it —yet. So we need a swift delivery system. We need as many systems affected as possible."

"Okay, so we need to identify the OS our targets are using. How can we accomplish that?"

"Hmmm, it shouldn't be too difficult. I subscribe to a service called ShowALLD. It scans every machine connected to the internet for out-of-date versions. I can correlate the public IPs that it has with our targets. It will take a day just to do that."

"Just make sure you're ready by Friday," Dahlia said as she disconnected.

Nigel found a quiet place to work atop a pile of boxes. He routed an extension cord he found in a nearby closet to his high perch. Skylights provided plenty of natural light, for now.

Nigel studied the flow of network traffic that led out of Jeremiah Mason's compound that his daughter Melissa maintained as a rehabilitation center.

There's something odd about this traffic—a dedicated circuit routes to the internet service provider, as expected. But there is another connection that keeps going offline. Time to get a closer look.

Nigel scanned the IP range where the Edinburgh facility

connected to the compound. At least seventy percent of all available addresses were in use.

Either someone has a lot of external connections, or a server farm is in use.

After some additional scans, Nigel outputted all the services that were in use. Most appeared to be mundane, well-known server ports that resembled web traffic. At least one connection used at least half of the entire facility's available bandwidth.

That is suspicious.

Nigel used the two-way radio feature on his cell phone to contact Melissa.

"Hey, Mel, do you have a server farm running at your facility?" Nigel asked.

"Not that I'm aware of."

"Is it possible Leviathan may still be accessing systems there? I'm seeing a large encrypted set of data flow from your compound to the internet."

"Any idea of who it might be communicating with?" Melissa asked.

"No, but I'm willing to bet it is connected to Leviathan, wherever it may be hiding."

"Can you break the encryption?"

"I already tried decoding some packets, but it will require more processing power than I have access to," Nigel replied. Then he saw something. "Wait, I see a connection that may be of interest." He pulled up the logs at the Edinburgh facility. "I think I have found a lead after all."

"That's great! I may have found a facility for Brody to perform Treeka's examination. It is a proper medical office in Brooklyn," Melissa said.

"So long as it has a decent internet connection and an actual chair for me to sit on, I'm all for a location change."

"Keep working on tracing that connection while I get us better accommodations."

Nigel resumed his reconnaissance.

Melissa entered the penthouse suite at the Roxy Hotel. She was about to disrobe and take a long hot bath when an incessant rapping sound boomed through the suite. When she answered the door, George was standing there with an urgent look.

"What is it?" Melissa asked.

He walked into the room and closed the door.

"You need to see this," he said.

George handed Melissa a tablet. It looked like grainy video footage of a woman. Melissa couldn't see the image clearly.

"So, what am I looking at?"

"This is some footage taken at your compound in Edinburgh. Now look at the next photo."

Melissa swiped to reveal the next photo in the series. She gasped.

"Is this the same person that attacked us in Edinburgh?"

"Yes," George replied. "The second photo was taken from a security camera in Chinatown last night. It showed a woman with white hair decapitating people near a noodle shop in the area."

"The first photo is grainy—are you *sure* it's the same person?"

"I had my top investigator authenticate both photos—it's the same woman!"

Melissa's heart sank.

Is this woman looking for April?

"Do we have any information about who she is?"

"Yes, she is known as Noz the Dark in the criminal under-world. I believe her name is Nozomi."

"Excellent work. Increase the guard—but I don't want an army of men following us around."

"I've got the perfect man in mind. His name is Klaus, and he is professionally trained and very discreet."

George rechecked the suite, and when he was satisfied it was secure, he left Melissa to her thoughts.

CHAPTER 11

MEANWHILE, somewhere across the Atlantic Ocean

Nasri Zubayr Hadad, otherwise known as the Sultan, sat in the stateroom of his magnificent yacht. It would be several days before he would reach his destination in Lisbon. He would spend the time gathering information about the meetings to come and continue to conduct meetings with his associates, when in range of the nearest satellite. Some of his new compatriots preferred the use of videoconferencing technology. The Sultan didn't care for such devices, but he understood the appeal.

"Bring in Seymour," the Sultan said to a nearby servant.

He didn't have to wait long. Even with the massive size of his superyacht, it didn't take long before anyone answered the Sultan's calls—especially Seymour.

That man is insufferable, the Sultan thought, *but he is a master at finding anyone.*

"Yes, Your Highness?" Seymour said, entering the room.

"I have a job for you. I need you to find this man," the Sultan said as he handed Seymour a folded note.

Seymour caressed the note, held it to his nose, and inhaled. A faint grin of pleasure could be seen on his face.

"What are you doing?" the Sultan asked.

"Oh, I just like the smell of your royal paper," Seymour replied. "The scent of your twenty-four-pound bond is particularly captivating."

"I will need that person in my presence by the time we dock in Lisbon."

"That's less than four days' time."

"Deliver, or suffer the consequences. Should I start reviewing resumes for my next chief of staff?"

"No, Sultan. Forgive my impertinence," Seymour said.

"Take the helicopter back to port—have a member of the Dark Angels take you. I think Gerry is available. This man must be in my presence in four days' time."

"I pride myself on my thoroughness, which takes considerable time—"

"He lives in the United States, somewhere in the Dakotas, I think. That should give you enough time to convince him. Oh, I almost forgot—give this to him. Tell him Nas gives his regards."

Seymour took a sealed envelope from the Sultan, and Seymour's expression changed.

"This feels heavy," he asked. "What's in it?"

"That's not your concern—bringing him here is."

"Yes, Your Highness," Seymour said as he hurried away.

The cyborg Nozomi made it to her safe house in lower Manhattan. She opened her satchel and pulled out an object that resembled a full head of hair. As Nozomi pealed back the layers of hair and fleshy scalp, she found what she'd was looking for: a data core. She tapped her temple three times. An AR interface appeared. She scanned the data core with the AR interface built into her left eye and confirmed the data core was functional. She uploaded the data core's metadata information via the stolen Wi-Fi connection that belonged to a neighboring apartment. The encryption slowed the data transfer, but she had time. She sensed Dr. Ash had been trying to reach her, but she was having too much fun extracting data cores. Soon she would have the treacherous Treeka's and her sister's information. Instead of a chirping noise, Nozomi's cybernetic perception abilities and connection to Dr. Ash's AI allowed her to detect when the doctor needed to speak.

I'd better call her back.

Nozomi accessed her communications menu and dialed Dr. Ash. She selected the audio-only option because she didn't want Dr. Ash to see the bloody mess she had made with the data cores.

"Hello, dear, it's about time you called me back," Dr. Ash said.

"I trust your body is holding up okay?" Nozomi asked.

"Yes, quite well. Have you been able to locate Delta-51?"

"She's no longer at the Edinburgh facility. Neither is anyone else," Nozomi said, chuckling.

"Nozomi, what you have done?"

"Let's just say no one from the Mason foundation will bother us any longer."

"Nozomi, listen to me carefully. I want you to bring Delta-51 in, but you need to promise me you will not kill innocents."

"I didn't kill innocents, I killed enemy combatants."

"Promise me, no more killing."

Nozomi thought for a moment.

"Alright, no more killing civilians, but if another gunslinger tries to take another shot, they will be sorry."

A thought occurred to Nozomi. *Do we need to bring Delta-51 in, or just her core?*

"What happens if I'm unable to bring Delta-51's body

back?" she asked. "I mean, what if there is an accident, and she is injured or dying? What then?"

"In such dire circumstances, we would want to preserve her data core," Dr. Ash replied. "But a word of caution: Delta-51 is unique. She has absorbed a powerful AI. If you learn it is still active, you need to consult me. Is that clear?"

"Yes, that is clear, Dr. Ash."

Thank you for giving me a loophole Dr. Ash. If Delta-51 doesn't come I'm stealing her core.

"I have a lead on Delta-51's location," Dr. Ash continued. "Her last known location is in New York, close to our meeting in Newport, which is in three days' time. I need you to rendezvous with me before entering the Bromwick Hotel. That is Mr. Chen's territory. With any luck, you will find Delta-51 by then."

"I will find her."

"She has a bond with a woman named Josephine Smith, who goes by Jet. I have sent Jet's dossier, along with her known associates, to your neural AR interface."

Nozomi reviewed the information. She saw a photo of Nigel.

Ooh, the boy is kind of cute. I bet I can seduce him. It will be fun trying.

"I will analyze and scout ahead for clues," Nozomi said. "Treeka might be with them."

"Treeka is to be returned unharmed. You have authorization to dispatch her sister and extract her data core," Dr. Ash replied.

I will extract all of their memory cores, and no one will be the wiser. Dr. Ash made me a hunter, and that's what I shall do.

"Affirmative, I'll provide another update soon," Nozomi said.

"There's one more detail that needs to be attended to," Dr. Ash said.

"What's that?"

"The data core is fragile—you need to transport it in a specialized container. It looks like a gray plastic bag. The outside of the bag will have some markings that resemble a lightning bolt with a circle and slash through it. It's very important the data core be transported in the proper container."

"If the data core is damaged, is there anything you can do to repair it?"

"I do not possess the technology to do so. I've tried partnering with chip makers before. It didn't end well."

"I'll be careful when extracting the core," Nozomi said.

"Thank you, young one. We are all counting on you to bring all your sisters home."

CHAPTER 12

LONG ISLAND, New York, October 20th

The Sultan's limo pulled up to the gravesite where his friend Tony Gratzano would be laid to rest. The dark gray skies emphasized his somber mood. He watched as Nico Gratzano, Tony's son, comforted his mother. The woman clung to Nico as the casket of her late husband was lowered into the ground.

"They will pay for this, Ma, I promise," Nico said.

Moments after Tony was laid to rest, the cloudy day turned into a torrent of wind and rain. The service was at the graveside, at the far end of the cemetery. Onlookers ran for cover under trees or inside open mausoleums. Nico and his mother took shelter in the crevice of a nearby tomb. The Sultan and the remainder of the funeral procession clustered together with black umbrellas; if someone had looked from above, the crowd would have resembled the carcass of a giant bat.

"Tony was a kind man, a family man, and he will be missed," the priest said.

Afterward, the Sultan waited until most of the mourners had paid their respects to Nico and his mother before approaching.

"Mr. Gratzano, I came to pay my respects," the Sultan said

to Nico. "Tony, your father, was a trusted associate, and he will be missed."

"I appreciate you coming in person, Nas," Nico said.

"Of course. If there is anything I can do to help the family, please let me know."

"I think you can help me," Nico said.

"Name it, and it will be done."

"Do you have access to the security footage at the dock? I would sleep better knowing we've exhausted every lead before giving up."

"I have cameras everywhere on my vessel, and I've already reviewed it."

"What about the dock?"

"I can obtain it. I'll put my best man on retrieving the footage. I should have it to you this evening."

"Much appreciated. When are you going back home?"

"I have business in Newport in two days. Not sure if you are familiar with it, but it's a seaport town about two hundred miles north of the city."

"I would be honored if you could join us for dinner tonight," Nico said.

"The honor would be mine."

"Vince, a trusted member of the family, will give you the details. And Nas, thanks again for coming—it means a great deal to me," Nico said.

Later that evening

The Sultan knocked on Nico Gratzano's door, and a woman answered. She was in her mid-twenties and was dressed in black.

"Can I help you?" the woman asked.

Before the Sultan could respond, he heard a familiar voice calling for him.

"Nas, welcome to my home. Would you let our guest in, dear?" Nico said.

The woman stepped aside. She had the starstruck look of someone who was in the presence of a celebrity. The Sultan entered, and everyone gave him a wide berth. He was dressed in clothes that people in New York weren't used to seeing. The djellaba made Nas look like royalty. Many of the Sultan's men stood guard at each of the house's doors.

"I'm Irene," the woman said. "It's good to meet you. Is Nas your proper name?"

"Nasri Zubayr Hadad is my birth name, but you may call me Nas, or the Sultan if you prefer."

Nico motioned Nas to follow. Moments later they were seated in Nico's study, which contained thousands of books and ancient-looking artifacts.

"I'm impressed with your library," the Sultan said. "There are many first editions I'm familiar with, and others I'm not."

"Yeah, Dad was obsessed with reading, and he made sure I had the best education. I learned so much from him. I'm going to get the person responsible for his death if it is the last thing I do!" Nico said.

"I have the camera footage you were interested in. It was taken just outside where my yacht was docked in Morocco," the Sultan said.

Nico looked at him expectedly. The Sultan waved a hand, and a Middle-Eastern looking man with a suit produced a small tablet and handed it to Nico.

"The image is dark," Nico said. "I can hardly see anything."

"Give it a minute. The video gets better, as we cleaned up the noise," the Sultan assured him.

Nico watched his father fiddle with the chair at some kind of gate. After several moments, his father turned. A tall, teenage-looking girl approached him from behind. For a long moment they appeared to be having a discussion. Suddenly the girl performed a full roundhouse kick to Nico's father's head. He fell to his knees. He held up his hands, perhaps pleading with the girl to let him go—but Nico wasn't sure. A moment later she kicked him again, and he went down and never got back up. Nico frowned as a rush as blood flushed through his face.

I'm going to hunt that little bitch down and kill her for what she's taken away from our family, he thought with rage, then demanded aloud, "Who is she?"

The Sultan gave Nico a sympathetic look and put a hand on his shoulder. "Her name is Josephine Smith, and she is close."

"How close? I want her dead."

"She lives in the tri-state area. I can help you find her, but I need to attend to something first. I hate to discuss business while you are mourning your father, but would you be willing to accompany me to a meeting with some of my associates in two days' time? It's concerning the opportunity we discussed before your father passed," the Sultan said.

Nico nodded. "We will take care of business first," he said, "and then this girl is all mine."

Freeman had just finished packing a duffel bag filled with clothes. For his plan to work, he needed to carry as little as possible. His plan was to come home early Thursday night, then stash his duffel bag and laptop at a friend's house before heading to the airport. He just had to excuse himself from dinner a little early before climbing out his window. Before his parents knew it, he would be back in Newport.

His red phone chirped.

What does she want now? he thought as he picked up.

"Freeman," Dahlia said, "I need you to do something for me before you head to Newport."

"What do you need?" he asked.

"An associate of mine needs a dark web contract put out on a young woman."

"A contract for what?"

"Death. What else?"

Freeman's mouth watered as a wave of nausea rolled over him.

This is crazy. I don't want to be responsible for killing someone.

"Freeman, are you still there?"

"Yeah, I'm listening."

"Well, can you do this or not?"

"Hiring assassins online is simply not possible. They are usually hoaxes run by law enforcement. I can do some research, but there are no guarantees."

"I know these sites can be elusive and hard to find, but I expect you to deliver," Dahlia said.

"Can you give me some information on the target? I need as much information as possible," Freeman urged.

"I'll send it to our usual encrypted channel," Dahlia said before disconnecting.

Moments later, Freeman checked his dark web mailbox. He had one new message from D.

He opened the message but couldn't believe his eyes.

Message Classification: Eyes Only
Subject: Eliminate target Josephine Smith.

Known aliases: Jet and JetaGirl
Known accomplices: Nigel Watson
Bounty Amount: 500 DigiBit

Wow, that is a crap-ton of Digibit. That's more than enough to get off this stinking island and my own place on the mainland.
A picture accompanied the dossier. The woman looked to be about his age.
Wait? Is this the same 'JetaGirl' I fought in the Colossal Machine? While I want her dead in the game, I'm not sure if I want to be responsible to killing a human being. Hmmm, perhaps I'll just check a few places. Once I've proven that dark web hit men don't exist, then I'll send a bill to D for a few Digibit for wasting my time.

After half a day of looking for a way to break the encrypted tunnel leaving Jeremiah Mason's former facility, Nigel found an unencrypted connection to a ProgHub server.
Someone uploaded an enormous amount of data to one of the ProgHub repositories.
Nigel examined one of the next generation firewall logs at the network perimeter of the Edinburgh facility. He adjusted his filters to capture all unencrypted web communications.
Time to crack a code repo.
Nigel did not know which code repo had the data from the facility, but according to the network logs, the attacker uploaded the stolen code to ProgHub. He consulted his library of exploits, a database of malicious code known to the hacking world, and found one that allowed access to the names of recent uploads. He wrote a script that helped narrow down the IP range used by the Edinburgh facility.

I should be able to find it a lot easier with the script.

Nigel loaded the exploit into the Datasploit program that hackers often used to break into systems. The exploit code worked as expected, and it provided a list of files and directories being uploaded. It also included the target repo.

Finally, something I can use.

When he tried to preview what was in the repository, he received a warning. He found and loaded another exploit that allowed him to download any private files. When he tried to access the files, he was asked for a cryptographic key. He scanned the files to learn more about the cipher and to his dismay discovered that something encrypted them with the highest elliptical curve encryption available.

I'm not breaking that anytime soon!

Nigel rubbed his eyes. He had been at this all day, and what did he have to show for it? His phone chirped; it was Jet.

We are going to send George out for some food. Melissa wants to meet up in the break room for a quick meeting.

I guess I can use a break.

He was about to depart from the stacks of boxes when an idea occurred to him.

Wait. I forgot to check the code signer. Maybe there's an exploit?

Nigel examined the security certificate on the ProgHub site. It was created by a third-party certificate authority called Digi-Northstar.

Didn't they get in trouble for certificate exploitation?

Nigel checked for exploits related to the certificate authority. There were plenty. Nigel downloaded the latest certificate blacklist and checked the ProgHub digital signatures, and it was flagged as being exploited by one malware variant of the Kracken_Hijacker.o13 code. This meant anyone who browsed the site could get infected if they didn't have protections in place. Nigel loaded his special image that contained his hacking tools, then loaded the site. It was time to hack!

This might take a while, so let's see what the others are doing. Nigel made his way to the break room.

It took Nigel ten minutes to get to the room that served as an impromptu operations center. Brody, Melissa, and Jet were waiting. George, Melissa's head of security, passed around sandwiches and bottles of water. Nigel tore into his sandwich like he had not eaten in days.

"I wanted to bring us together for an update on Treeka's condition," Brody said. "The longer her body is in the shielded room, the more guarded she has become. It's almost as if she is becoming a different person. When I first met her, she wanted to exact revenge on the people responsible for her sister's condition. But now she's becoming unresponsive."

"Do you think she was being controlled somehow?" Nigel asked.

"All I know for certain is her body is acting erratically the longer she's in the shielded room."

"I may have found something very interesting." Nigel opened his computer. Everyone tried to look at the small screen at once. "Someone from the Edinburgh facility sent an encrypted payload to a vulnerable ProgHub site. The attacker replaced the original certificate with a changed one. The minute we try to connect to it, we will become infected."

"Then we use a sandbox, simple as that," Jet said.

"In theory that would work fine, but we still need to decrypt the payload once we download it. I'm running a Dataspolit exploit on the site's certificate. If it works like I expect, we will have full access to that code repository."

"Wait, I'm confused. Who did you say uploaded the code from the Edinburgh facility?" Melissa asked.

"I don't know for sure, but I suspect it was Delta," Nigel said.

"Why would Ms. Mason's cyborg daughter do such a thing?" Brody asked.

"If it's Delta, then she is trying to fulfill her mission—"

"April is inside the cyborg body with Delta," Melissa said, cutting Nigel off.

"If that is true, then April may try to warn us."

Everyone seemed to be considering Nigel's words as they finished their meals. No one spoke for a long time.

CHAPTER 13

WORKING in a cramped corner of the shielded room was exhausting. Nigel and Jet shared a space meant for one.

"I have found a place for Brody to perform his examination," Melissa said.

It's about time.

Nigel looked up. He had been working for days with minimal breaks. The hotel suite Melissa had provided was more than adequate, but Nigel found it more productive working with everyone in proximity. Melissa had supplied Nigel with a new laptop more powerful than his old one; he could compile code, decompile, and reverse engineer other code at the same time: something he could ever have done with his old laptop.

"I was going through the scans Brody provided. Both Treeka and Meeka have embedded control code fragments," Nigel said.

"What does that mean?" Melissa asked.

"That someone could control them like strings on a puppet. We have to assume they can be tracked as well," Jet said.

"That's why I insisted the room be shielded," Brody said as he strode into the room.

How does a geneticist know about that? Nigel wondered. *There's something about this guy I don't trust.*

"There is no way we can access the information directly on the chip without a proper neural interface. There is one on the back of Treeka's head, near the base of the spine. But the problem is we don't have a suitable connector to interface with her. Plus, I have no idea what her bootstrapper would look like," Nigel said.

"Boot what?" Melissa asked, confused.

"Sorry, I'll explain, "Nigel said. "A bootstrapper is an interface that allows the computer to load an operating system. When you turn on any computer, you usually see some text, and then you are presented with a login prompt."

"Nigel, if you could construct a connector, I can help with the neural interface," Brody said.

"Yes, I think that would work. I need access to a maker lab. I should be able to build one. I'll draw up my specifications, then find the nearest maker lab."

"What's a maker lab?" Melissa asked.

"It's a special workshop that will allow me to build the connector. Have you heard of 3D printing? It's like that, but with additional equipment," Nigel replied.

Melissa nodded; she was out of her depth, but she was interested. Nigel wanted to help her understand this entire process. Some of it he didn't understand, but that was what Dogs in a Pile was for. It was an advanced search engine designed for technical people. It was surface web available, but Nigel preferred the dark web version because it offered more options.

"Assuming we build an interface, there's still the matter of figuring out her operating system. Assuming she had one at all," Nigel said.

Nigel didn't really understand how a cyborg was put

together. He understood the mechanical parts of fusing machine with human tissue but was lost when thinking about interfacing a human-created boot loader with a human brain. Nigel hoped Brody knew something about neurology.

"Let me figure out the neural interface," Brody said.

Treeka walked into the room. Except for her black boots, she was completely naked. Nigel couldn't help but stare.

She's not whole. What happened to her skin? Half of it around her waist is . . . missing. The rest of her is perfect.

"If you need to examine me, I will submit to anything required," Treeka said.

Everyone in the room gaped at her lack of modesty and willingness to help her sister. Brody appeared to be looking at Treeka with a little too much interest.

"Here—wear this, you must be cold," Melissa said as she handed Treeka a robe.

Treeka put it on, but much of her body was still visible.

"Half of her torso is . . . metal," Jet said.

"As soon as we relocate into a proper medical facility, then I'll perform a full physical examination," Brody said, smiling.

Dirty old man. "When can we move into the new facility?"

"I expect to get the keys as early as tonight," Melissa said.

"Excellent, I need to get started as quickly as possible. Treeka's sister is in a walk-in refrigerator at a trusted location—I cannot keep her there much longer," Brody said.

"Does the new medical office have an area to keep Meeka's body? What about proper shielding from electronic signals?" Nigel asked.

"It's in an abandoned funereal parlor in Brooklyn, so it is suitable for our purposes. I've had my people set up a triage center for the medical examination, and there's a small office that is shielded from electronic interference, built to your specifications," Melissa said.

"Good, I'll work with Brody. I need to know more about Treeka's neural interface."

⚙

Later that evening Nigel, Jet, Brody and Treeka entered the rear entrance of the abandoned funeral facility. A short hallway led to a gigantic examination room with many tables. Dozens of instruments were arranged on various tables. It looked more like an operating room than a mortuary. Nigel took over the office near the makeshift operating room. His first priority was to get online and track down anything she could find about Tomiju Kiyomizu, the cyborg's birth name, gathered from Treeka's long-term memory.

"I need to scan Treeka's short-term memory for any anomalies or clues to where this Dr. Ash is located," Nigel said.

"That will be part of the examination. I'll examine her physically first—"

"Don't you think it's important to scan her memory first? I get that it is important to check on her physically, but I need to get started looking for clues."

Treeka gave Nigel a calculating look.

"I'll let Dr. Brody decide. He is the only doctor present, and I trust him," Treeka said.

"As soon as I'm finished with my examination, I will let you know. For now, you should try to get some rest," Dr. Brody said.

"I think we all can use some rest. Do you want me to take you back to the hotel?" Melissa said to Nigel.

Jet didn't wait for a response; she grabbed her backpack.

"Come on, Nige, you can prepare from the hotel. I'm exhausted," Jet said.

"Okay, fine," Nigel relented. "But I want to come back here first thing in the morning."

"Why don't we meet back around ten a.m.? I still need to rest, and we can compare notes in the morning," Brody said.

Melissa yawned. "Agreed, it's getting late and we all can use the rest."

Nigel, Jet, and Melissa left without another word to Brody.

Brody checked the door and double locked it.

"Are we ready to begin the examination?" Treeka asked.

"Yes, my dear. I need to check you inside and out," Brody told her. "Lay down on the examination table."

Treeka removed the robe Melissa had provided earlier, then laid bare for Dr. Brody.

Dr. Brody came close and separated her legs.

"I need to be thorough," he said. "I don't want to leave a single detail to chance."

"Is it necessary to look down there?" Treeka asked.

Dr. Brody smiled.

"Try to relax. You may feel a pinch, but nothing should hurt. It might even feel good," Dr. Brody said as he caressed her face.

He's using you for his own needs, sister, a voice echoed in Treeka's head.

"Meeka—she's awake."

Brody's expression changed to a look of confusion—then horror—as Meeka appeared in front of him and slashed at his throat with a knife.

"Hey, easy with that. No one is going to hurt you," Brody said as Meeka appraised him like a predator sizing up its next victim.

"Stand down, sister," Treeka said.

"How are you awake? I checked on you just hours ago," Brody said.

Meeka smiled. "It seems I awoke at just the right moment. Greedy old men have taken advantage of my sister enough."

Don't harm him, he helped you sister, Treeka replied telepathically.

He has the look most men have when they approach a naked woman. His animal lust will take over, and he will ravage you, Meeka replied.

You've changed, sister. The old Meeka didn't want to kill innocents, Treeka said.

Dr. Brody snatched Meeka's forearm, trying to wrestle the blade from her. She moved with the precision of a cat. Meeka wasn't at full capacity, but she continued to strike Brody with increasing power. It was like she was feeding off of his pain and suffering; Dr. Brody confirmed this when he screamed in pain. She slashed at his face. Blood oozed from the gaping wound.

"Stop this now, sister," Treeka said. She leaped off the table, then shielded Brody.

"Move," Meeka ordered.

"I will after you put down the knife. He is not the one who hurt you."

Meeka looked unsure.

"He's no danger to you—we have to get that bad code out of your head. Dr. Brody wants to help us," Treeka continued.

"He just wants to help himself," Meeka shouted as she plunged the knife into Brody's chest.

"No!" Treeka shouted.

Meeka fled into the night.

Treeka pursued her sister. The cool night air and her nakedness reminded her she was not ready for another confrontation.

Dr. Brody was lying in a pool of his own blood.

What have you done, sister? Treeka telepathically asked her sister.

Treeka watched as a sticky substance oozed out of the hole of Brody's chest. Brody shook.

"Find something to stop the bleeding," Brody said.

Treeka looked for anything she could use to stop the draining. She opened various cabinets and tossed their contents to the floor. She was about to give up and look elsewhere when she spotted a small white box; it was nearly weightless, so she examined it further. The word "gauze" written on it. Treeka tore into the box and removed all the small white sponges. When she examined the wound, her cybernetic interface appeared over her vision. The knife was still lodged in Brody's chest. Her interface changed her vision to a makeshift X-ray machine. She could see the knife as it penetrated the area just below his ribcage. It didn't appear like it had punctured any vital organs, but it was close to his heart.

"It doesn't look like the blade hit anything important, but I'll try to stop the bleeding," Treeka said.

"Be careful with the knife—"

Brody's screams echoed through the lab as Treeka removed the knife. She ripped a hole in his shirt, exposing the grievous-looking wound. She was about to jam the gauze over it and apply the tape when a system message appeared on her visor:

Warning: Remember to disinfect the wound before applying to bandage to prevent infection.

Treeka looked around for something to help clean the wound. She found a bottle with clear liquid labeled "isopropyl alcohol" and poured it over the wound. More screams emitted from the man as she finished dressing the wound.

"I need to go after Meeka," Treeka said.

"Stop her before she hurts people," Brody whimpered.

Treeka put on her soiled black leather outfit, then entered the chilly fall night.

###

Nigel, Jet, and Melissa sat in the back of the stretch limo.

"I've never been in a car as nice as this before," Jet said.

This car is like the one Natasha picked me up when I was just an intern. All those years ago. That weekend of testing helped shape me into the man I am today.

Nigel closed his eyes as the thought of his murdered friend surfaced. He had buried it deep within him.

"What's wrong, Nige?" Jet asked.

"Nothing, I'm just tired."

Melissa looked at her watch and said, "It's past midnight, and we all need rest, so let's plan on meeting at the hotel restaurant at 8:30 for breakfast."

"That sounds good to me, the later the better," Jet said.

"How well do you know Dr. Brody?" Nigel asked.

Melissa seemed surprised at the sudden change of subject.

"Not well," she answered, "but he is highly regarded in the genetic engineering community."

"He's also wanted by Interpol," Nigel said.

"What?" Melissa said, confused.

"I did a background check, so I could check his credentials when I received an Interpol warning. Nigel positioned his laptop so both Jet and Melissa could see it.

Wanted:

Nicolai Brody

Genetic Engineer

Wanted for eight counts of unauthorized genetic modification, three counts of sexual assault, and one count of bribery.

Melissa was glued to the screen.

"That bastard—how did he? I'll have some serious questions for Jensen, my chief of staff, tomorrow, he vetted him. I will put a stop to Dr. Brody's involvement," Melissa said.

"I don't think it's wise to let him know we are on to him. We don't have the necessary expertise in genetics to replace him," Nigel said.

"He looked very pleased to see the cyborg with no clothes on too," Jet said.

Nigel remembered seeing Treeka naked, and silently admitted he hadn't been immune to its effects.

I can only imagine what Brody has in store for her.

Nigel shook off the thought. Jet snuggled against him. He closed his laptop then, just before closing his eyes.

Sometime later, Nigel awoke as one of the limo doors opened. He shook Jet until her eyes opened and met his. She gave him that special smile that always seemed to make his heart flutter.

"We've arrived. Please exit the curbed side of the vehicle," the driver said.

Nigel looked around. "Where's Melissa?"

"She retired for the evening. I suggest you do as well.

"Come on, Jet, let's put you to bed," Nigel said as he coaxed her out of the vehicle.

CHAPTER 14

NIGEL AWOKE to the sounds of the city. Although it was the middle of the night, New York never slept; there was always someone awake. As he tried to regain sleep, an errant thought invaded his mind.

What is Dr. Brody's true motivation? Does he want to help Treeka and her sister, or himself?

Nigel got out of bed and gazed out at lights of Times Square; the vibrant lights lit up the surrounding streets as if it were day.

If I can't sleep, I should get that connector made for Treeka's neural interface.

Nigel found a maker lab—called Maker Station—about eight blocks away. He confirmed it was open twenty-four hours as he got dressed. Jet was still sleeping, and he looked at her.

How did I get so lucky?

He left Jet a note, grabbed his jacket, then left to brave the cold early morning air.

Thirty minutes later, he arrived at Maker Station. There were several people working at various stations.

More people than I expected at this hour.

A gigantic clock made from electronic circuits and other computer parts was hanging over a reception desk.

It's past three a.m. I don't think it will take long to make the connector. With any luck, I will be back in bed with Jet before dawn.

A woman a few years older than Nigel sat behind a reception desk reading a small magazine called *Dark Encounters*. As she raised her head to get a better look at Nigel, she smiled.

"What can I help you with?" she asked. Then she put an index finger on her lips and licked it.

"I need to use the lab," Nigel said.

The girl turned the page of her magazine before resting it on the counter. Something was off about the woman. If her braided black hair, black lipstick, and fingernails weren't enough, she had several piercings.

"It's fifty an hour for full use of the lab plus materials. I need the first hour upfront in cash," she said.

Nigel handed it over. "Can I get a receipt?"

The woman shoved the cash in an area behind the counter. "Follow me."

I guess I can get that receipt later.

Moments later, Nigel was seated at a workstation. He let the woman show the machine's use, then reviewed his schematic.

He entered the exact specifications of the connector's outer plastic shell. As soon as he pressed the "execute" button, he watched the machine inject some blue material into some kind of mold. The machine shook as it made the part.

As the machine continued to work, he gathered the remaining parts he needed:

A surface mount resistor with a resistance range of one kilo ohm.

Rosen core solder

Variable range soldering iron (12- to 18-watt range)

Micro PCB

I forgot the nanowire FET specs. They are on my laptop. But I've studied the spec enough. I think I can figure it out.

Nigel made an educated guess on the specification for the proper nanowire FET. He needed something with an appropriate drain rating. He wanted to avoid a rapid decay if possible. He decided on a circuit with an exponential decay because it allowed for the decrease of electrical signal at a proportional rate, which meant electrical energy for Treeka's neural interface wouldn't fry the circuit attached to her cranial interface, which would be disastrous.

It took Nigel longer than expected, but he put everything together. His phone chirped. It was a text from Jet.

Hey, Nige, where are you?

He looked out a nearby window. The streets were lighting up.

The sun is rising, Nigel thought before texting back.

I'm at the maker lab, didn't you get my note?

Nigel watched the blinking dots showing Jet was replying.

Oh, I see it now. You should have texted me instead, lol, she wrote.

I'll be back soon, Nigel answered.

He gathered his newly created cyborg connector, cleaned his workstation, and then provided a materials list to the woman at the desk.

"An additional $37.50, please—for the extra thirty minutes on the machine, plus $12.50 in materials," the woman said.

Nigel paid, then turned to leave.

"Wait," the woman said.

Nigel turned to see her with a thin paper in hand. Nigel took the paper.

"If you can figure out how to create a better sex toy, let me know."

What did she just say?

"I'm sorry, I didn't get that last part," Nigel said.

"I said have a nice day. I work the night shift. Come back anytime," she answered, smiling.

A knock on the door awakened Jet. She read the note Nigel had left as she headed toward the door. She looked through the peephole to see April standing in the hallway.

"Jet!" April said as she opened the door.

"April, it's great to see you. Come in."

April gave Jet a bear hug. "It's so good to see you." Then she cried as Jet put her arms around her.

"Don't be frightened," Jet said. "I'm here for you."

April wiped the tears away.

"My mum told me to leave you alone, but I had to see you. I'm sorry if it's early, but the guards wouldn't let me visit last night."

"That's okay, April, but you're going to have to be a little more careful in the future. Your mom told me about what happened at your home."

"It was awful. This woman with white hair almost got us. I was so scared."

Jet held April for a long moment.

"Can I stay here for a while?" April asked.

"You can stay for a little while, but Nigel's coming back, and your mother will wonder what happened to you if you're not back soon."

"That's okay, I left her a message."

"How have you been holding up? Your mom said you haven't been speaking or interacting with people as much as you should," Jet said.

"Can you keep a secret?"

"After everything we've been through, you know I can."

"After you and Nigel shut down Delta, she came back. She tried to escape. Later, she took over my body. I didn't know what was happening when she did."

"How did you find out?" Jet asked.

"Nurse Marge said something about how bad I was becoming. But I didn't remember acting bad—I'm a good girl." April paused before continuing. "I found something bad on my tablet that I tried sending to you and Nigel."

"I don't think we got it, April."

The cyborg frowned. "I thought I sent it, but the merge—or nexus, as Lev calls it—may have mixed things up."

"Lev? As in Leviathan?"

"Yes, she is part of me now, and so is Delta. I hear all of them in my head."

Jet gave April a worried look.

"Wait, you mean Delta and Leviathan can hear us talk?" Jet asked.

April nodded.

Jet was speechless.

"Delta doesn't want to harm anyone, does she?" Jet was worried.

"No—she promised she is going to be good. We want to help people now," April said.

Careful, April, I don't like where this is going, Delta warned.

We can trust Jet, she's one of the good ones, April said.

I've switched us to a private channel. I've been doing some research. After analyzing our collective memories, I've determined Leviathan is not telling us everything. I found a note labeled "The Cabal" in a secret drawer the AI doesn't know I have knowledge of, Delta said.

What was in the drawer? Damaris asked.

A detailed diary of everything that has happened since we fought our way out of Edinburgh, Delta replied.

Is that a bad thing? April said.

The information is not suspicious, but there is information about a rendezvous point with Dr. Ash, Delta said.

She's dead—you killed her, April said.

Yes, because she failed us. And she was interfering with Grandfather's plans. During my research, I learned Dr. Ash's consciousness lives inside another AI I've tried to take control of. It's possible she may gain possession of another cybernetic body. She may try to control us, or attempt to use us as a weapon, Delta said.

I'm afraid that isn't in our best interest, Damaris said.

What are we going to do? April said.

We get help from your friends, Delta said.

Jet and Nigel? April asked.

Yes, but we need to keep it from Leviathan. The nexus that was formed caused Leviathan to detach from us; I'm not sure if it is aware. We need to be aligned in case Leviathan turns against us, Delta said.

Leviathan knows all of our thoughts—we are omnipresent. How are we going to control our thoughts? Damaris asked.

We partition our minds. I did this just before the nexus event. Leviathan was starting to get suspicious, I think, Delta answered.

I don't understand how we can hide anything from Leviathan, April said.

It's easy, little one, you store this knowledge in this special box. Delta held out a virtual hand, revealing a music box her grandfather had given her so long ago.

That may work. We store all memory of this conversation in our own version of the box until it is needed. But how will we know when it's time? Damaris asked.

I will know when it's time, and I will give you back those memories. Soon the AI will be connecting to the one of many wireless networks in the city. Once that happens, we may not be able to control it without help. That's where your friends come in, Delta said.

"April, are you okay?" Jet asked, alarmed. She'd just watched April have a conversation with herself.

"Yes, I'm alright."

"Were you talking with your friends?"

"Yes, we have agreed we can trust you."

"You mean you and Delta?"

"And Damaris," April said.

"You have two other consciousnesses inside your head?"

"Yes, and Leviathan is also there, but . . ."

Jet stared at April as if she was an alien.

"We don't trust Leviathan. That's why we need your help," April said.

"I'll help, but I'll need to tell Nigel."

"We expect you to, just be careful. I'm afraid of that white-haired woman." April's gaze shifted to the door. "We have to go, but we will try to get a message to you," April said as she left.

Thirty minutes later

Jet did her best to fall asleep after April's visit, but it was no use. Her mind was wound up, and she didn't think she would be able to sleep.

Maybe I should log back into the Colossal Machine and resume my quest?

Jet didn't want to continue her adventures without Nigel and April, but that old man who called her the redeemer was so damned compelling. It didn't take long to convince herself. She unpacked her portable VR interface for the Colossal Machine. It wasn't as immersive as the full setup she had at the loft, but she wanted to get her mind off recent events. Moments later she was transported back to the Garden of Light.

Jet found herself outside a set of massive double doors made of bronze. Jet always enjoyed how much detail the developers of the Colossal Machine put into the game world. She had read somewhere the artists and level designers weren't allowed to mass produce any of the game details. Virtually everything was hand-crafted. Just as she was contemplating her next move, the double doors opened inward. She was bathed in the bright light emanating from a golden luminescence called the Sphere of Fate. The old man had guided her to this level—which Nigel had compared to the Hanging Gardens—for a reason, and she wanted to find out.

"It's good to make your acquaintance, JetaGirl," the old man said.

How does he know about my in-game handle? Jet wondered. *I didn't tell him, and the game's AI constructs usually have to be told.*

"It's good to meet you, meister," she said.

"Come. The council wishes to palaver."

Jet followed the old man through the massive chamber. There were a number of columns made from brilliant alabaster so bright Jet couldn't look directly upon them for very long. The floors appeared to be made of polished marble. In the center of the room, an enormous golden ball emitted the brightest luminescence she'd ever seen in the game.

"The council's chambers are just beyond the great seal," the old man said, pointing onward.

"Are you coming?" she asked.

"What the council has to say is for you to hear, not I. Remember, once you pass the seal you may not return."

"Why? If I can't come back, then where will I end up?"

"Such details are not for a simple guide such as me."

Jet took one last glance at the magnificent room before her. Then she examined the great seal the old man was referring to. She didn't see it at first, due to the bright ball mere feet behind her. As she gazed upon the golden pattern, she realized the seal was a series of four inverted triangles.

The seal is a magical barrier, it's another test of the Magi.

The spaces near the intersection of the points had circles with some kind of runic inscription Jet realized the runes were familiar.

It's a spell ward. Those runes are the incantation. I must learn its significance.

As Jet traversed across the great seal, she realized she was shivering. Her teeth rattled together, reminding her of that frozen coyote in those old cartoons. The feeling passed as soon as she passed the seal. She turned to wave at the old man, but she only saw a curtain of light behind her.

I guess there is only one way to go now.

A short passageway led her to a gigantic, cavernous room with no apparent exit. A wooden crate just large enough to admit one person was in the center of the cavern.

This looks out of place.

"I bet this is a test," Jet said to the empty room.

She heard a slight echo as she spoke. The walls were as smooth as the marble she had stepped on earlier. She touched it, and to her surprise the surface was coarse. Then her eyes were drawn to the center of the box. Then examined a triangular-looking device made of metal with two holes. Surrounding it was a silver plate about the size of a gigantic serving platter. Upon further examination, Jet realized two wooden dowels running through its center held the crate in place.

This looks familiar, the silver platter is a compass!

The platter around the triangle-shaped device resembled a compass, but instead of the usual directions she was used to, she saw five textured slices engraved onto the platter connected to a point in the middle.

I bet I can travel to the council in this contraption.

Jet examined the slices. She recognized the symbols on each slice. A series of pillars and a giant eye represented the Timemaker's Terrace. She recognized a series of rivers with a gnarled hand pointing to the water as the symbol for the Garden of Light. The slice that represented Darkow was as black as pitch. The stony slice she knew as Strombach. A ruddy, reddish slice with slimy-looking creatures carved into it she knew all too well as the Kingdom of the Mad Queen. In the center, where the tip of each slice merged, was known as the Nexus Circle.

How do I activate this thing?

She touched the Nexus Circle. The device vibrated. She thought she could hear a low humming sound. The center of the triangular device opened, and the dowels retracted. A black rectangular box raised with four prongs on top of it. It looked like a ring missing its diamond.

I wonder if I need to activate this thing, just like the keys to a car?

The crystal attached to the end of her staff glowed. She examined it for a moment as it became brighter. She removed it from her staff, then placed it in the four-pronged clasp.

Nothing happened at first. Then the cavern shook, and the top of the crate opened. It was like a giant opened a box and found her inside it. She saw several stalactites fall into the opened crate. Other rocks and debris peppered the box from above. The sound was deafening. A small chair-like bench raised from the floor. She sat in it without thinking. Then the vehicle jolted, like she had just shifted a car into the wrong gear. Moments later there was a snapping sound, then darkness.

"In-Por-Ot-Bem," Jet said, the crate illuminated.

After a few moments and a little more tinkering around, she realized the slices could be controlled. When she touched the Darkow slice, the crate seemed to change directions. Jet did not know for sure, but she surmised it was traveling toward Darkow. She pressed the Garden of Light slice, and was jolted in the opposite direction.

Now where am I going?

She thought about it for several seconds as the device powered down.

She touched the crystal, and the device turned on again. From the glow of her light spell, Jet noticed there was a blank gray area in the center, that bound all slices together. It had no symbols or anything carved on it. When she pressed that slice, the device roared into motion. After a few moments, the crate stopped, and an image of a box with a beam of light shining on it appeared.

What the hell is this?

When she did nothing for several seconds, instead of the device turning itself off, the sides of the crate opened, revealing a starry darkness. The next sensation was most unusual; a pulling force. It was like she was being sucked out of the crate by a giant vacuum cleaner.

What the hell?

Then a menu overlay appeared:

<<>>
System Message: Solve the equation
What is your answer?
You have two clues available.
<<>>

A shaft of light shining on a three-dimensional cube appeared to be floating in space. She brought up her menu overlay, then hovered a virtual hand over a green button labeled "clue." When she pressed it, the following message appeared:

<<>>
System Message: It is the world's most famous equation.
What is your answer?
You have one clue available.
<<>>

I hate math! Does it have something to do with light?
She examined the light shining on the floating cube. After giving the problem some thought, she typed the following into the box provided:
E=hv
Nothing seemed to happen.
That is the equation for photon light. Why didn't it work?
Moments later, two giant fists appeared and seemed to be heading in her direction. They didn't seem to have an arm attached, but they were massive. She barely avoided getting pulverized.
Time for a new hint, Jet thought as she selected the "clue" button again.
A portrait of Albert Einstein appeared, floating in midair.

Then it all came to her. She typed in $E = mc^2$ into the game interface. Then the crate jolted into action. Jet grasped onto the nearest object: the compass. She had no frame of reference, but she anticipated the crate was going much faster than it had when she first entered. The sides of the crate evaporated. She gasped upon an expanse of stars.

The crate seems to be able to fly through time and space—I didn't know this was a part of the game.

Moments later, rays of light shot across the starry field. As the stars faded, the beams of sunlight replaced them. The crate picked up speed as it shot through the void and into the light beyond.

Sometime later, Jet awoke on an engraving in the floor. Further examination revealed the engraving was a mirror image of the seal she saw before the encounter with the crate. Jet noticed the runic language was backward.

The seal is the same, but different. It's like I'm looking at it in the mirror.

She took a moment to get a frame of reference, pulling up the in-game map. She appeared to be in the middle of a void. Nothing was visible, but yet she appeared to be standing in the middle of an enormous library. Around her, arched staircases led to an upper mezzanine area she couldn't see. She heard voices coming from above. They sounded almost musical.

Sounds like a debate, or an opera.

Jet ascended one of the enormous staircases. As she climbed, the distance was misleading; what appeared to be thirty feet was like three thousand in this realm. After a considerable amount of climbing, she made it to the level above the seal. Jet looked toward the area where she'd started her ascent;

the seal the old man had warmed her about was engraved on the floor. It looked more magnificent from her current vantage point.

Is it glowing?

The voices were getting louder. She couldn't make out the words, but she followed their captivating and melodic song. Jet traveled deeper into what she thought was the inner sanctum; she didn't know what else to call it. The hallway narrowed, then opened up into a chasm lined with every book imaginable. She became dizzy as she tried to find the bottom of the crazy bibliotheca. The voices were louder here.

I can't understand what they are saying.

Jet couldn't find a way down into the chasm of books, but she caught a glimpse of a reflection. She strode toward the reflection. She maintained a laser focus on whatever was causing the light to reflect. Moments later, the old man appeared from nowhere.

"Congratulations, JetaGirl, you have passed the final test," the old man said.

Where did he come from?

"A test of what?"

"Faith. Now come, the council awaits."

The old man appeared to be walking on empty space ahead of her. Then she looked down; she hadn't noticed she was no longer standing on the ledge, but rather seemed to be floating— no, gliding—over a chasm. She decided to walk normally, as the last thing she needed was to fall to her death then have to restart the level—or worse, lose in-game progression.

"This way," the old man urged.

Jet followed the old man into a vast chamber. Many rows of seats were arranged in a semicircle. Nine figures sat around a gigantic chair.

"Soon you will be judged. I'm here to answer questions you

may have. But choose wisely, as you only get two," the old man said.

"Why am I being judged?" she asked.

"You are the only player who hath made it past the puzzle of the ancients and onto the encounter with the dungeon master. You are worthy of being elevated to the position of Grand Magi."

Jet's heart was beating so fast that she had a tough time forming another question.

"How many Grand Magis are there?"

"If you succeed, you will be the only Grand Magi alive."

The old man let Jet take in the splendor of the judging chamber.

"Now I must leave you."

"Wait—you never told me your name!"

"My name is Icarius, and I'm the dungeon master."

It was six a.m. when Nigel got back to his hotel room. He had only gotten a few hours' sleep, but was rested enough. Jet was stepping out of the shower, a towel wrapped around her.

"Are you hungry?" Jet asked.

"I can eat," Nigel blurted.

Seeing Jet with just a towel to cover her stirred up something in Nigel. He didn't want to do anything except be with her.

Snap out of it, Nigel!

"Give me a few minutes to get ready," he said.

"There is an interesting crepe place a few blocks from here. Let's try it," Jet told him.

Two hours later Nigel and Jet were finishing breakfast at a cafe near Bryant Park. Nigel had just finished paying when his phone chirped, and he looked down as his lock screen filled with dozens of texts. Most of the texts appeared to have nonsensical patterns of alphanumerical strings. Nigel recognized some information as part of a root certificate, and he recognized the format. He caught glimpses of other texts from some of his contacts, but they got obscured by the dump of other information.

What's going on?

Nigel showed his phone to Jet. "Did you get any of these?"

Jet checked her phone, then shook her head.

"I don't know what any of that is, but Melissa has been texting a lot. I had my phone on silent during breakfast," he said.

Nigel sorted his texts and every message had the same timestamp. After a cursory check of the metadata for the messages Melissa sent, he noticed his phone seemed to have been lagging, since her last message was more than an hour ago.

"I got Melissa's messages at the same time as these others, so perhaps my cell phone provider is having trouble?" Nigel asked no one in particular.

"Let's get back to the hotel, I have a strange feeling about this," Jet said.

Nigel paid the bill, and then the teens ran the seven blocks back to the hotel; it took them longer than Nigel was expecting, due to the sheer amount of people on the street. He thought about going around some slow pedestrians, but that would require entering the street, and judging by the way these drivers were behaving, he didn't want to risk getting run over.

"Let's cut through here," Jet urged.

Nigel followed Jet through a narrow alley. They dodged several cardboard boxes with sleeping bags and blankets strewn about. His legs shook as people crept out of boxes, crates, and dumpsters. He stared in stunned silence at the homeless hoard as it prepared for battle. The alley seemed to get smaller, and Nigel was beset by many hungry faces. Grimy hands extended toward Nigel, who reached into his pocket for spare change. They swarmed him as he attempted to give a homeless person some coins.

"Come on, Nige," Jet said.

Nigel pushed through the crowd. Moments later they entered Seventh Avenue, just south of Times Square. He could see the hotel nearby. Despite being less than a block from the hotel, it took more than five minutes to reach the entrance. Melissa and George, her driver, greeted them at the hotel entrance.

"We have a situation—I'll explain as we drive," Melissa said.

"I need my stuff," Nigel said.

"No need, my men packed for you."

An enormous balding man that didn't seem to have a neck held out Nigel's suitcase and backpack.

If my newly crafted interface is damaged . . .

Nigel, Jet, and Melissa filed into the back of the limo as the man who resembled a Neanderthal dressed in a suit loaded their luggage into the trunk.

"Why the urgency?" Nigel asked.

"Something has happened to Brody," Melissa said. "He's been attacked."

"Is he alright?" Jet said.

"I don't know the full extent of the damage. Jensen did not give many details. But I do know is last night, after we left, our medical facility was raided. Brody was injured and Treeka is missing, along with her sister."

"Just before we saw you, I received hundreds of text messages," Nigel said.

"Like these?" Melissa said, handing her phone to Nigel. The messages looked similar to Nigel's but were different.

"What about you, Jet, any messages?" Nigel asked.

"Nothing! What could it be?"

"I'm not sure, but it looks like a core dump."

"A core dump?" Melissa said.

"When a server crashes, it creates diagnostic files and writes them to disk. The purpose is for programmers to analyze it to figure out what's wrong," Nigel explained.

"Will it help if you fetch the messages from my phone?" Melissa asked.

"Yes, but I'll need to connect it to my laptop to retrieve them. I'll need the phone and some time."

"Let's do that, but we need to secure our facility first."

Moments later, the limo dropped them off at the rear entrance of Melissa's new medical facility. It looked like the intruder kicked the door out from the inside. Blood was smeared on the walls, and it pooled in several areas on the floor. Brody was on the floor holding his stomach, bleeding from his wounds. A broken and bloody cellphone appeared nearby.

"What happened?" Jet asked as she hurried to Brody.

"Attacked by Meeka . . ." Brody trailed off as he lost consciousness.

Later that morning

Nigel was working in the office while Jet helped Melissa. He had been trying to decipher the fragments of code on his cellphone for hours.

"Back to help me?" Nigel said in a playful tone.

"I've been up to my elbows in blood, cleaning up after Brody's attack," Jet snapped.

"What's wrong?"

"Sorry for snapping. While you've been here, I've been helping Melissa with the cleanup. Aren't you concerned about Brody?"

I don't feel anything for that man. Besides, he's with a doctor now—there's not much I can do for him.

"When you're ready, I'll show you what I have so far."

"Just give me a minute to clean up," Jet said as she headed toward the bathroom.

Nigel downloaded the mysterious code from Melissa's phone first. It looked like a series of functions and methods from a popular programming language known as PSnake.

It's almost as if the sender dumped an entire ProgHub repository and texted it to us. Is it related to Delta somehow? Nigel wondered.

"Figure out the code yet?" Melissa asked.

"The code looks like it is part of a much larger program. There are different modules of it scattered about, so I need to examine everything before I can figure out the code's purpose," Nigel said.

"Like a puzzle?"

"Exactly like that. We just need to find the hooks that connect these pieces. For example," Nigel pointed, "it looks like this part of the code is referencing contacting an external server —the IP address is not hard-coded, and there is no name resolution, which means something will need to update it via another mechanism. Such as passing a value via a variable," Nigel explained.

"That's not standard. Someone obviously wants to hide it, or the server's name changes so often it needs to be a variable. Either way, that is suspicious," Jet said.

"Yeah, or the function is getting updated by another module. We need more time to decipher this."

"Can I have my phone back now?" Melissa asked.

"Oh, yes—I've already downloaded everything off of it, so here you go," Nigel said, handing her the phone.

I need to check the ProgHub server. Perhaps there will be additional clues there.

Nigel checked an online scanner called ShowALLD, checking its database for a compromised ProgHub server. The scanner was useful for finding compromised sites because it routinely scanned every program on that server connected to the internet. It reported information about each scanner, and if it responded with information, it would log it. A lot of security researchers used the data to help companies close security holes. But the bad guys also used the service for malice.

"Judging from the preliminary ShowALLD scans, it looks like this code is linked to the code egress from the Edinburgh facility," Nigel said.

"Could there be a message somewhere in this jumble of code and data?" Melissa asked.

"It's possible, but I need more time to find it."

CHAPTER 15

NEW YORK CITY, October 21st, 10:03 p.m.

Solomon Friedrich walked across the yard of the metropolitan correctional center. The bite of the chilly fall air was a bitter reminder of what his life had become. A chilly breeze blew his wispy white hair around in a haphazard fashion.

Maybe I can meet my grandson someday.

Solomon sighed. His grandson was five and had never met him.

I shouldn't get my hopes up, that's what I get for trafficking in nuclear material.

A push thrust Solomon out of his thoughts. He looked back at a burly guard named Smalls, if his name tag was to be believed.

"Playtime is over, it's time to go, Sol," Smalls said.

The guards lined him up behind two other prisoners, and Solomon followed a man who looked like a human tank and another smaller skinny man. The guards left the prisoners chained in a featureless hallway while Smalls discussed something with another corrections officer just out of earshot.

"Hey, buddy, are you with us?" the skinny man said.

"What?" Solomon said.

"Bubby and I are making a break for it. Watch for the sign."

Before Solomon could respond, the guards herded the men onto an oversized and reinforced bus. They separated the prisoners. The guards placed the large balding man in the back of the bus, Solomon in the middle, and the smaller man in the front. Soon the bus was moving toward the Hudson.

"How long until we reach USP Canaan?" Smalls asked.

"A few hours, maybe less," the driver said.

Solomon held his breath as they entered the Holland Tunnel. The idea of having so much water above his head was a little unnerving. He released a long breath once the bus cleared the city.

About an hour later, the skinny man turned in Solomon's direction. He nodded his head, Solomon looked toward the back of the bus. The larger man appeared to be staring straight ahead toward the front of the bus. If he was communicating with the skinny man, it wasn't obvious.

"I don't feel so well," the smaller man said.

"You look fine to me. We will call ahead for a doctor," Smalls said.

The skinny man clutched his stomach. "Argh, the pain!" Then he started foaming at the mouth.

What the hell is going on here? Solomon wondered. *Is this part of the diversion?*

"I think he needs a doctor, he is foaming at the mouth," Solomon said.

"Pull over," Smalls said.

"There's no room. Hold on—I'll try to find a place to pull over," the driver said.

Moments later, Solomon noticed the bright red glow of

flares burning on the road. Cars were strewn about haphazardly.

An accident?

"Something doesn't feel right—you better call it in," Smalls said.

"Dispatch, we have an accident and a sick prisoner, request local help," the driver said.

Moments later, Solomon was thrust into a world of confusion. The bus rocked, throwing Solomon into the side of the bus. Blood squirted everywhere as the skinny man's head bashed against the window. The glass shattered inward, pelting everyone with an array of shards. The bus was rolling off the road. Solomon covered his head. His hands, neck, and arms were distressed in flames of agony. The bus came to a stop. The world became blurry, then faded.

Sometime later . . .

Solomon awoke to a flurry of pain and confusion. He opened his eyes. Smalls was checking on the skinny man; he wasn't moving and appeared to be dead. Seconds later, the guard started bleeding from his neck and chest, and then his head exploded.

What the hell is going on?

Another yelp came from the driver, and then silence. Solomon tried to turn his head around to get a better view, but pain shot through his neck and back. The world of consciousness began fading away.

Solomon tried opening his eyes, but the intense light above interfered. He blinked as he adjusted to the bright light.

"Doctor, he is waking up," a female voice said.

Doctor? Solomon thought.

"He can take one more dose, but no more. He is too important, and I will not let him expire before his work has begun," a man's voice said.

Solomon watched a man in a white suit, but he couldn't see his face because he was wearing a mask.

"I know who you are . . ." Solomon tried to say.

They placed something over his mouth and nose. The world blurred again.

Bromwick Hotel, the next morning, 5:54 a.m.

Ezekiel opened the door to Chen's master suite. It was the largest in the Bromwick, and it took most of the top floor. He put the tray on a battered antique desk.

"Do you want to dine at your usual spot at the desk, or would you prefer to enjoy your breakfast in bed this morning?" Ezekiel asked.

"I'd prefer the bed this morning, if you don't mind."

Ezekiel set up the breakfast tray so Chen could have everything in easy reach.

"Is there anything else, master?"

"Sit—I would appreciate the company this morning."

Ezekiel took the chair from the desk and positioned it so he could be of service in case his master required it. Chen opened the lid to his breakfast. The steam escaped from his two poached eggs and dry toast.

"I'm not sure if you know the history of this place, but the

Bromwick Hotel is one of the oldest in the region. Its roots go back to the days of George Washington," Chen said.

"Many ghosts reside in this hotel."

"Indeed, that's one reason why I have invited all the members of the Cabal to discuss our problem. This place has power and serves as a reminder for those who wish to betray us, unless they want to become ghosts themselves."

Ezekiel nodded.

"The roots of our organization go back to the same year America was founded," Chen said. "Two months and three days, if I remember correctly. Do you remember which city the Cabal was formed?"

"Ingolstadt?" Ezekiel asked.

"That's correct. Our group is called the Cabal, but do you know its original name?"

Ezekiel thought for a long moment.

"Quintessence Society?" he replied.

"Excellent, you know your history well. The Quintessence Society started with five principal members. It is fitting there are only five members who remain," Chen said as he chased a runny egg with a piece of dry toast.

"Societal norms have changed since the forming of our group. People are different," Ezekiel said.

Chen thought about this for a long moment.

"Yes, people are different, but not in a good way. We need a reset—it's time to revisit the work Jeremiah started. Perhaps people will treat each other with respect again after losing everything they perceive to be important."

Ezekiel didn't respond at first; he seemed conflicted. Then he asked, "How confident are you with Jeremiah's plan? A pair of teenaged hackers defeated him."

"Many of Jeremiah's decisions were flawed because he let his emotions get in the way. So I have hired some of the world's best computer programmers and hackers. Jeremiah's plan is ready. We just need a scapegoat," Mr. Chen said.

"Something tells me you've already accounted for this contingency."

"I have indeed," Mr. Chen said, smiling.

CHAPTER 16

LATER THAT AFTERNOON

Mr. Chen decided to wait for his guests in the parlor of the hotel. It was massive and could hold at least thirty people. Like everything in this hotel, it was old and built to withstand the test of time. Mr. Chen liked to think he shared that distinction. He checked his carefully prepared agenda.

I need the full support of the other members of the Cabal, Chen thought. *I cannot do this alone.*

"The guests are arriving," Ezekiel said.

"Excellent, I will receive them in the parlor."

Moments later, four women entered the parlor. The first woman strode into the parlor with an air of confidence. Her long black hair was braided and fell to one side. She had a very intense look about her. She looked deadly and unforgiving.

The Black Heart has arrived.

"Dahlia, it is good to see you again," Chen said.

"Chen," she asked, "how is paradise?"

"It's magnificent as ever, but I'm glad to be back in the Bromwick."

"I agree it's good being back in this historic place, but I

always feel I need to watch my back here. Like there's always something lurking in the shadows," Dahlia said.

"Yes, but you are always protected within these walls."

"Hell, having such a high position and nefarious reputation is an invitation to danger."

"I suppose it is. Care to introduce me to your crew?"

Chen analyzed how the three women were positioned at strategic locations around the room, like they were prepared for almost anything.

"The woman to my right is Blanka. She is my primary lieutenant, and my most capable commander. When my . . . son died, Blanka took the initiative. She has been training with me since she was a toddler. By the time she was a teenager, she had defeated one of the world's deadliest assassins. She has completed many solo missions with minimal resources or help."

Chen gave her an appraising look.

I'm impressed. She is both a beauty and a beast in one dangerous package.

"The girl with the long red hair is Vedrana. She has trained with me since she was five. Blanka has taken her as a mentee, and she shows much promise."

Something stirred in Chen at the sight of Vedrana, an almost insatiable lust he had not experienced in a long time.

She is a dangerous beauty. When cultivated, she will be one of D's deadliest of assassins.

"The girl at the door with the short-cropped hair is Eva. She grew up with Vedrana and is one of my deadliest pit fighters. She has defeated foes with her bare hands."

Chen gave Eva a respectful nod.

Any of these women would be a worthy foe. Combined, they are a force to be reckoned with.

Ezekiel gave Chen a nod, then left the room.

"I know I'm the most recent addition to the Cabal, but I'm

concerned about the timeline for the plan's execution," Dahlia said.

"That is one item on the agenda. We lost years' worth of progress when Jeremiah went off task. He was foolish to use Dr. Ash's technology for personal gain. He paid for that mistake with his life. We were all lucky when Nas recommended you to the Cabal," Chen said.

A moment later, Ezekiel reentered with the Sultan. He had three men with him.

"*Marhaba*, Nas, it's so good to see you," Chen said.

"*Shukran*, Chen," the Sultan said.

"*Ahlan*, Nas, it's good to see you again," Dahlia said.

"Hello, D, the pleasure is all mine," the Sultan said.

The Sultan introduced his lieutenants.

"Nico Gratzano is my new first lieutenant, and his father was Tony Gratzano, my former lieutenant, who passed away. Nico has not only taken over the family business, but he also has the confidence of all families on the Eastern Seaboard," the Sultan said.

Loyalty is important in our line of work. Having a mobster who controls unions is important for our plan to work, Mr. Chen thought.

"The other two men are my other lieutenants," the Sultan continued. "I believe you already know Seymour, but the older gentleman with him is General Frank Kurtzen—he commands the preppers in all of North America, including Canada and Mexico."

"A pleasure to meet you, General," Chen said.

Kurtzen returned Chen's greeting with a stony look.

"Is Tage here?" Dahlia asked.

"He will be with us—I believe he just checked in," Ezekiel said.

Why is the kid nearest the school always late to class?

A moment later, Mr. Tage entered with two men. One was a middle-aged, and the other was much older, perhaps in his late sixties.

"Mr. Tage, so glad you could make it," Chen said, trying to keep his tone neutral.

"Greetings, Chen," Mr. Tage said.

"Please introduce your lieutenants to the group."

"The young man you see before you is Rick Watson, and before you ask, he is Nigel Watson's father. The other man is Solomon Friedrich. He's a former inmate at New York's metropolitan correctional facility and a nuclear physicist. I suspect his skills will come in handy during our proceedings."

"Wait—how long has Tage been a member of the Cabal?" Dahlia asked Chen.

"For a long time," Chen said.

"You mentioned I replaced Jeremiah Mason as a member of the Cabal," she said.

"Yes, that is correct. From your tone, I sense this might be a problem for you?" Chen asked.

"No problem, it just makes sense now."

"What does?" Mr. Tage asked.

"That you pretended to not know who Jeremiah was. The assault on his island fortress cost Black Iris dearly."

No one said anything for a long moment.

"I'm sorry for not bringing you into the fold—I had to keep my cards close to the chest because I only knew you by reputation," Mr. Tage said.

"Let us put this unpleasantness behind us. We all have sworn a blood oath to our cause," Chen said.

"Who is the fifth member of the Cabal? You mentioned five principal members before, during my initiation process," Dahlia asked.

"The fifth member has arrived and will be with us shortly. We will start without her," Chen said.

Everyone took their place at the long conference table, which was large enough to seat twenty.

"As you all know, I've called an in-person meeting of the Cabal to address a matter of grave importance," Chen began. "The chaos event planned early this year never happened. As a result, it delayed all other planned events."

"One mistake Jeremiah made was hiring such an unstable hacker for the delivery system. If he had planned half as well as he did for that cyborg, then the plan would have succeeded," Dahlia said.

"Yes, Jeremiah was a fool for not listening to me," a woman's voice said.

Everyone turned to look at the newcomer. It was a woman in her sixties. She was accompanied by a woman in her mid-twenties whose white hair provided little contrast to her white leather outfit.

"Dr. Ash, I'm glad to see you are back on your feet after your . . . ordeal," Chen said.

"You're supposed to be dead," Dahlia said.

"My human flesh was dead for a brief moment, but the diligence of Nozomi, my lieutenant, made it possible for my transfer back into this vessel. In hindsight, I should have prepared a cybernetic body, but I'm attached to this form," Dr. Ash said.

Her eyes seemed to be looking at everything at the same time. The pupils were constantly moving; they reminded Chen of a camera trying to refocus.

"Now that the pleasantries are out of the way, let us begin," Chen said. "In less than a year's time, Melissa Mason has used her father's significant wealth to form a philanthropic organization to help those in need. The Mason Foundation's charter doesn't mention cyborgs, but that is their primary concern. She has hired some of the best minds in artificial intelligence and cybernetics to assist her cyborg daughter. April Mason has information buried away that we need. I believe Dr. Ash can shed some light on how we can leverage that information to put our plan back on track."

"Delta-51 was the first cyborg to be integrated with one of the most powerful artificial intelligences ever created," Dr. Ash said. "The AI's hunter-seeker functions are suppressed by the Mason Foundation's imprisonment of the cyborg."

"Why can't we storm the castle and take her by force?" Dahlia asked.

"They keep April in a guarded castle in Edinburgh—it's walls are defensible. Our forces are needed elsewhere," Chen explained.

"I'm afraid we've already tried that approach. Nozomi nearly took out every guard single-handedly," Dr. Ash said.

The room fell silent as all eyes fell on Dr. Ash.

"How long have you kept this from us?" Mr. Chen demanded.

"It's been a few days. Ms. Mason was supposed to be en route to New York. She escaped with Delta-51 before Nozomi could complete her mission. With Leviathan's help, I've received some information, but I could not reestablish an uplink to the AI," Dr. Ash said.

"If she's in New York—isn't that good for us? We just need to figure out where she's staying, then take Delta by force. Seems simple enough," Mr. Tage said.

"Perhaps, but she will be on high alert considering Dr. Ash's earlier attempt. This weekend she will host a benefit gala. Security will be tight. But . . . perhaps some or all of her bene-factors will decide they don't want to invest in her foundation.

We can give her more trouble than she can handle. The possibilities are endless," Mr. Chen said, chuckling.

Mr. Tage smiled. "Leave it to me, Chen. I know just the person for the job."

"I suggest we get back to the matter at hand. Have we been able to determine why the AI stopped updating?" the Sultan asked.

"I'm not sure, but if we can't re-establish the link, then I'm afraid we have lost the receiving infrastructure code. I believe the source died with Gregor," Dr. Ash said.

"I don't think that is completely accurate," Dahlia said.

Chen urged Dahlia to continue.

"I now have the loyalty of one of Gregor's apprentice hackers, Freeman, and he is on my payroll. I believe he lives close to you, Chen," Dahlia asked.

"Good to know, in case I need my men to pay him a visit," Chen said.

"No need, he's coming here."

"Excellent, I can see you are already surpassing my highest expectations."

Ezekiel gave each principal member a folder.

"The information you have before you contains the key elements of the plan, but we still need to work out some finer details. I'll let Mr. Tage explain our secret weapon," Chen said.

Ezekiel handed Tage a remote control. He fiddled with the buttons until a projector and screen lowered from the ceiling. The blinds also closed, leaving the room in a semi-darkened state. A picture of an island appeared. It looked inhospitable and appeared to have some sort of concrete structure that resembled a prison.

"This island is beautiful for several reasons. You wouldn't know it from these pictures, but the island contains a valuable energy source powerful enough to run the city of New York for years to come."

Mr. Tage let the weight of his words sink in.

"This island looks like it is home to a prison. What is this energy source?" Dahlia asked.

"I was just getting to that. Almost forty years ago, an accident at a nuclear plant in Russia caused panic in Europe and set back my work by a dozen years. If it wasn't for my steel business, I would have been forced to declare bankruptcy because I was in the middle of building my own nuclear fusion plant off the coast of Milford, a city just north of here. I had given up on the idea of supplying energy to the Eastern portion of the United States and put the island up for sale. About a year later, a lucky accident changed everything."

Mr. Tage poured himself a glass of water and drank slowly.

"What accident?" Dahlia asked in an impatient tone.

"About sixty-five million years ago, a meteorite formed the island where I was building my nuclear plant. In the early 1990s, an enormous meteorite event was visible over the Atlantic Ocean. A small meteorite hit the surface of my island. Scientists wanted to study it, of course, so I charged them for the privilege. When the lead scientist told me he found something important, I listened. He theorized the new meteorite event had caused a chain of events that made my island a viable energy source. I discouraged him not to write about his findings. It's funny how a nonstop cash flow into a single scientist's projects will get you. It has taken thirty years and a great deal of money to perfect it, but we have discovered an alternative energy source."

"Unbelievable," the Sultan said.

"The best part was developing the transfer mechanism," Mr. Tage continued.

"Tell us more about the transfer mechanism," the Sultan asked with renewed enthusiasm.

"It's a special cylinder that is lined with the material from the meteorite. I'm told it will contain the basis for the energy source. Then my people will replicate that energy source on the island."

"What island?"

"Jeremiah's, of course. As soon as Mr. Tage persuades Ms. Mason to sell, then our plans will be set into motion," Chen said.

"How do you plan on doing that, Tage?" Dahlia asked.

"Good question—it's one reason I wanted the Cabal to meet in person. We are all here to help Mr. Tage figure that out," Chen said.

Mr. Tage shifted uncomfortably in his chair and looked at his folder.

"Playing with your pet rock is not the only reason we need nuclear material. The current and most advanced cyborgs require protein to function. To mass-produce cyborgs for the military, we will need a more sustainable energy source," Chen said.

"Integrate nuclear material in a cyborg—are you mad?" Solomon said.

"It will work with the proper shielding, and we need only a small amount," Dr. Ash said.

"We need some uranium-235, or a similar isotope for the new cyborg energy source; we can also use that as a catalyst to make use of Tage's energy source," Solomon said.

"How much of the material do we need?"

"About the same amount that is needed to make an atomic bomb: about fifteen pounds of the material." Solomon scratched his beard stubble. "Or—if we have enough material, we can make polonium."

"Where are we going to get that?"

"The most logical is a nuclear reactor or an enrichment facility. The most common way to make polonium is from uranium, but we might be able to bombard certain metals with atoms."

"Solomon, you may be on to something here. I should be able to change the cyborg's chemistry to be compatible with Polonium easy enough," Dr. Ash interjected.

"Yes—bombarding the metal bismuth with a certain number of atoms would have the desired effect without acquiring a nuclear weapon. It sure is a hell of a lot safer," Solomon said as he started scribbling on a nearby whiteboard.

"Wait, I don't follow—what's a bismuth?"

"It is a chemical element with the atomic number 83," Solomon said, as if it were common knowledge.

"So, if I understand correctly, if we steal at least fifteen pounds of uranium, we can activate the power source for the meteor and use the bismuth for the cyborgs?" Mr. Tage asked.

"Something like that."

"I don't have the slightest clue what you are saying. Just tell me what I need to steal," Dahlia said.

"We need a contact at a nuclear facility that will sell some uranium-235 or uranium-238. I'll give you the amounts of each material we need," Solomon explained.

"How are we even going to get the material out of the reactor?" the Sultan asked.

"It would be best to raid the stockpiles of plutonium. The security measures would be less stringent than at a nuclear reactor," Solomon suggested.

"Where do we get access to these stockpiles?"

"I would start doing some simple internet searches. Many countries may even list these sites on their civil engineering websites. If that doesn't work, then stealing a playbook is another option."

"I think I have an idea where to look," Dahlia said.

"Where?"

"According to the search I just made, Russia has more than one hundred metric tons of the stuff. Which is going to be stored in many facilities in the country. All we need to do is find the least secure facility," Dahlia said.

"Easier said than done, but I know someone who is up for the task of helping us," Mr. Tage said.

"Who?" Dahlia asked.

"Our former level-five intern, Nigel Watson."

Rick perked up at the sound of his son's name.

"I don't think he is going to help us," Dahlia said.

"Nonsense, all we need is a little persuasion. Remember how he was looking at Natasha back at Tage Manor? We just need to send in one of your beauties and he will be eating out of their hands."

"Why don't we send in a more experienced operative?" Dr. Ash said.

"Who do you suggest?"

"Nozomi is beautiful and knows how to take care of herself in a fight," Dr. Ash said.

"Do we even know where the boy is?" Dahlia said.

"He's in New York with Melissa Mason. Nozomi has been tracking Delta-51 for some time. It was Delta who led us to him. It was a happy accident for us all," Dr. Ash said.

"I volunteer to go with Nozomi. I know how my son thinks and can help her," Rick said.

"I suggest we vote on it," Dr. Ash said.

Mr. Chen was following the conversation with some interest. "All principal members of the Cabal will vote on enlisting

Nigel Watson's help in finding an insecure location for the plutonium," he said. "Who's in favor?"

Mr. Tage and Dr. Ash raised their hands immediately. Dahlia considered for a moment before raising hers. The Sultan and Mr. Chen were the last ones to raise their hands.

"Well then, it looks like we are going to enlist a young hacker's help. We will discuss this in more detail at the beginning of the morning session. Now, the hour is late, so I suggest we retire in the main dining hall for an excellent meal prepared by my executive chef," Mr. Chen said.

The Bromwick guests were treated to a seven-course meal. Mr. Chen was known for hiring the best in culinary excellence. The guests were treated to hors d'oeuvres, several choices of soup and salad, a choice between fish, meat, or fowl, dessert, and a mignardise that everyone seemed to enjoy.

"The petit fours are superb," Vedrana said.

"I'm glad you approve, my dear," Chen said, smiling.

Rick stared at Vedrana with some interest. His gaze skirted to her chest and remained there for several moments.

If I didn't know any better, I'd think Tage's lieutenant has designs for our young assassin. You better watch your step, my friend, or D will gut you like a fish, Mr. Chen thought.

"Why aren't you eating, my dear?" Rick said to Nozomi.

"I don't eat what you eat," Nozomi said.

A moment later, Nozomi unzipped the leather on her left side, revealing perfect flesh. Then she tapped her side until a panel popped out of her. She removed a cylinder-looking device, replaced it, then put the used cartridge back into her purse.

A moment later, Nozomi's expression changed. It was less intense, and more subdued.

"Much better now. Thanks for the reminder, handsome," Nozomi said, winking at Rick.

Rick's face turned red; then he refocused his attention on his meal.

"Mr. Tage, once you transport the new energy to the island, how do you plan on igniting the catalyst for it?" Dr. Ash asked.

Mr. Tage thought about it for a moment.

"Yes, we do need a reaction large enough to ignite the energy in the meteorite. We will need some material from a nuclear reactor, I think," Mr. Tage said.

"It's not like anyone is going to let you take some uranium from a power plant. Do you have a plan of action?" the Sultan asked.

"Not yet, but I hope to lean on the Black Heart for some tactical assistance."

After dessert and coffee, Mr. Chen invited the principal members of the Cabal for a nightcap. The lieutenants retired to their respective rooms.

Mr. Chen handed everyone a glass with two fingers of his finest brandy.

"This is the best drink I've ever had," Mr. Tage said.

"I have spared no expense for our meetings. Tomorrow we lay the foundation that will change human history, and while I think it's important to involve our lieutenants, it's paramount we meet privately," Mr. Chen said.

"Does this have something to do with the nuclear material?" Dahlia asked.

Mr. Chen smiled.

"I understand you are an expert in covert operations. I would like your assistance in getting this into a nuclear power plant," Mr. Chen said as he removed a flash drive from his breast pocket.

"What's on it?" Dahlia asked.

"I'm told it's a zero-day virus. It will allow us to control certain systems found in nuclear power plants."

Dahlia considered this for a moment. "We should determine the second-shift workers with certain social inadequacies. Then, with the help of one of your beautiful assassins, we can implant it," she said.

"They must persuade a complete stranger to insert a device at the plant," the Sultan said.

"It's not complicated. I'll have Vedrana frequent an establishment our target visits. It could be a bar, coffee shop, or whatever and establish a rapport. When our target makes a move on our girl she will play hard to get, but then, when the time is right, she will show him some seductive photos. The next time they meet, she will get more intimate and then offer the flash drive with the promised photos. He will want to view them as soon as possible, so when he returns from his dinner break, he will be dying to insert the infected drive into a computer."

Mr. Chen rubbed his chin.

"It will take a long time for this rouse to work. Especially since the target is across state lines," Mr. Chen said.

"Let me worry about that. Where is the target?" Dahlia asked.

"Eastern Ohio, near the Pennsylvania border."

"Not a problem, I can perform the reconnaissance. What is the timeline?"

"The sooner the better."

"I'll make it a priority then." Dahlia finished her drink in one gulp. The small table shook as the glass slammed against the polished wood. "Time for bed. See you . . . gentlemen in the morning."

Mr. Chen watched Dahlia leave.

"You've been quiet tonight, Nas. I would like to hear your thoughts," Mr. Chen said.

"This plan requires a lot of coordination to get it right. There are easier targets," the Sultan replied.

"There are, but the timing for this attack is good if we want to blame others," Mr. Chen said.

"I don't follow—who is going to get blamed?" Mr. Tage said.

"Our good friends, the Red Falcon hacking group." Mr. Chen smiled like he was the only person privy to a private joke.

Everyone's phone chirped in unison.

"Oh my! A nuclear power plant in southern Ukraine has exploded," Mr. Tage said.

"They were hacked," the Sultan said.

"All is going to plan. In a week's time they will strike the Ohio Valley Nuclear Reactor," Mr. Chen said.

"Won't nuclear facilities around the world be under a heightened security warning?" Dr. Ash asked.

"Not the Ohio Valley facility," Mr. Chen said, laughing.

"This is not part of the plan, Chen!" the Sultan said.

"It is now. Relax—I have everything under control."

"This has the potential of harming hundreds—if not thousands—of innocent lives, and we can't take the risk," the Sultan said as he headed for the door.

"Nas, please hear me out. It's not our wish to harm innocents—the Cabal will see to that."

"I hope so, Chen. If this puts our plan at risk there will be hell to pay, and not just from us," Mr. Tage said.

"Are you worried the Red Falcon group will figure out who is setting them up? Because it sure seems like a setup to me," a gruff male voice said.

Mr. Chen turned to look in the direction of the voice and saw General Kurtzen, who was leaning on his bookcase and cleaning his nails with some kind of knife.

"Tell me, how are they going to know? Members of that

group have been vocal about nuclear disarmament for years," Mr. Chen said.

"That may be so, but why would an Eastern European hacking group want to target a nuclear power plant in Ohio?"

"The general brings up an excellent point," the Sultan said.

Chen furrowed his brow in concentration. "Red Falcon has disrupted other nuclear facilities before."

General Kurtzen started swiping on his phone. "I think you need to rethink this, Chen. So far I've found no evidence that the Red Falcon group has any involvement in any nuclear meltdowns."

"Chen, I think you need to reconsider this course of action. The damage in the Ukraine is done and there will be a lot of press about it. I'm confident that with the collective brainpower in this room we can figure out another way to gather the required material without inciting disaster," Mr. Tage said.

"Nonsense, this needs to happen." Mr. Chen slammed his glass on the table. The ice in the glass rattled.

"Why does this need to happen? I've already proved we don't need material from a reactor," Solomon said.

Chen inspected the room, thinking, *I want to make these people millions, but they only care about collateral damage.*

"What are you not telling us? What business of yours stands to gain if the Ohio Valley Nuclear Reactor melts down?" the Sultan demanded.

"It's simple, he needs jobs for the environmental cleanup companies he just acquired. It's a good move—ballsy, but profitable," Nico Gratzano said.

Mr. Chen raised a glass. "To your late father Tony, a shrewd businessman who knew when to exploit a great opportunity when he saw it coming."

The room fell silent. Nobody seemed to be in the mood to celebrate.

CHAPTER 17

NOZOMI RETIRED to her suite at the Bromwick. It contained many antiquities which gave it an old, but elegant look. She had preparations to make.

"Hey beautiful, you leaving so early?" a man's voice said.

Nozomi shot a glance in the direction of the voice.

Mr. Tage's man, she noted. *What was his name, Russ? Roy? No . . . Rick!*

Rick Watson stood about ten feet away. He was holding two drinks. "Care to join me?"

Nozomi closed the distance and pushed Rick against the wall hard enough to send a nearby painting and his drinks crashing to the floor.

"What do you want, little man?" she demanded, pushing him.

"Ooh, baby, I like it when a woman plays rough."

Rick grabbed Nozomi by the throat. She froze, didn't offer any resistance. He kissed her.

"Are you sure you have it in you, little man? Then come get me!" Nozomi said in a playful tone.

Rick watched as Nozomi unlocked her room, then entered. She left the door open.

See if the big man has the balls to play rough with me, Nozomi thought.

Moments later, she encountered the embrace of two greedy hands pawing her like an animal. He pulled at her white leather outfit, trying to find an entrance. She smiled as he attempted to pull at the leather.

"If that's how you treat all of your woman, no wonder why your ex-wife dumped you for that FBI agent," Nozomi said, laughing.

"Take your clothes off," Rick said.

"I'm not an object for you to use, little man."

Rick clasped a hand over Nozomi's neck and squeezed. Nozomi backhanded him so hard he lost his grip and stumbled. A moment later she leaped on him and ripped his shirt off.

"If we are going to play, it's on my terms," Nozomi said as she punched him in the stomach.

"Stop it, you crazy bitch," Rick gasped.

"Shall I stop?"

Rick looked around the room like a desperate man.

"No . . . Don't stop . . . Mistress."

Nozomi smiled, then opened a drawer and took several pieces of leather out and threw them to Rick.

"I need to prepare. Put these on and be ready when I return."

Nozomi left Rick, who looked like he was having trouble untangling the leather outfit. She took out a red leather duffel bag and entered the next room of her suite. Nozomi removed her white leathers. She paused when she saw a red leather suit, mask, and pointy high heels hanging in the open closet.

Rick is in for a treat.

She rejoined Rick, who was sitting in the center of the floor, half-naked.

"I'm ready to play," she said. "Are you a big enough boy to teach me a lesson?"

Rick stared at her in stunned silence.

She took a clump of his hair and pulled it back.

Oh yes, he will pay for his mistreatment of others. People like him never learn.

Nozomi's cybernetic interface filled her vision; Dr. Ash was trying to contact her.

"I'm in the middle of something, can it wait?" Nozomi said.

"Judging from your tone of voice, I take it you're not alone?" Dr. Ash said.

"You know me so well."

"You can have your fun later, meet me in my room as soon as possible."

Argh, I was so looking forward to making this worm pay.

"Sorry, lover, duty calls. Our playtime will have to wait."

Rick reached out but could only touch a leathery thigh.

Perhaps I have an extra moment before meeting Dr. Ash.

Nozomi removed her whip and started lashing Rick. His screams and cries for more put a smile on her face.

Twenty minutes later, Dr. Ash opened her door to find Nozomi. She was wearing her usual white leather outfit.

"What couldn't wait?" Nozomi said.

"There has been a recent development. Meeka has been spotted."

"Where?" Nozomi demanded.

That bitch is like a cat with nine lives. I'll put her down for good this time, Nozomi thought.

"In New York City, Chinatown."

"How did you find her?"

"I'm locked out of Leviathan, but I still have access to my mainframe in London. I received an alert about a mass killing in Chinatown. I wouldn't have cared, but the news article described the assailant as an Asian woman in her early twenties wielding a samurai sword," Dr. Ash explained.

"Who was her target?"

"Members of the Gratzano and Chen crime families."

"Any idea why they were meeting?"

"Not yet, but I suspect our host is not telling us everything. Keep an eye out as the conference resumes."

"I will, Mother. I always have your back."

"There's one other development. Without direct access to my lab, there is little I can do to reverse engineer the data cores. Give this to the doctor you met. I don't trust him, but if he can get us closer to our goal, an information trade might prove useful," Dr. Ash said as she gave Nozomi a tiny flash drive.

"I'll set up the exchange."

Freeman assembled the last piece of code for his planned attack. He had been working on it for hours and didn't feel comfortable working in new environments.

By now all of my bots should be in place. They will help me spread the nasty zero-day exploit code, Freeman thought.

He connected his computer to the gigantic flat-screen television that took up most of one wall of his hotel room. After considerable fiddling with the televisions controls so his computer would connect to it, he brought up a dashboard and sent the results to the big screen.

"I hate traveling," Freeman said to his empty hotel room.

At least this hotel is pleasant. It's old. But it has one hell of a Wi-Fi connection.

A rapping at his hotel room door interrupted his train of thought. He tapped a few keys on his keyboard and a video feed of his hotel door appeared. An older woman dressed in black, and a young red-haired girl appeared. He opened the door.

"Hello, Freeman," the girl said, "may we enter?"

Freeman locked eyes with her. His heartbeat rose and other parts of his anatomy went rigid at the sight of her. She appeared disinterested.

"Yes . . . come in," Freeman said.

"Are you ready to deliver?" Dahlia asked.

"Ah . . . yeah, I can monitor the malware's progress from here. I'll also monitor various dark web news feeds for chatter about the worm," Freeman said.

"Worm?" the girl asked.

"A worm is a piece of software that scans infected machines' connections for other connected machines. If it finds a compatible match, it will infect it. Once it is installed, the process replicates. When enough machines are infected, I can send the instructions to detonate. Once that happens, all infected machines will destroy all data on the machine, rendering it useless."

"How long will it take to delete everything?"

"It will wipe the machines in seconds. If it disrupts enough computers, the affected businesses cannot function. I have excluded certain medical devices that run the High Tower OS. We don't want to kill people in hospitals," Freeman said.

"Exclude nothing, we need to affect as many businesses as possible. We need to keep the worker bees busy while we collect our prize," Dahlia said.

Do I want to be responsible for the deaths of innocents? He shifted uncomfortably at this thought.

"Is that a problem?" Dahlia asked.

"No . . . not a problem," Freeman said.

The red-haired girl gave him a faint but noticeable smile. Freeman's heart soared at the girl's reaction. An excitement overcame him as a tingling sensation embraced the more sensitive areas of his body.

Maybe I can get close to her later? I would love to touch her—

"Freeman, are you with us?" Dahlia said.

"What?"

"You seemed to fade out for a moment. I need you sharp."

"Sorry, it's jet lag, I'm more than ready. I was born for this," Freeman said.

"Just be sure not to become overconfident. You don't want to end up like Gregor."

Freeman nodded, then held out a red flash drive.

Dahlia took the drive. "What's this?"

"Here is the other code you asked for. All you need to do is plug it into any free computer connected to the target's network."

"So, this will hack any network we plug this into?"

"It's designed for one target. Once the drive is on the network, then the distraction will begin. Then I'll download everything off of our target's network."

"Good. Make your final preparations. We will come back when it's time," Dahlia said.

"Will I see you at the celebration later?" the red-haired girl said to Freeman.

You better not screw this up if you want to get close to that girl again, Freeman thought, responding with a smile.

CHAPTER 18

Nigel and Jet worked in the security office of the medical lab facility Melissa rented for Dr. Brody. Without the doctor or his staff, the facility was quiet. The only other people in the building were Melissa and her guards. Nigel hadn't finished exploring the lab but had an idea for its size.

"I'm on the right track, but I need more time for analysis—"

"Nigel, come quick!" Jet said.

Nigel hurried to her workstation. "What's the matter?"

"Look," Jet said.

He followed her gaze to one of many monitors on the desk. Nigel was looking at something that could only be described as a dancing bear dressed in a tuxedo wearing a top hat. The bear appeared to be bleeding from many wounds. A caption appeared below that read:

Don't wallow in this bear's despair, embrace the fun of the circus of the mind.

The bear faded, and another figure appeared. It looked like a man dressed like a magician. He waved a wand and another image appeared. It was an animated teenage boy tied to a chair. It reminded Nigel of Peter's video.

This is crazy.

The image of the boy squirmed and wrestled. They tied his arms and legs to unseen posts. A message with enormous letters appeared on the screen.

Do you want to save this boy?
For YES text 212-555-7283
For NO text 212-555-5455

"Where is it coming from?" Melissa asked.

"Something has infected this network," Jet said.

"That means—"

"Someone is inside the building with us," Jet completed Nigel's sentence. Her eyes widened at the realization.

"I'll have a look," Nigel said.

"Take Klaus, the tall built guy with blond hair," Melissa said.

"How many men do you have here?" Jet asked.

"Two. Klaus, and you already know George. He's the guy that's been driving us around," Melissa said.

Nigel grabbed two handheld radios from a nearby table. "In case you need to get in touch."

Jet gave him a thumbs-up signal. Nigel tested the radios, then headed toward the building's entrance. Nigel flipped a nearby wall switch. The lights weren't operational. He could see well enough without them, so he proceeded down the wide corridor.

Is it my nerves, or has someone turned off the lights? Maybe it's just a fuse? Nigel thought.

George was standing next to the medical lab entrance.

"George, do you know where Klaus is?" Nigel asked.

George responded with a shrug.

Man of few words—that's okay, I will find him myself.

The lab's entrance was a large open area; a reception desk

was visible opposite the double doors. There were three exits from Nigel's current position. Since Nigel had just come from the hall next to the reception desk, he checked the hallway to the right of the entrance.

Not very well lit in here.

Nigel used the flashlight feature on his phone as he navigated the hallway. There were a few doors that led from the main hallway—all locked. At the end of the hallway was another closed door; Nigel could turn the doorknob, but it wouldn't budge. He pushed harder. It was like someone had put something in front of the door. As he continued to push, he opened it enough to slide through. As soon as he did, the door slammed shut. It was pitch-black. Even with the aid of the flashlight, he could only see a few feet in front of him.

How big is this lab? I wish I had explored it earlier.

Nigel checked to see what was blocking the door, and to his horror he found Klaus. He was slumped over, and his white shirt was stained with something brown. He shook Klaus. The man's head flopped back, revealing dead eyes.

Nigel's mouth went dry. He grabbed the radio and tried to speak, but no words came. As Nigel tried to form the words, his lips moved, but it was like someone had switched his vocal cords off. Memories of Hunter flooded back. The man's mischievous grin and knife paralyzed him and often caused a great deal of anxiety for Nigel, especially in stressful situations.

"Nigel, I didn't get that," Jet said on the other end of the radio.

He took in several deep breaths. After a few moments, he could speak.

"I found Klaus, and I think he is . . . *dead!*"

Nigel cringed at his words; he'd said the last a little louder than he intended.

"Dead? How?" Jet replied.

She sounded shocked as the awful truth gripped him. Nigel examined the body. His throat was cut. He turned and grabbed the door handle and yanked it as hard as he could, but it wouldn't budge. It was locked.

The door must have auto locked! Nigel thought, on the verge of panic.

His hand was shaking so much the door handle rattled.

I must find another way out of here. Is the killer still here?

Nigel hugged the wall, looking for another way out of the room he was in. Although he couldn't see the open area, it reminded him of an airplane hangar.

What was this place before Melissa converted it into a lab?

The room filled with light, and Nigel let out a yelp of surprise. He was in an enormous warehouse; it was so vast that he could barely see the other side. Various shelves and barrels made it difficult to navigate the area.

Is the killer still here? he thought again, panic rising.

Nigel walked for a very long time; then he saw another door leading from the warehouse. He ran toward it. His heart was racing, and he thought he could hear footsteps behind him. He quickened his pace. He flung the door open so hard it slammed against the wall. A long, featureless hallway appeared before him. It wasn't as lit as the warehouse, but he could see well enough without the aid of his flashlight. He picked up his pace and, before he reached the end, he noticed a door. When he opened it, he froze when he saw the silhouette of a female.

"Hello, Nigel," the figure said.

"Who . . . are you?"

"A friend."

"Whose friend?"

"Is Treeka here? I'm her friend."

"What did you say your name was?"

"My name is Nozomi."

At that moment, the hallway illuminated with light. The woman was shorter than Nigel; he estimated she was about five feet tall. Her white hair provided little contrast with her white leather outfit.

Where's Treeka? I haven't seen her since last night, Nigel thought before telling her, "She's not here."

Nozomi's eyes lit up.

"Ahh, thank you for confirming," she replied.

Nozomi closed the distance and, before Nigel could react, her lips locked with his. Her mouth was soft and inviting. She slipped her hands across his body and found his tender spot. He pushed her back.

"Don't you want me?" Nozomi said.

"What? I don't know you. What the hell are you doing in here, anyway?"

"Men cannot resist my charms," Nozomi said as she unzipped her leather outfit.

Nigel froze as she undressed before him.

She's beautiful, but who is she? And what the hell is she doing? Did she kill that guy? This is all too weird.

"I can tell you want me. I'll do anything you want, and boys your age seem to want a lot. I will provide that—and more—if you help me."

"Help with what?" Nigel said.

Why are you playing along? he asked himself. *She's psychotic.*

Nozomi embraced Nigel again. He returned her embrace.

She's different . . . oh, I want her. But I can't . . . Jet!

Nigel pushed Nozomi back. She gave him a murderous look. Nigel's heart got stuck in his throat. He didn't breathe for a very long time. After a moment, Nozomi's expression changed to the look of desire.

"What's the matter? Am I ugly? Do you like guys instead?"

"No, it's none of those. I think you're beautiful. I . . ."

Just as Nozomi reached for his belt, the radio came to life.

"Nigel? What are you doing with that woman?"

He recognized the voice: it was Jet.

Holy shit, the surveillance system must have reactivated.

Nozomi laughed, grabbed the radio, and squeezed. It broke into pieces and crumbled into a ruined heap at Nigel's feet. Nigel heard footsteps. He could see George rounding a corner, gun drawn. Nozomi charged him, and the gun went off. Nigel's face was peppered with fragments as the wall burst into pieces.

Was I shot?

Nigel touched his face, and while he was bleeding, he realized he hadn't been shot. The wall next to him had been. He couldn't believe what he was seeing. A naked Nozomi was fighting George. She disarmed him, and then George landed several punches that would have caved in the head of a normal woman. It seemed like Nozomi was getting hit on purpose. This all made no sense.

"Playtime is over," Nozomi said as she hit him hard in the throat. George dropped to his knees, grasping his throat.

She disassembled the gun and threw the pieces aside. As George was trying to gasp for air, Nozomi strode to her outfit and grabbed a small knife from her belt.

"No!" Nigel said.

Nozomi gave him a playful smile. "Don't worry, lover, I'll be with you soon," Nozomi said as she plunged the knife into George's chest while maintaining eye contact with Nigel.

Blood spattered over Nozomi's naked body. She smiled as George's blood covered her body. She continued stabbing long after he was dead.

Nigel slipped out the door and ran into the warehouse. He had to get to Jet, and to safety. He ducked behind some barrels.

"Nigel, come out. Don't you want to play?" Nozomi taunted.

What now? I hope Jet stays away from this psycho. She's an assassin.

"Come on, Nigel, I just want to talk. I promise."

Nigel snatched a glance. Nozomi skulked about the warehouse in her white leather outfit.

At least she got dressed. I wasn't sure how long my willpower was going to last. She's deadly, but captivating.

"If I come out, will you promise to leave my friends alone?" Nigel said in a weak voice.

"I promise—you have my word, Nigel."

Nigel stepped from behind the barrels. Nozomi sauntered up to him.

"See, I'm not here to harm any of your friends, I just want to talk to Treeka."

Resigned, Nigel led Nozomi to their impromptu command center; Jet gasped as they entered.

What a sight we must be, Nigel thought.

The blood on Nozomi had dried. It looked like a ruddy brown smear.

"I will not harm you, I promised Nigel," she told everyone. "I just want to talk to Treeka."

"She's not here," Melissa said.

"Where is she?"

"Why do you want to know? So you can kill her too?" Jet spat.

"I'm forbidden to kill Treeka, Dr. Ash wants her back."

"Back where?" Nigel asked.

"To our mother, Dr. Ash," Nozomi said.

"That's impossible, Dr. Ash is dead, I saw her body," Jet said.

"I secured Dr. Ash's body. She lives once more."

"What are you talking about?"

Nozomi brought Nigel and Jet up to speed with current events. She described how Dr. Ash's consciousness had been downloaded into a machine before being reunited with her human body.

"What if Treeka doesn't want to go with you?" Melissa asked.

"It's not her choice. She belongs with her family. And besides, I need help training the new recruits."

"New recruits? What are you talking about?" Nigel said.

"We have orders for hundreds of assassins, and Dr. Ash doesn't need Treeka running amok undoing all the work she's spent a lifetime cultivating."

"You might as well let us go, Treeka isn't here—"

"But I'm willing to bet you know where I can find her, or you have some clue as to where to look."

"I'm not telling you anything," Melissa said.

With the reflexes of a viper, Nozomi grabbed Melissa by the hair and raised a knife to her eye.

"If I poke out your eyes," Nozomi said, "you will never see anything again. Well, perhaps Doc Chop can give you a cornea implant. He runs a rogue cybernetic clinic and asylum. I hear he's quite good."

"Get your filthy hands off my mum!" a female voice said from behind them.

Nozomi turned to find another cyborg who was about the same height with cropped white hair. A wicked smile formed on Nozomi's face.

"Well, if it isn't the little bot who likes to pretend she's a real girl." Nozomi sniffed the air. "I can smell your data core, sister." Nozomi pushed Melissa to the floor and strode toward the teenage cyborg. "What's your name, little one?"

"April Mason, but together we are Legion." April's voice sounded like several voices talking in unison.

"There's more than one of you in there? Tell me I'm wrong," Nozomi taunted.

"No, just one. Delta."

Nozomi raised an eyebrow. "You're the one that killed Dr. Ash's human form?" she asked.

Delta smiled, then charged. Steel rods extruded from her wrists. Nozomi dodged the first blow, and then Delta belted her. The rods cut into Nozomi's face just below the eye. A pink milky goo oozed from the gaping wound.

"You will pay for that," Nozomi snarled.

With cat-like reflexes, Nozomi flung two blades in quick succession. Delta dodged the first attack, but the second blade plunged into her arm. A white liquid oozed from the wound.

"The Delta experiments were weak—you shall be a distant memory." Nozomi unsheathed her sword and got into a fighting stance.

"You can't beat her! Run, April," Jet cried.

"Jet?" Delta said in April's voice.

The teenage cyborg looked uncertain, then ran to Jet and embraced her. Nozomi watched with some fascination.

"Don't worry about us, you have a bigger part to play in all of this. I need you to be safe," Jet said.

Delta looked at April; she looked very much like a little girl. Jet kissed the young cyborg on the forehead, then motioned Delta to get behind her.

"Hand her over, Jet, she belongs with her own kind. This is your last warning. Release Delta into my custody, or I will do something drastic."

Delta walked to Nozomi. "I surrender—just leave my friends alone," Delta said with April's voice.

"Alright, now come here," Nozomi said, fetching a pair of handcuffs from a pouch on her belt.

Delta stopped, just out of Nozomi's reach. Then she started convulsing and dropped to the floor.

"What's wrong with her?" Nozomi said.

"I think Delta is coming," Melissa said.

Nozomi attempted to handcuff Delta. She got one loop around a wrist, but before she could secure Delta's other hand, Delta struck Nozomi so hard she flew halfway across the room and hit the wall hard enough she nearly went through it; a stud in the wall prevented it.

Nozomi recovered, then leaped on Delta. The cyborgs seemed to be fighting to the death. Nozomi was taking a lot of damage, but Delta was getting the worst of it. Nozomi dodged Delta's attacks, then punched Delta. Delta fell flat on her back, and Nozomi picked up a desk and flung it at Delta, who tried to dodge it, but was too late. She was pinned against a wall and didn't move. Nozomi kept kicking the desk. White liquid poured from her mouth.

"No, don't hurt my baby girl," Melissa pleaded.

"She's already dead—she just doesn't know it yet," Nozomi said.

Delta collapsed on the desk. She seemed to lose energy. Nozomi reached for a compartment on her belt. Moments later she kicked the desk aside, then took out some thin wiring and garroted Delta. White milky liquid streamed from Delta's neck like a fountain.

"Stop it, you're killing her," Jet said.

Nozomi ignored Jet as she pulled the wire tighter; it looked like she was trying to decapitate Delta. Nigel grabbed Nozomi from behind, and she backhanded him.

Nigel tumbled to the floor.

"Nige!" Jet screamed.

"Sorry, lover, it's a shame I had to mark up that pretty face," Nozomi said.

She just tossed Nigel around like he was a doll, Jet thought with panic. *He's not moving.*

Delta was trying to get up, but Nozomi resumed her grip on Delta's neck, which was streaming with white liquid. Nozomi pulled out a small glass tube and filled it with the white liquid pouring from Delta, then put it back in a pouch on her belt.

"I only need the memory core. We will transfer you into another body," Nozomi said.

Nozomi continued to pull on the wire, and more liquid sprayed from Delta's throat. She grinned as the white goo spattered her face.

I'm not letting this crazy bitch kill April.

Jet looked around for anything she could use to attack Nozomi. Then she saw it: a small knife that Delta had dodged during the fight. Jet palmed it, then got into position. Nozomi positioned her foot on Delta's back to gain a firmer grip while she continued pulling the wire; Delta screamed, then made an awful gurgling sound. Jet plunged the small knife into Nozomi's back. Her leather outfit provided some resistance, but she penetrated it. Jet's hands were covered in a pinkish, sticky goo.

That should slow her down . . . I hope!

Nozomi screamed in aggravation. She turned and twisted, trying to reach the knife. Jet kicked her. Nozomi fell to her knees, desperate to reach the blade. Jet grabbed one of the giant LCD screens and slammed it over Nozomi's head, and an awful audible cracking noise emitted. She went down. Jet hurried to Delta and, after some effort, removed the piano wire from her neck. The wound was grievous. April was back now, and she was sobbing.

She's switching between Delta and April so rapidly it's hard to tell them apart.

"Get something to stop the bleeding," Jet yelled to Melissa.

Melissa slowly emerged from behind a desk. During the fight, she threw everything she had readily available at her daughter's attacker. Nothing seemed to phase Nozomi, she was like an unstoppable force.

"Why does she want to hurt us?" April said as tears rolled down her face.

Jet's heart ached at the sight of the Delta-51 body. She did not see a mindless killer—only a little girl. Jet wished the Delta consciousness would have kicked in before. This was not a fair fight.

Moments later, Melissa returned with some duct tape. Jet wrapped her neck with the sticky substance.

At least she's no longer hemorrhaging.

Jet gave April a hug.

"Thanks, Jet. I was so worried she was going to hurt you guys," April said.

"We took care of her—"

"Watch out!" Melissa screamed.

Before Jet could react, Nozomi plunged a knife deep within Jet's back. Nozomi covered Jet's mouth as she twisted the blade. She removed it then plunged it again, trying to rupture a kidney. Nozomi's grip muffled Jet's screams.

"Let's see if Nigel still wants you after I cut your face off," Nozomi hissed.

"*No*, I will not let you hurt my family!" April yelled.

Using the strength of the cyborg's body, April hit Nozomi in the face, and a crunching sound emitted. Nozomi fell lifeless to the floor. April picked up Jet and ran out of the room. A trail of blood followed.

"April, wait, I need to call an ambulance," Melissa yelled.

Melissa rummaged through the pile of ruined office equipment looking for an undamaged phone. She started to dial when Nozomi sat up. Her head was twisted around at an awkward angle. She screamed as she pulled her head back into place.

"Where did she go?" Nozomi asked Melissa.

Melissa stared back. "Your face!"

Nozomi picked up a monitor and surveyed the damage in the reflection. "Time to visit the surgeon, I suppose." She flung the remains of the monitor at Melissa, who ducked just in time.

Nozomi followed the trail of blood out of the office.

CHAPTER 19

MEANWHILE, back in Newport

Mr. Chen sat at the head of the conference room table in the parlor of the Bromwick. He prized punctuality as much as loyalty. Just before important meetings, he always remembered what his father told him: "Our family has controlled most of Hong Kong's drug trade for twenty generations. We would not have accomplished this without the loyalty of the people we serve."

Mr. Chen never forgot these words, and he intended to pay tribute to his father's memory with strength and conviction. It was his duty to punish a world that had forgotten the true meaning of honor.

All the Cabal leaders arrived early for the meeting and appeared ready.

"Thank you for your punctuality. The first order of business shall be one of alignment. For this I request only the principal members of the Cabal attend the first meetings. Scheduled breaks will be provided to coordinate with your lieutenants. Mr. Chen watched as the room cleared.

"I know we have regular online conference meetings, but I wanted to go over the plan in person. Some of you had reservations about Jeremiah's plan and its execution. He led the group known as the Timeslicers, which is under Cabal control."

Mr. Chen paused for emphasis then continued.

"Mr. Tage, care to give us an update on the island? I understand you've had a bit of a breakthrough?"

"I felt it was best to share the news with only the principal members of our organization. My scientists have figured out a way to get enough of the meteorite transported to Jeremiah's island. We have achieved a stable catalyst, and the alternative energy source is powering the entire chain of islands in the area, including Príncipe and São Tomé. In exchange for supplying energy, we get military support and certain assurances, including full control of the eight hundred and eleven square miles of the island housing Jeremiah's former compound."

"I did not know you were that far ahead of plan, but it's all for nothing if we can't get Melissa Mason to sell her interest," Dahlia said.

"She will soon enough," Mr. Chen said.

"What do you mean?"

"Some of our associates are convincing her to sell as we speak."

"What are the terms?" Mr. Tage asked.

"The shell company for the Cabal will purchase it for 14.3 billion in cash and real estate. We are prepared to give her a state-of-the-art research facility in Upstate New York as a bonus. The Mason foundation can do a lot with seven billion."

"What if she refuses?" the Sultan asked.

"Let's just say she will be motivated once she receives the offer."

"If the catalyst has started, then why do we need the nuclear material?" Dahlia asked.

"We still need it for our cyborg production," Mr. Chen replied.

"Do we have enough volunteers?" Mr. Tage asked.

Mr. Chen laughed. "We now have more volunteers than we have cybernetics to fill. A lot of workers are keen for the endurance upgrades. We are funding all expenses."

"When will we be ready for Project Reckoning?" the Sultan asked.

"Most of the pieces for Jeremiah's massive doxing operation are already in place. Once the scapegoat provides the delivery mechanism, we will be ready," Chen said.

"Who's the scapegoat?" Tage asked.

"Just a mediocre hacker that Dahlia hired. He thinks he's one of the elites, but I have it on good authority he is akin to a cyber thug who bullies others for personal gain. He's under the illusion he is controlling the code, but all evidence will lead back to him."

"What will happen once all the pieces are in place?" Dr. Ash asked.

"The code Jeremiah designed with the aid of a now-deceased hacked named Gregor acts like a worm and parasite. It feeds on internet infrastructure while making as many copies of itself as possible. Anything connected to a host computer is susceptible to attack. Jeremiah's worm adapts to any operating system. Once the worm spreads, it will affect much of the world's internet infrastructure in minutes," Mr. Chen explained.

"Does this virus follow some route, or does it just attack things at random?" Dr. Ash asked.

"The code has some advanced adversarial techniques, but it's almost impossible to predict how it will react in the wild. It is expected certain services like ATMs will be offline. If it runs on the High Tower OS, then the disruptions will even be greater, but it's impossible to tell what the actual impact will be until it launches."

"My people are ready. General Kurtzen has at least two years supplies in each Cabal bunker location just in case the anarchy disrupts travel," the Sultan said.

"Don't worry, all of you should have enough time to be safe in your bunkers when the worm attacks," Chen assured them.

"Black Iris has stockpiles of gold, platinum, and silver. Not to mention several warehouses filled with essential supplies for trading," Dahlia said.

"You shouldn't have bothered to hoard supplies—general internet access will still be available, albeit a little slow."

"Just make sure we are at our safe locations when the virtual bombs go off," Dahlia chided.

"The main event is a week away. Your junior hacker will help us with testing, but no real damage is expected to happen until next week," Mr. Chen said.

Ezekiel announced that lunch was served. Moments later, the principal members headed in the direction of the banquet hall.

"A moment, sir?" Ezekiel said as he pulled Chen aside. "We have a situation with the Dark Angels."

After months of extensive training, Titus and his Dark Angels better deliver the engineers he promised. Time is short, Chen thought.

"What's wrong?" Chen asked.

"The computer worm they promised isn't working as expected," Ezekiel replied.

"What's wrong with it?"

"It wasn't very good at hiding. Apparently, it spread like it should have, but had a problem at calling the other parts of itself. The code opened the required network ports, but it sent too many packets with little information. During the field tests, analysts detected it too soon."

"I don't understand all of this technical stuff—just give me a recommendation on how we need to fix it," Mr. Chen said.

"The lead engineer needs help. This problem is beyond his expertise."

"So much for hiring the best and brightest. We need to solve this soon, or we'll lose our window of opportunity."

We might have a real problem, Chen thought. *I don't think Dahlia's hacker has the skills we require. But what about that other kid Dahlia mentioned?*

Two hours later

Mr. Chen stood at the entrance of the parlor watching the principal members of the Cabal return from lunch with their lieutenants following close behind.

"I trust everyone had a pleasant lunch," Chen said.

"More than good, it was superb," Mr. Tage said.

"Excellent, because we have an additional problem we have to solve."

Mr. Chen let his words hang for a moment.

"What sort of problem? How does it affect the plan?" Dahlia asked.

"There is a problem with the code that Jeremiah's hackers wrote. It's susceptible to detection."

"Another to add to Jeremiah's long list of mistakes," Mr. Tage said.

"We need someone to fix this worm, so it isn't detected until it captures every piece of data we require in supporting the doxing operation."

"Nigel is a capable hacker—we should get him on that job," Dahlia said.

"Where is the boy? Shouldn't he be here already?" Chen said.

"Rick Watson, Nigel's father, is retrieving him as we speak," Mr. Tage said.

***

Vedrana arrived at Chauncy's Bar and Grill close to the Ohio Valley Nuclear Reactor. Based on the research the hacker known as Freeman had provided, she was looking for a man in his late twenties, overweight with glasses. Vedrana was dressed in formal business attire, and she had unbuttoned her blouse, revealing ample cleavage. A man fitting her target's description was sitting at the end of the bar near the wall. She caught quite a few looks as she removed her thick coat. She squeezed behind her target and took her time hanging her coat on a nearby hook. The man shifted in his seat at the bar. He appeared to be enjoying his sandwich and beer, but he stopped eating when she was close. Vedrana took a seat with a barstool between them. She leaned over the bar to fetch a menu. The man reached it before she could.

"They don't have enough menus at the bar, allow me," the man said, handing her the menu.

"Thank you," Vedrana said as she touched the man's hand.

He jumped.

He's attracted to me—I will use that against him, Vedrana thought.

She browsed through the menu. Every menu item seemed to have the word "fried" in it. She saw nothing that appealed to her. A man with many stains on his shirt and a dirty towel in his hand came over.

"Identification, please," he said.

Vedrana opened her purse and handed him a Romanian passport.

"It says here that your twenty-first birthday is at the end of November, almost a month away. Sorry, you will need to sit at a table instead."

"Come on, Joe, it's not like she asked for a beer. She wants to eat lunch without waiting for a table," her target said.

The bartender looked conflicted for a moment.

"You're supposed to be twenty-one to sit at the bar, but since your birthday is so close, I will let you have some lunch, but no drinking."

"Fine, just a club sandwich and a ginger ale, please," Vedrana said.

The bartender left without acknowledging her order.

"Don't worry about Joe," her target said, "he's a good guy. He got busted a few years ago for allowing underaged drinking."

"Thanks for saying something, I don't have time to wait for a table. I need to get back to work," Vedrana said.

"Haven't I seen you here before?"

"Yes, I come in with my girlfriends, but today I'm alone."

"My name is Ambrose. It is good to make your acquaintance."

"My name is Gwenneth," Vedrana said.

"What a lovely name. I noticed you are not from around here. What brings you to our corner of the world?"

"I have an interview scheduled with a man at the power plant. I'm hoping to secure an internship."

"I work there as an operator. Right now I'm a level two, but I'm up for a promotion to level three soon. Who are you meeting with at the plant?"

Vedrana pulled out her smartphone and pretended to pull up an email. She felt Ambrose's gaze.

"I'm meeting with Cole Lewis."

"I know Cole, he's real smart. He went to the University of Michigan and graduated with honors."

"I'm attending the University of Pittsburgh, about an hour's drive from here."

Moments later, the bartender placed the most disgusting club sandwich Vedrana had ever seen in front of her. The fries were dripping with grease. About halfway into the meal, Vedrana moved the plate then emptied the contents of her bag on the bar.

"Where is it?" Vedrana said in a frantic voice.

"What's the matter?" Ambrose asked.

"My resume and project are missing."

"I'm sure Cole has that in electronic format."

"My resume, yes, but he doesn't have my project. I was hoping to impress him with it. I've done so much work in the field, and now it's gone."

"Is there a way I can help?" Ambrose said.

"I have the project and resume on this flash drive. Is there a copy shop nearby?" Vedrana said as she removed the drive from her purse.

"I don't think so . . . But tell you what. I'll take it to my office, then print it out for you. What time is your appointment?"

"At two p.m."

He looked at his watch.

"Plenty of time," he said. "I'm going to leave now—meet me in the parking lot of the plant in an hour?"

Vedrana gave Ambrose a prolonged hug. She pressed her body against his and said, "Thank you."

Ambrose froze at the sudden contact.

An hour later, Vedrana pulled up the Ohio Valley Nuclear Reactor. She checked in at the guard shack, got her visitor badge, and then proceeded to the guest parking area. A few moments later, she noticed Ambrose leaving the facility with some papers in hand.

"Ambrose!" Vedrana said.

"I printed both files, but a bunch of extra stuff printed with the project file. It looked like random characters, so I recycled them. Let me know if the pages are intact."

She leafed through the papers. He watched her every move.

"It's all here—thanks, Ambrose."

She gave him another hug.

"Hey," he said, "maybe we can grab a drink sometime, if . . . you want."

I have him now!

"I would like that," she replied. "See you around, Ambrose."

He smiled, then walked back into the facility.

CHAPTER 20

APRIL RAN down the streets of Brooklyn looking for a local hospital, clinic, or some place that could help Jet. There was not a hospital in sight and her external communication system was damaged preventing access to her mapping interface. Moments later she spotted an animal clinic; she noticed a sign that said the surgeon was on staff and barged in.

"I need a doctor," April said.

The receptionist glanced at Jet with the knife sticking out of her back.

"What happened? Come back here," the receptionist said.

Delta followed the woman into the back of the animal hospital. Dogs barked at the intrusion. She laid Jet on a metal table.

"She needs help," April said, pointing to the knife.

Moments later, an older man came into the room and examined Jet. Jet's shirt was wet, and blood oozed out of her.

"We need to stop the bleeding, but she needs a proper hospital. We run an animal clinic. There is little I can do for her here," the doctor said.

Another woman in her early twenties entered the room

with fresh towels and started preparing a tray on wheels. April watched as the woman laid out several surgical instruments.

"Help her, doctor, I don't want her to die," April pleaded with the veterinarian.

A hand squeezed April's shoulder. It was the receptionist.

"You need to give the doctor space," she told April. "He cannot operate with you hovering over him like that. Besides, you need to give a statement to the police."

"Police?" April said in a frightened voice.

"Yes, you were involved in a crime, and the police need to take a statement so they can find the person responsible."

"You will not call the police. The doctor is going to help my friend, and then we are going to leave," Delta said in a menacing tone.

The receptionist's eyes widened. She looked as if she'd seen a ghost.

"I'm scared," April said as the tears flowed.

The receptionist gave April a tissue, but still looked like she thought April was going to attack her.

"I just got her back, and I can't lose her," April cried.

"It's okay, Dr. Maxwell is taking care of her. I won't let anything happen to her," the receptionist said while looking longingly at the phone.

Nigel opened his eyes to a beautiful woman. Melissa was holding something wet against his forehead.

"Welcome back," she said. "I was worried you got hit a little too hard."

"Jet!" Nigel said as he shot up and scanned the ruined office.

"She's been injured, April took her . . ."

Nigel looked at Melissa, her eyes glistening with tears.

She's even more beautiful when she's upset, he thought, then stopped himself. *What? Why am I having these thoughts? That cyborg hit me a little too hard. Need to find Jet.*

"Let's go!" he said.

Nigel tried standing, but lost his footing and fell on top of Melissa. He lingered there for a long moment as something stirred deep within him. He loved Jet, but he also had a deep and sudden lust for Melissa.

I think she feels it too.

Melissa confirmed his thoughts by kissing him on the lips. He surprised himself by kissing her back.

"I've wanted to do that since that night at Tage Manor," Melissa said.

A noise emitted from the entrance to the room, Nigel stiffened as he saw Nozomi staring at them.

How long has she been observing us?

"Touching. I can't leave you alone with anyone, Nigel. You are a dog," Nozomi said, grinning. She picked him up by the scruff of his neck. "On your feet, soldier. Someone is here to see you."

Melissa reached out for Nigel, but Nozomi pushed her to the floor. "I'll deal with you later."

"She stabbed Jet," Melissa blurted to Nigel.

Nigel froze. "Why?" Nigel's eyes filled with tears.

"Stop being weak, I just cut the chain to the ball dangling from your neck. Now you'd better come with me if you have any chance of seeing her again—boy!"

Nigel hesitated; Nozomi handcuffed him, then gave a shove. Nigel stumbled, but she kept pushing until Nigel was out of the lab building. Nigel looked around. They were in a small parking lot. He could see a busy street through an abandoned lot about two or three blocks away. A moment later a van pulled up and the side door opened. He looked inside and couldn't believe his eyes. Rick Watson was dressed in black and holding out a hand.

"What the hell are you doing here?" Nigel said.

"Hey, Nige, I suggest you come peacefully. Noz here is stronger than she looks. And twice as flexible," Rick said, laughing.

Nigel gave Rick a look of utter contempt.

That bastard makes me sick!

"I bet you are wondering where your girlfriend is. Have a peek," Rick said as he held out an oversized phone.

Nigel snatched the phone. He couldn't believe what he was looking at. Based on the angle of what appeared to be traffic camera footage, April was carrying Jet into some kind of animal hospital. The video switched to a black-and-white security video of inside the animal hospital. Nigel couldn't hear anything, but saw Jet being taken into a back room.

"It looks like an animal doctor is going to take a knife out of your girlfriend's back. I'm sure that's a tricky procedure. One wrong move, and then she could bleed to death."

"I can barely see her face in the video," Nigel replied.

"You're not the only hacker we know, Nigel. I suggest you decide quickly if you want to help her," Rick said.

Nigel clenched his jaw and threw the phone at Rick. His father ducked just in time.

"My employer has many doctors. He will ensure she is taken care of. That procedure looks tricky and probably requires a blood transfusion. What is the vet going to do? Get blood from one of the dogs?"

"Help her," Nigel said.

"Get in," Rick said.

Nigel froze, but he couldn't seem to decide. Nozomi got close and whispered into his ear, "Get in before I finish the job."

Nozomi shoved Nigel into the van, then shut the outside door. The van jumped into motion. Nigel nearly fell over.

"Is she not joining us?" Nigel asked.

"Noz?" Rick said. "Nope. She will want to take her pound of flesh from the Mason girl. Besides, she's helped enough. We need your computer skills more."

"She better not hurt Melissa."

"Whoa, now that's my boy! How many girlfriends do you have?" Rick said, chuckling.

Nigel flushed, as his right hand formed into a tight ball.

"I'm just kidding, lighten up, Nige."

Nigel rocked in his seat as the van sped on the streets of Brooklyn faster than was safe. He couldn't believe how quickly the situation had changed. His heart ached at the thought of Jet not getting the proper medical attention. Rick picked up the phone and dialed a number.

"We got him. You can pick up the girl now," Rick said as he disconnected the line.

I hope I don't regret this. Hold on, Jet, I'm coming.

The van changed direction and started heading back into the city.

⚃

About thirty minutes later, Nigel found himself atop one of New York's newer skyscrapers, watching a helicopter land. Most boys would enjoy taking a helicopter ride with their father. Nigel could only think of reaching Jet.

"Where are we going?" he asked.

"You're needed in Newport," Rick replied. "Once our business is complete, then we will send you to your girlfriend."

"If she's hurt, then you will be sorry. I don't care if you are my father. I will end you!" Nigel said.

Rick helped Nigel get into the helicopter and took a seat next to his son.

Two hours later, the helicopter landed on an older hotel that possessed some historical significance in the Newport area. Rick rushed Nigel to Mr. Chen's parlor doubled as a conference room. The room fell silent as the duo entered. Nigel remembered Dahlia and Mr. Tage, but he didn't know who the others were.

"Can I get these removed?" Nigel said, raising his bound hands.

Mr. Chen approached Nigel and gave him an appraising look. "Of course, my apologies for any mistreatment you may have experienced. Are you hungry? Can we get you anything?"

"You need some hacking done. I provide that, and I'm free to go—right?"

"Of course, you're not a prisoner. You're just helping out your dear old dad's employer. We will even take you back to New York. I just need a day's worth of your time."

"Let's get on with it, then."

"I will provide you a computer and a place to work. If you're hungry—"

"If it's all the same to you, I just want to get started," Nigel said.

"Very well, your father will show you to your workstation."

Nigel followed his father to the elevator. As the doors

opened, a woman taller than him was exiting the elevator. He watched her exit the elevator and head toward the lobby.

"Nigel, are you coming?" Rick said.

Nigel snapped out of it and joined his father in the elevator.

"She's beautiful, I know. Just remember what's at stake, son."

What's wrong with me? Nigel wondered.

As soon as the elevator opened, two men who resembled sumo wrestlers in black leather approached the elevator to greet Nigel.

"Chen instructed me to get a place for the kid to work. Got anything a teenaged boy would like?"

One of the sumo wrestlers removed a picture of some awful-looking flowers opposite the elevator, revealing an electronic safe. He put his index finger on a sensor and then opened the safe. He tossed Rick a key with an oversized keyring.

"Put him in there," the sumo wrestler said.

Rick led Nigel to Room 1313. Other than the old furnishings, the room had many modern features. A gigantic flat-screen adorned the largest wall. A desk, bed, and chair were the only furnishings.

"I will bring you a computer soon. Wait here until then," Rick said as he left.

Nigel turned on the flat-screen. A menu appeared with a picture of the hotel. A message appeared below:

Welcome to the VIP floor. As a distinguished guest, you have access to many of the hotel's facilities. We invite you to take advantage of the VIP lounge.

A moment later the door opened. Rick was juggling several boxes, trying not to drop anything. He placed them on the bed.

"Mr. Chen has the latest in computer hardware. Let us know if you need anything," Rick said as he left Nigel.

Nigel tore into the boxes and inventoried the equipment.

Let's see if any of this is usable.

Nigel turned on the laptop and inspected the contents. The laptop contained High Tower OS (HTOS). Usually when setting up a new computer, a welcome screen with instructions appeared; he was greeted with the graphical user interface of the OS instead. He checked the system for any additional profiles that might give him a clue as to who had used the computer previously. The system was bare.

Someone has used this before. I should find out what was on it.

Nigel rebooted the computer, then held down the "Control" and "R" keys to bring up the computer's recovery mode. Nigel found the recovery option and was presented with a new menu:

Please select the partition you would like to recover.
Drive 0 Partition 1: Recovery
Drive 0 Partition 2: SYSTEM
Drive 0 Partition 3: OEM Reserved
Drive 0 Partition 4: DRV Reserved
Drive 0 Partition 5: PrimaryHT-OS
Drive 0 Partition 6: SYS_RECOVERY

Nigel selected Drive 0 Partition 5 and selected the recovery option. The following menu appeared:

High Tower OS Setup:

This partition may contain important files or other data you may need. Restoring will destroy its contents. Would you like to proceed?

Nigel clicked the "Yes" button.

The system seemed to take a very long time to complete the restoration process, but he was happy a recovery partition was still intact. The existence of the recovery partition told him data was automatically saved during a routine system snapshot; Nigel knew from experience the OS had this enabled by default. Except for the gusts of wind outside, the room was quiet. He noticed a door leading to another room.

An adjoining room?

Nigel decided to check if it was unlocked. It wasn't, but he could hear some mumbling, like someone was speaking into a microphone. He pressed his ears against the door—nothing! He tried using the built-in microphone on the laptop to try and pick up the mumbling from the other side of the wall, but it didn't work. After some further examination of the laptop, it appeared someone had cracked open the laptop case.

The microphone on this laptop is damaged. I need a smartphone.

He picked up the phone mounted on the wall next to the bed.

"How can I help you, Mr. Watson?" a man's voice said.

"Send Rick up, I have a request."

Rick will provide a smartphone without a SIM card to prevent me from calling someone. That's fine because I just need the smartphone.

Moments later, a loud rapping noise brought Nigel out of his thoughts. He answered the door.

A woman a few years older than him greeted him. She was dressed completely in black and was several inches taller than Nigel. Her skintight black leather outfit displayed ample cleavage, which he found himself staring at like a young kid in a candy store.

"Can I help you with something?" the woman said in a thick Eastern European accent.

Nigel flushed. "Sorry—I was expecting someone else."

This is the woman I saw exiting the elevator earlier.

"I was told you needed something. If that is false, I will leave."

She's direct and to the point, and . . . she looks annoyed. I better watch what I say.

"I need a smartphone," he said.

The woman gave him a disapproving look but didn't answer.

"I need it to enable the multifactor authentication I'll need to download the hacker tools to the laptop," he explained.

The woman left without another word.

I must have offended her.

Nigel finished restoring the laptop. He noticed two system profiles: "Guest" and "FreeBird." He selected the FreeBird profile. To his surprise, it logged into the graphical user interface without even prompting for a password.

Whoever this FreeBird is, he doesn't have good security.

Nigel examined the contents of the user's document folder, and it was blank.

Let's see how good FreeBird is at hiding data.

Nigel checked the contents of the "Recent" and "PreFetch" folders. They contained information. Nigel examined the PreFetch folder contents first. It contained cryptic-looking file names that Nigel recognized as hashed files; a hash was a way to obscure the actual file name with a random series of alphanumeric values. There were too many of these values to check them manually, so Nigel sent all the file names to a text file. Once he separated all other metadata, he examined the computer for a suitable browser and, to his delight, found the multipoint online remote privacy (MORP) browser.

A hacker or someone who wants to keep their actions hidden must have used this computer.

Nigel launched the MORP browser and went to a security analysis website called MaliciousTotal and uploaded the hashes. A listing of several known hacking tools appeared, including the Belch Suite, an invasive and advanced toolkit so expensive only corporate clients and criminals could afford.

Now to dox this wannabe hacker!

Nigel downloaded another tool to analyze the master file table on the former hacker's computer. From that he constructed a timeline of when the hacker tools were downloaded, installed, and executed.

Time to check the logs.

Nigel checked the system, security, application, and network logs. About an hour later he found the trail he was looking for. All the traffic generated by the MORP browser was not logged by design, so he relied on other system activity to determine the hacker's identity. He examined the browser cache on the built-in High Tower OS internet page rendering tool and found what he was looking for: a Stick-yBin login.

Nigel rechecked the logs on the laptop and found something interesting. The hacker had modified the laptop's network settings to monitor every network packet that flowed through the system. This meant the hacker would be able to scan each bit or byte as it entered or exited the system. With this information, Nigel would be able to trace every move the hacker made.

A banging noise broke him out of his technical trance. He opened the door and the attractive woman he'd met before was holding out a cell phone.

I'll look at her eyes, not her chest, Nigel reminded himself.

"Is this what you need?" the woman asked.

"Yes, it is—thank you," Nigel said as he closed the door.

"Wait," the woman said as she stopped the door from closing. "When we first met, you showed interest in my body, and now you don't even look. Am I not attractive?"

Why is she asking me that?

"I'm in the middle of doing some important work for Mr. Chen. That's all that matters right now," Nigel said.

The woman forced her way into the room and pushed Nigel to the bed.

"The other boy wanted my body," she said. "I'm curious why you don't."

What other boy? Nigel thought.

"I'm in love with another—"

The woman's embrace interrupted Nigel. Her passion took hold of his mind and body, and he was under her spell. He wanted her—but he couldn't stop thinking about Jet. He went stiff and stopped responding to her advances.

"What's the matter?" she asked.

"What are we doing? I don't even know your name. I just . . . want Jet to be safe," Nigel said in a wavering voice.

He didn't like what he heard.

I'm weak!

Nigel buried his hands into his face, and he lost control of his tears; he couldn't help it. In an instant, the pain of losing her wounded him. The enormity of it all threatened to crush him. After an endless moment, he opened his hands. He expected the woman to have vanished, but he found her sitting on the bed. Nigel looked into her eyes, and he expected to see resolve; instead, he found compassion. He wasn't sure, but it looked like his outburst had affected her. Nigel wiped away the tears.

"My name is Blanka. Please forgive me if I had offended you."

Why is she apologizing to me? This is crazy!

"You have not offended me. I find you attractive, but my heart belongs to another. I'm the one who is sorry," Nigel said.

Blanka looked at him for a very long time. Nigel wasn't sure what to make of the situation. She got up and offered a hand. He took it. Her grip was firm, but something shot through his system as he touched her. He couldn't explain it, but it was just as strong as when he'd first kissed Jet. He stared into her eyes one last time.

Blanka kissed him gently on the lips, then departed.

CHAPTER 21

BROMWICK HOTEL, 11:46 p.m.

Freeman's red phone chirped. It was Dahlia again.

She's been calling me every hour.

"We need you in the war room."

Before Freeman could respond, the phone disconnected. Moments later, Freeman entered the conference room where he'd first met the Cabal. He scanned the room for the red-haired girl, but she wasn't present. He only saw the deranged adults who called themselves the Cabal. To Freeman, it was like an old person's clubhouse. Dahlia, the woman who hired him, was present with two young apprentices. The middle-aged man known as Mr. Chen, his massive Polynesian-looking bodyguard, was an imposing force. Freeman didn't want to go up against someone so formidable. The man who looked like a sheik, an old man known as Tage and several other mean-looking men all stared at him like a piece of meat on display.

"Good, you're here. I need you to give a status on the deployment of the malware," Dahlia said.

"It's ready to go," Freeman replied. "All we need to do is press the 'go' button." He plugged in a wireless communication device that synchronized the enormous conference room monitor and his dashboard, which showed a world map, appeared.

"What are the orange dots on the map?" Mr. Chen asked.

"These are the malware distribution hubs. They will send commands to the dormant machines," Freeman explained.

"How many of those do we have?" Mr. Tage asked.

Freeman pressed another key on his laptop and the screen filled with red dots. There were so many that the entire map was red.

"Wow, it will affect everything!" Gratzano said.

"All industries will be affected in some way. Businesses won't be able to function without their computers. Many will consider this the start of a cyber war," Freeman said.

"Can you explain to the group what will happen once the malware detonates on the machine?" Dahlia asked.

"When an infected machine receives my encoded message and decodes it, first it will check for updates. Then, unless the update contains other instructions, the computer will remove all data and system files. The system will be useless after that," Freeman said.

"Then we need all agents in place before this detonates," Mr. Chen said.

"Vedrana and Eva are in position and awaiting further instruction," Dahlia said.

"Good. What about the cyborgs?" Mr. Chen asked.

"They are awaiting instructions. We have them outside the Ohio Valley," Dr. Ash said.

"Are you sure the Ohio Valley Nuclear Reactor will be offline?" Solomon asked.

"Yes. Vedrana was able to coerce an employee into inserting an infected flash drive. Now we own all systems within the Ohio Valley Nuclear Reactor," Dahlia said.

Mr. Chen rubbed his hands together. "Excellent!"

"When do we launch?" Freeman asked to no one in particular.

"Soon. We will monitor local and international news from this room," Mr. Chen said.

Nigel examined the phone Blanka had given him. A message telling him no SIM card was present mocked him.

I need to get out of here! Let's see what's on this phone, anyway.

The phone was unlocked, and there were only a few apps on the phone. It ran a mobile version of HTOS. He checked the apps inventory, and two authenticator apps were installed on the phone, but nothing else seemed to work.

Time to root this phone.

As Nigel hooked the phone to the computer to start the process known as rooting, his thoughts drifted toward Blanka.

Was she playing games with me, or was that real?

He stared at the boot screen as he loaded the hijacked operating system. Instead of the usual happy robot, the phone showed several lines of text as it booted. It looked like a computer screen, except on a much smaller scale. He typed some commands, and then after a brief moment, the display changed from the text display to an enormous icon of a cable. From his computer Nigel loaded a transfer program that allowed him to manually copy programs. He transferred a text messaging app designed by Pretzelverse to let players communicate with others when not logged into the game. Nigel had found a way to exploit the program to let him talk to his friends without a game channel. He connected the phone to the hotel Wi-Fi. During his reconnaissance of the Bromwick's Wi-Fi network, he realized the hotel's Wi-Fi blocked most communications ports at a firewall level. But he had modified the Pretzel-verse chat app to use nonstandard ports last year when he was in fear for his life from a hacker group known as the Collective.

Time to see if Milo still has the app on his phone.

He dialed, and after a few rings, Milo picked up.

"Hello? Nige?"

"Hey, Milo. I wasn't sure if you still had this app on your phone."

"Well, I sort of forgot about it. If it wasn't linked to the contact I had for you, I probably would not have picked up. How is Jet?"

Nigel's mouth went dry. He tried to speak, but his lips wouldn't obey.

"She's—we're in trouble," Nigel croaked.

"Okay, Nige, slow down, let's talk this through. Maybe I can help or call the police for you."

"No—no police, not yet."

"Okay, just let me know how I can help then."

Nigel filled Milo in on most of the events since they'd spoken a few days ago. Milo was silent. He let his friend finish.

"What can I do to help?" Milo asked.

"I don't know what Chen has planned, but it's something big. He has some kid leading a cyberattack. But based on what I've seen, he couldn't hack his way out of a paper sack. If that kid messes things up, there's a chance it could disrupt cellular and other phone services. Do you still have your ham radio equipment?"

"You bet! I would never give that stuff away."

"Get it ready, we might need—"

The door to Nigel's room opened, and Nigel disconnected the line. It was Blanka.

Why did she barge in like that?

She made sure the hallway was clear, then closed the door.

She stood there for a long moment with her back to him. Nigel hid the phone in his pants pocket. Blanka turned, then looked toward the ceiling. She jumped on the bed, then yanked something out of the wall just above the bed. She tossed it aside, then looked around the room. Nigel picked up the device she'd discarded; it was a small spy camera.

My room is bugged?

Nigel shot Blanka a glance. She put a finger over her lips to show silence. Nigel took her lead and waited for her to finish ransacking the room. She wedged a chair under the door handle.

"What's wrong?" Nigel asked.

"I've disabled this room's eyes and ears for now. Mr. Chen wanted me to convince you to work with these Dark Angels. I don't know who they are, but I have a bad feeling about this."

That's the group Milo wanted me to look into.

"I've heard of them," Nigel replied.

"Mr. Chen seems like the type of man who plans for the unexpected. I just wanted to warn you before you get forced into something," she said.

Nigel was about to respond when a banging at the door interrupted his train of thought.

Blanka unzipped the top of her leather outfit, revealing even more cleavage.

"What are you doing?" Nigel asked in a low voice.

"Giving them a reason to not be suspicious. Now get on the bed and remove your shirt."

No sooner than Nigel had finished positioning himself, Blanka opened the door. Mr. Chen entered.

"Forgive the interruption, my dear. May I speak with Mr. Watson, alone?" Mr. Chen said.

Blanka winked at Nigel before leaving. Nigel put on his shirt.

"She is quite the looker, and I know you're young, but don't you wish to see your beloved?" Mr. Chen asked.

The question took Nigel off guard. He spoke, but he stumbled on his words.

"Of course I do," Nigel blurted.

"I have a favor to ask, and then we will reunite you with her."

"What do you want?"

Mr. Chen smiled. "Thank you for the courtesy of being direct. I shall return the favor. In short, I need your skills."

Moment of truth, Nige. It's better to see if he is truly a man of his word.

"To be clear, after I help you, I'll be set free?" Nigel asked.

"You have my word, and I always keep it," Mr. Chen replied with a smile.

"What do you need me to do?"

Mr. Chen smiled as he made himself comfortable in Nigel's desk chair.

"How good are you at hacking the physical security of a data fortress?"

"I've been known to get into tight places."

"If you are as good at breaking in as you are at fixing code, then you shall be reunited with your girlfriend soon."

"What am I breaking into, and what do you hope to achieve?"

"The details are on this," Mr. Chen said, handing Nigel a flash drive.

"Hey, as much as I want Jet back, I'm not breaking into some building until I know why," Nigel said defiantly.

Chen gave Nigel a wary look.

"I don't have to tell you that data is the lifeblood of our society. We no longer manufacture items—not in any meaningful way. Instead, we manufacture data and allow corporations like the phone companies to resell it to the highest bidder. We have become the product. Jeremiah knew this and wanted to use the data to dox millions, then profit from the ensuing bounties."

"That makes no sense. Based on the malware I fixed, you are planning something bigger than a data heist."

"Yes, you are a smart boy. This was to be the latter of a two-pronged attack, but due to changes beyond our control, the plan needed to be altered."

Nigel pondered this for a long moment. Despite the chaos Chen's attack would cause, he had to admire its simplicity. The man had gone to great lengths to make this happen, but if it was the only way to get Jet back, he could do it a thousand times over.

"How long do I have to prepare?"

"You have until tomorrow afternoon to review the data and plan of attack."

Mr. Chen left Nigel to his thoughts.

Nozomi looked out the window of the limo as her unwilling guest squirmed in the opposite seat.

"We will have you out of those bonds if you cooperate, and only if you do," she said.

Moments later, the limo pulled up to the side entrance of the Bromwick Hotel. Nozomi untied Melissa Mason and removed her gag.

"Remember what happens to your daughter if you don't accept Mr. Chen's generous offer."

Nozomi pulled Melissa out of the limo and urged her into the hotel. The hotel staff got out of her way as she prodded Melissa through the lobby and into the conference room where the Cabal was meeting. Everyone stopped talking as the newcomers approached.

"She's ready to cooperate," Nozomi said as she pushed Melissa into the conference table.

"What happened to your face?" Dr. Ash asked Nozomi. "Come here so I can examine you."

Nozomi let Dr. Ash examine her.

"Your auto-healing has stopped working," Dr. Ash said. "I need to find a suitable facility to make the repairs."

"Don't bother, I've been meaning to pay Dr. Sylvester another visit."

"Yes, please do it. We can't have you walking around with half a face."

Nozomi handed Dr. Ash a vial. "This is that sample you wanted."

"From Delta-51?"

"Yes. Sorry I couldn't bring her in."

"Just take care of yourself, dear, you are my finest creation," Dr. Ash said as she rested a hand on Nozomi's damaged face.

"Ms. Mason, welcome to the Bromwick. Please take a seat. Would you like a refreshment?" Chen said.

Melissa shook her head, then picked one of the vacant seats. She gave Dahlia a wary look, as if the Black Heart was preparing to attack. Moments later, Ezekiel placed a folder and pen in front of her. All eyes were on Melissa as she examined and signed all paperwork.

"In the morning, the transaction goes into escrow. As soon as that process finishes, you will be seven billion dollars richer," Mr. Chen said, smiling.

"When can I see my daughter?" Melissa said.

"Soon, my dear, but while you wait, I suggest you make yourself comfortable in one of the penthouse suites."

CHAPTER 22

NEW YORK CITY, October 23rd 1:32 p.m.

Titus Flavia pulled up to the tallest windowless building in Lower Manhattan. He backed his BlueSphere Communications truck onto the ramp that led to the loading bay. He didn't expect any resistance since the parking permits on the truck were in order, and he didn't expect the van to be reported stolen for quite some time.

It's time to get Norris and his team of engineers on the horn. I just hope that commando is worth the money, Titus thought.

"Dark Angels, I'm in position. Set your radios to the encrypted frequency," Titus said.

"Affirmative. Are the engineering teams in position?" a gruff male voice asked.

The twenty-nine-story building, often called the *local blight*, got its name partially because of its bleak exterior. The brown building was devoid of all exterior distinguishing features. The building was shielded against physical attack with a triple-insulated layer of lead and concrete. The exterior of the building could withstand a direct atomic bomb blast; even the so-called bunker busters couldn't penetrate its physical security layers.

"The engineers are in position, but the teams are blocked. Project Titan Rising has taken the main communications center. Our engineers need access to that area to disrupt the ring," a younger man said.

"Norris, are you running point?" Titus said.

"Yes sir, the engineers are in position, but they tell me there's a problem. A high-priority project has been moved up and the communications room is blocked. I'm also babysitting a tourist," Norris replied.

"Then I suggest you unblock it. I'm sending Atticus in to disrupt the party. Your tourist is a hacker of some renown. I'm told he knows these systems inside and out. How much of a window does your team need to get the worm installed?"

"At least ten minutes to get in and out."

"It will be tight, but I think we can pull this off. Once Chen starts the main event, we will have an opportunity for distraction. Once our worm is in the system, the defenders of this monstrosity will have their hands full," Titus said.

"The entrance of the building is heavily guarded. We do this, and there's no way out," Norris said.

"No, there's another way," Titus said.

Titus rummaged through his backpack and pulled out a well-worn map. It was held together by tape and it looked ancient. Titus examined it as if his life depended on it.

One miscalculation, and then we are killed, or worse —caught.

"There's one way out of the building that doesn't require leaving through the front door," Titus said.

"I'm listening," Norris said.

"How many engineers are in the building?"

"Six engineers, and seven including the tourist. The rest are hiding in the network closet next to the operations center."

"After the engineers implant the malware, can you make it to the roof for egress?"

The radio went silent.

Nigel gazed upon a building that looked out of place in a trendy part of lower Manhattan.

"Put this on," a grizzled-looking man with a thick mustache said.

As he put a communications worker uniform on, he wondered how he got here. Just hours before, the commando picked him up from the Bromwick. He felt like one of those computer geeks in movies that aids an assault team. Nigel couldn't believe it. To save Jet, he had to storm a fortress with an extraction team no less.

I shouldn't have let Chen coerce me into this.

"Titus, are you there?" Norris said.

"It looks like we are on our own," Nigel said.

Moments later, an alarm sounded. The Titan Rising staff that were previously impeding the Dark Angels progress evacuated the communications room.

"Engineers at the ready. You have less than ten minutes, and an expert mentor. Get to work!" Norris said.

Nigel sprang into action and made it to the operations center at the same time as the engineers. Each engineer took control of a terminal.

"Intrusion prevention systems offline," an engineer said.

Nigel was impressed at the level of commitment and discipline of the Dark Angel engineers. Every member knew their job well.

I'm not needed, so why am I here?

"The malware isn't deploying," a female engineer said.

"Sally, is the flash drive recognized?" another engineer asked her.

"Yes, it's mounted, I checked twice! If we can't load this, then it's time to leave while we still can."

"Sally, check the boot log file," Nigel said.

"Why would I do that?"

"Because it may give you clues about disabled peripherals. Check while we still can."

Sally checked the log file. "I'm getting a dependency failed message."

"Give me the values of the last four characters."

"x8ox."

"That message means all drives except for boot are disabled. We need to restart and reenable it."

"How do I do that?"

The alarm was stopped.

"Four minutes remaining, people—probably less than that, since the alarm stopped," Norris barked.

"Move," Nigel said as he nudged Sally aside.

Sally watched as Nigel proceeded to reboot the system.

"Forget launching the malware, you won't be able to log back into the system," Nigel said.

Once the computer started, Nigel quickly began tapping the F8 and F12 keys repeatedly. Soon a blue screen appeared. Nigel navigated to the external menu selection. He enabled all USB ports, then saved the configuration. A system message asking for a password appeared.

"See, what did I tell you? It's not happening today, it's game over!"

Nigel quickly tried a few passwords, but nothing worked. Another system message appeared:

This is your last attempt before the system is reformatted.

Nigel ran his fingers through his hair: a habit he got into when nervous.

"No, it can't be," Nigel said as he typed in a series of characters.

Thank you, the system configuration has been saved. Have a nice day.

"You have little faith, Sally!" Nigel said, chuckling.

"Two minutes people, hurry up already," Norris said.

Nigel didn't have the password to log in to the system, but he remembered a backdoor that affected certain versions of HTOS, so he tried various keystroke combinations. He pressed the uppercase "G" key six times, followed by the "F" key, then repeated the "G" and finished with the "E."

A terminal window appeared. He had full shell access, which meant he could do anything he wanted without logging in. Nigel typed the following:

Sudo fdisk -l
The following menu appeared:
DeviceBootStartEnd Sectors Size ID Type
/Dev/dsk1*829115571554515bFAT32

Nigel typed in the following commands to launch the malware:
/Dev/dsk1/fanciest_bear_launch
Moments later, a series of dots appeared.

"One minute, people," Norris reminded.

The engineers began to scatter.

"You should go too," Nigel said to Sally.

"No, I want to see what you do next," she answered.

"Thirty seconds!"

A second or two later, a blinking cursor appeared. Then another message was displayed:

Your PC is now stoned!

"What's that? Did it work?" Sally asked.

"Yup, Mr. Chen will start receiving his precious data momentarily. Our work is done, let's roll," Nigel said as he removed the flash drive.

Nigel and Sally ran toward the Norris's hiding spot, but he was already gone.

"Meet us on the far side of the floor, we are climbing the tower," Norris said.

Nigel and Sally positioned themselves between two racks of servers. Nigel headed toward the exit sign across the room. When they got to the end of the row, he noticed a door to his left, the exit sign was to the right. Nigel started for the exit when a banging sound emitted from the floor. He looked back to see men with all manner of weapons pouring out of the door. Soon Nigel and Sally were surrounded.

"Stop! Hands where I can see them," an authoritative voice said.

Sally got on her knees and put her hands on her head. As Nigel raised his hands, he formed an exit strategy. About five feet away, a red button encased in glass beckoned him. The words "Emergency Stop" was just above the button.

I bet that button shuts off the power. I must get to it, somehow.

He leaped toward it. Some men opened fire. The shots were deafening. Nigel's ears rang, but he was still alive. The searing, white-hot pain shot through his shoulder. It was the most excruciating pain he had ever experienced.

I can't feel my arm!

Nigel attempted to smash the glass, but his right arm was useless.

"Hold your fire!" a man shouted.

Nigel was able to smash the glass with his left hand just

fine. His fist not only penetrated the glass, it smashed the button, obliterating it. Moments later, the entire room went dark. Nigel ran away from the men and he fled toward the exit.

"Nigel, you copy?" Norris said.

The words amplified through Nigel's earpiece.

"Yeah," Nigel replied. "I've been shot, I think."

"You need to get to the stairs."

Nigel looked back. The guards had surrounded Sally, and men were running after him. Nigel made it to the farthest stairwell. He flung open the door with his good hand. Norris and a group of engineers were huddled behind the stairs leading up.

"Is Sally with you?" Norris asked.

"They caught her," Nigel said.

"Bolt that door, now!" Norris shouted.

Two engineers opened a case about the size of a medium suitcase and removed some kind of machine; to Nigel, it resembled a drill. An engineer tried closing the door, but the men on the other side finally caught up. Several other engineers joined in, trying to keep the door closed. The engineer with the machine shot into the floor. A thick nail was sticking out, blocking the door.

"That will serve as our locking mechanism. Now hurry to the next level. According to the plans I have, we need to cross the floor every other level. We will bolt the doors as we ascend."

Norris shoved a map into Nigel's good hand. "Navigate us up the tower."

Nigel guided Norris and his group of engineers through a series of stairwells and hallways he was certain were unoccupied. After they ascended a few floors, Nigel collapsed.

"Go, I'm just going to slow you guys down," Nigel said.

"We leave no man behind," Norris said as he rummaged through his pack.

He instructed Nigel to take his shirt off, and then inspected the wound. "I think the bullet went through, but you are losing blood."

Norris took out some antibacterial ointment and bandages. After he patched Nigel, he took out a hypodermic needle and shoved it into Nigel's arm.

"Come on, soldier," Norris urged, "the battle is not over."

"The pain," Nigel said, "it's gone."

Norris smiled, then patted Nigel on the back. "Only the best for my team, kid."

Nigel guided Norris and the remaining engineers through the various levels of the windowless building. There weren't many people on these levels, and the machines would provide cover. When the group reached the twenty-sixth floor, Nigel noticed a lot more security cameras. They had been able to avoid the few security cameras before, but this floor had way too many.

"Wait, if we don't disable those cameras, then security will pinpoint our location," Nigel pointed out.

"What do you suggest?" Norris said.

"Does anyone have a laptop?"

An engineer took a laptop out of a backpack and gave it to Nigel. With his good hand, Nigel navigated and could use the hacking tools on the engineer's laptop to access the local network. Nigel inserted a shiny red metal flash drive into the laptop. A terminal window displaying green text on a black window appeared. A system message also appeared:

Operation BedBug 2.0 successful. You now have eyes in the sky. Remember to use this power with care.

With the aid of the helper program operation BedBug provided, he could control the camera system. He recorded a two-minute snippet of footage, then would play it back as Norris's team slipped in undetected all the way up the tower.

Guard post, Windowless Building, New York

Bryon Kowalski loved his new gig as a night watchman. His security clearance allowed him to take employment at one of the most secure facilities on the east coast. The best part was Jeremiah was dead, and he would not interfere in his life again. He often wondered if he should pursue the relationship he had with Jeremiah's daughter. He hadn't reached out when he heard of his death. On some level the man still terrified him.

When the time was right, Bryon planned to visit his daughter—well, she wasn't his real daughter, but he thought of her as one. His friends at the Dark Angels had gotten him this job; hell they'd done more than that, they had saved his life. Being on a platform in the middle of the Black Sea with no one to talk to for weeks at a stretch was almost too much to bear.

At least I'm not on that dammed platform again, he thought.

The phone rang. He glanced at the caller ID. *Security from the twenty-third floor. I've never gotten a call from anyone that high. That area is top secret.*

Bryon picked up.

"Is this the main desk?" a voice asked.

"Yes, it is, can I help you?" Bryon replied.

"I just wanted to make sure—there have been a lot of systems problems in the tower, and we never have problems."

"What's the emergency?"

"We caught a group of intruders on a frame of video. One moment there were the machines and an empty row of metal racks, and the next a group of at least three were visible. The strangest thing is they looked like teenage kids."

"Are you sure someone didn't bring their kids to work or something?" Bryon suggested.

The guard hesitated for a moment.

"No, this floor is supposed to be locked down to all non-essential personnel."

The phone went dead.

Moments later, his phone rang again. It was IT Security. Bryon picked it up.

"Are you the duty guard?" a male voice asked.

"I am," Bryon replied. "Who is this?"

"I'm Frank from Cyber Incident Response. We need to lock down the building to all visitors. Lock all entrances—we have a communications breach."

"I hate to break it to you, Frank, but I think it goes beyond communications. The guard on the twenty-third spotted a group of kids. Anyway, I will need an authorization code to start any lockdown protocol."

Bryon heard a click as the phone went dead.

Hmm, I guess there was a communications problem. I don't know why he called me—he should have called the security operations center. Is it down?

Bryon called the operations center himself. If there was a real security issue, they needed to know about it. The line was dead. Now the phone system was nonoperational. He grabbed one of the handheld radios and switched it to the secure channel—dead.

What the hell is going on here?

Bryon took out his cell phone, and the display read: *No Service*

"Shit, something is happening."

After a few more agonizing moments of indecision, Bryon decided to initiate a full building lockdown. He unlocked a small safe behind the desk and took out a red envelope that contained a single key. After locking the doors of the main entrance, Bryon hurried down a darkened hallway. He unlocked another nondescript door, then entered. It was about the size of a janitor's closet, except instead of brooms, it contained a rack of wires and equipment locked behind a glass cabinet. He used his special key to unlock the cabinet.

What's next? he wondered.

He couldn't remember the procedure he had learned during his onboarding ritual. That week had been a blur and involved many sleepless nights. He remembered stressing about the exam required at the end of that week. When he'd asked what would happen if he failed the exam, his instructor had given him a look of contempt.

"If you cannot pass the exam after a week of training, then someone made a poor hiring decision," the instructor had said.

The drawer!

He tried pulling on the edge of the blank area of the cabinet; it didn't budge. He punched the cabinet out of frustration.

I'm going to get fired for sure. I need this job since Jeremiah ruined my reputation in the industry. I'm glad that bastard is gone.

Then the blank panel he'd tried to pull popped out. He was then able to pull the drawer the rest of the way out.

Stupid trick panel.

He opened the panel. A black screen with green text appeared. He typed in his username, then entered the password when prompted. A system menu appeared with two options:

1) *Start Lock Down Protocol.*
2) *Exit.*

He pressed the number one button, which then asked him for his login to confirm. Once he did, a siren with a female voice emitted from unseen speakers. The light inside of the room went out, and the only illumination came from the equipment and LED lights on the network sockets.

The power is out too?

"Building lockdown started. Please gather in your designated emergency area," the female voice said.

He took out a portable flashlight, secured the cabinet, then made his way back to the guard post. Gates were lowering from the ceiling. He heard a massive clunking sound as the last gate descended. The bars reminded him of a prisoner locked in an isolation cell.

Communications are out—I can't leave. What now?

Stewart Norris attempted to open the door leading to the roof. It was locked.

"We're trapped," an engineer said.

Norris looked in the direction of the voice. The engineer looked like he was in high school. He had a frightened look that Norris knew well.

"We have other options," Norris said as he removed his pack.

Voices were ascending to their location. Norris removed his sidearm and thrust it into the hands of a nearby engineer.

"I need to prep the door, shoot anyone who interrupts us," he said.

"I would do it, kid, but my arm is messed up," Nigel told the engineer.

The engineer looked frightened, but Norris ignored the look and focused his attention on his pack. He removed a brick of clay wrapped in plastic. He untangled some wires with some clips and buried them into the brick. Then he peeled something off the other side of the brick and shoved the brick against the door near the lock. Next, he unwrapped the wires and strung them from the door to a safe location in the stairwell.

"They are here!" the engineer's voice said in a shrill tone.

The kid held the gun toward the ascending men, who held automatic-looking weapons. Norris grabbed the gun, then shot the closet man in the face. Two other men retreated. He shot toward them, then holstered the weapon when he was sure they were gone. He ascended the half-flight of stairs that led to his pack.

"Keep you heads down," Norris said.

Norris grabbed a black box with two metal posts with over-sized knobs. He loosened the knobs enough to wrap the wires around the posts. After he tightened the screws, he looked around. More men were ascending to their location.

It's now or never, Stew, he told himself.

"Get your heads down," Norris yelled.

The group of young engineers obeyed.

He huddled against Nigel and the frightened kids who had braved one of the most secure facilities in the United States, then pressed the button. The noise was deafening. Norris looked up to see a missing door; part of the wall was missing, as well.

I guess I used too much explosive.

"Move!" Norris shouted.

The group of young engineers rushed past, heading toward the smoking doorframe. Norris grabbed the automatic weapon his victim had dropped. The men kept coming, and this time they were carrying shields. Norris started shooting anyway. One of the bullets ricocheted off one of the shields and hit one of his legs. White-hot pain stung his shin; he could still move it, so his shielded boots must have absorbed some damage. Two of the shielded men were mere feet away. They were awkwardly trying to hold their shields and weapons as they climbed the stairs. Then Norris flung himself at the men, both of whom fell on their backs. He flung away their shields, unsheathed his knife, and then started stabbing the men. He didn't know how many times he'd stabbed them, but the wall and floor were spattered with blood. He snapped out of it when he heard one of the kids scream something.

"The helicopter is here!"

It took Norris longer than normal to climb to the blown door. Pain shot through his leg as he moved it. The engineers were ascending a ladder attached to the helicopter.

I didn't know the Dark Angels had a Blackhawk.

The massive satellite dishes on the roof prevented the helicopter from getting any closer. Behind them, a small group of men filed out of the blown doorframe and started shooting at the helicopter as Norris made it to the ladder. He freed a grenade from his belt, pulled the pin, and then threw the explosive in an arc that seemed to be too high.

I hope I calculated correctly—

"Argh," Norris screamed as bullets peppered his armor. It was if someone was hitting him with a hammer.

Moments later, the grenade exploded just above the men's heads. Body parts and gore splattered the area where the guards had been. Norris hung on as the chopper moved away from the building. Seconds later they were flying over the East River. Norris barely made it to the interior of the chopper as it accelerated quickly into the fall evening air.

Minutes earlier

As Gerald Scott piloted his chopper across the Manhattan skyline, he put on his aviator glasses to block out the glare of the late afternoon sun. His dream of becoming a full member of the Dark Angles was becoming a reality.

"Get ready back there," Gerald said.

"I was born ready," Seymour said.

Gerald didn't care much for his passenger, but he had helped him get into the Dark Angels and that had to account for something.

There it is!

The windowless building gave the Manhattan skyline an eerie look, as it was the only building without a light source. As the sun dipped under the western horizon, many buildings already had their internal structures illuminated from various light sources. The building he flew toward was quite the contrast; it looked like a black hole in comparison to everything else.

They better be ready—I won't be able to stay long.

Moments later he saw several people on the roof of the windowless monstrosity.

"Lower the rope, Seymour," Gerald said.

Seymour untied the wench that controlled the rope and begun to lower it.

Gerald got as close as possible to the rooftop of the windowless building. He had to be careful because there were many antennas and satellite dishes on the roof, which made any expeditious extraction impossible.

Gerald switched frequencies, trying to gauge if he had been spotted. The radio was dead.

Something must be jamming the signal.

As the engineers began climbing the ladder, Gerald heard screams. He looked out the window and one of the engineers was falling to his death.

"Someone's shooting at us—take evasive action," Gerald said.

"I'm on it," Seymour said.

Seymour opened one of the back seats in the helicopter and removed a semiautomatic weapon. He checked the clip and chamber. He looked toward the rooftop for signs of an attacker.

"Eleven o'clock," Gerald said.

Seymour started firing in the eleven o'clock position at another helicopter. Moments later, an explosion illuminated his target. Seymour helped the engineers into the helicopter.

"We have wounded," an engineer said.

Seymour looked down. Apparently one of the engineers had been shot, and his arm no longer worked. He lowered a harness attached to a steel cable. Norris helped him into it and hoisted the kid to the helicopter.

"Thank you," Nigel said to Seymour.

Seymour nodded.

"Norris is on the ladder—let's get out of here," Seymour said.

Gerald flew eastbound out of Manhattan. Moments later, Norris hoisted himself into the helicopter.

"That was too close. You should warn Titus. All hell is breaking loose in there," Norris said.

"My radio is dead—it's either out, or someone is jamming us," Gerald said.

"Was the malware—or worm, as you call it—active?" Norris asked.

"It was active the minute it was uploaded. Anything that worm crawls into will be infected," an engineer said.

"Any computer?"

"No—the worm exploits a flaw in the High Tower OS subsystem. Since most of the world's computers use that operating system, it's a matter of time before everything is infected."

The radio came to life.

"What is your status, flying angel?" a male voice asked.

"Identify," Gerald said.

"I'm the one with the cold breeze on a summer's night."

"Titus?"

"Affirmative."

"Heading to the roost, one casualty."

"Sally was taken," Nigel said.

"Correction, one casualty and an MIA," Gerald said.

"That's regrettable. Damien will want to break his daughter out. I will prepare myself in case he needs persuasion on why that's a bad idea. I'm en route via the underground," Titus said.

"See you soon, old friend," Gerald said.

CHAPTER 23

DESPITE ITS AGE, the Bromwick had many amenities, and the conference room was no exception. As the late afternoon gave way to evening, the conference room glowed with blue and white lights interior designers called mood lighting. After several days of meetings, the principal members of the Cabal looked exhausted.

"We have accomplished a lot over the past two days, and regrettably, tomorrow will be our final day together before we test our delivery system. I want to ensure everything is perfect before we proceed," Mr. Chen said.

Ezekiel barged into the room. "You all should see this."

He activated the projector systems and brought up one of the local news channels. A massive skyscraper with no windows appeared. Spotlights shone on the monolithic structure; the shadows and impending darkness made it look more imposing.

"What is this place?" Mr. Tage said.

"It is where all the information we require gets spilled, like the lifeblood of a wounded solider," Mr. Chen said.

"You knew about this?" Dahlia asked.

"It wasn't supposed to happen until our testing of the

malware was complete, but our parallel strike will be even more effective now."

"You knew about it, and kept it from us?"

Like a viper, Dahlia moved in for the kill. Ezekiel held a massive hand out, trying to stop her.

"I knew you were fighting a war on multiple fronts, but you should have let us in on this one," Mr. Tage said to Chen.

"This is an outrage! You have broken our trust. I demand you fill us in on everything—no more secrets," the Sultan said.

Mr. Chen held a hand out. "Calm down, I thought you would be happy at the news. Project Reckoning has begun."

"And what about getting the material needed for the cyborgs?" Dr. Ash said.

"We strike the Ohio Valley Nuclear Reactor tomorrow. The news of this dark data hub breach will be all over the news for days. When they hear the news that the facility has been spying on them for decades, the public outrage will be palpable. We will steal the bismuth material we need to ensure the creation of polonium. Just make sure you all are ready," Mr. Chen said.

"I already have a dozen cyborgs waiting nearby. I didn't have enough skin to make them perfect, so some metal might show in places, but they are immune to radiation. We just need to make sure the hack gets deployed," Dr. Ash said.

"Speaking of which, how is our young hacker doing?" Mr. Tage said.

"Which one?" Mr. Chen asked.

"Freeman is still on for the test, and we have Nigel waiting to assist," Dahlia said.

Sally Wilde sat in a small featureless interrogation room deep inside the legendary windowless building. A table attached to a wall and two chairs were the only furnishings. Her right arm was handcuffed to a ring embedded in the nearby wall; its elevated position made her arm ache from the lack of circulation.

I have done it. Father would be proud. I just hope the stories of the government spooks are not real. I hope Nigel and the other engineers got out—

The only door to the room opened. An older man with a thick stack of papers entered. He dropped the bundle on the table. The commotion interrupted Sally's train of thought.

This guy is trying to scare me. No way my capture has generated that much paper.

The man was dressed in a typical black suit that screamed FBI agent.

"You don't seem very comfortable," the agent said, looking at her restraint.

He placed a key in front of her. Sally stared at it for a long moment.

"Go ahead," he said, "make yourself comfortable. I'll wait."

The man watched her every move. After a moment, Sally grabbed the key with her free hand. She almost dropped it, but she straightened it with her mouth, then unlocked the cuff from her right hand. The agent watched the handcuffs dangle on the hook.

"My name is Agent Ralston of the FBI, and I'm here to help you, Sally."

Yeah, I bet! You want to know where my father is!

"What's in the stack?" Sally asked.

Agent Ralston placed a pack of cigarettes on the table. Sally was drawn to them like a fish to water.

"Cooperate, and maybe I will let you have a smoke. Heavens knows I need one."

He took out one of the cigarettes, put it in his mouth, and lit up. He blew the smoke toward the ceiling so it wouldn't get in her face. Sally realized she was staring at the cigarette. She forced herself to look away and licked her lips.

"Isn't it illegal to smoke in government facilities?"

"It would be if we were sitting in one."

"Wait—isn't this windowless monstrosity containing a secret surveillance operation?"

Agent Ralston laughed. "Did you father tell you that?"

He's a Fed—I'm sure he knows all about Daddy!

"Who owns the building, then?" she asked.

"Didn't you notice the NET logo signs as you snuck in? This building belongs to Northeastern Telecommunications, but there are government agents working within the confines of these walls."

Sally shifted in her seat, trying to find a more comfortable position. She hated to admit how much she needed a smoke.

I should have never taken up that filthy habit—another consequence of my sweet sixteen party, I suppose.

Agent Ralston pushed the cigarettes a few inches in her direction.

"I'm a minor child," she said. "The only evidence you have is trespassing. Soon you will need to let me go."

"Yes, you are a minor, but at the end of the month you turn eighteen. I'm sure you don't want to spend it in a cell."

"I'm not saying anything."

Sally crossed her arms and gave Ralston a defiant look. His eyes moved to her right arm.

"Interesting tattoo," Ralston said. "Where did you get it? Those yellow eyes are creepy!"

Sally looked surprised at the sudden change of subject. She

examined the tattoo on her forearm as if noticing it for the first time. "Daddy calls me his crimson dragon."

Agent Ralston took another drag, then used the bottom portion of the table to extinguish it.

"Come on, Sally, you don't need to protect the group you work for. I can get your sentence reduced to five years from the twenty-to-life you are facing. And, when you get out, you will have a government job waiting for you. Don't you want to put those hacking skills to good use?"

Sally's eyes widened. "Twenty years for trespassing?"

"That's only one of your charges. The district attorney for the southern district wants to charge you with domestic terrorism. That carries a minimum of twenty years without the possibility of parole. I know you want to make the smart choice here."

"I don't get it! Why the harsh punishment for trespassing on a non-government facility?"

"Telecommunications companies were reclassified as critical infrastructure more than twenty years ago. We consider an attack on one of these facilities an attack on the United States. I will give you time to think on it."

Agent Ralston took the handcuffs, cigarettes, and the enormous stack of papers and then headed toward the door.

"Wait!" Sally called.

Agent Ralston turned to face her.

"Aren't you going to cuff me again?"

"That won't be necessary," he replied, "we have eyes on you. Just think of all the good you can do."

He paused for emphasis, then left.

Nigel watched as the sun set over Manhattan; the view from the helicopter would have been pleasant under other circumstances.

People got hurt today, and it's my fault.

The spotlights that shone on the windowless building reminded Nigel of one of many World War II movies he and his brother Ralphie would watch together. All of that seemed a lifetime ago.

"You did well, kid. Welcome to the Dark Angels," Norris said as he gave Nigel a pat on his good shoulder.

Nigel grunted as a fresh wave of pain shot through his arm. It seemed to settle in his shoulder.

Norris examined Nigel.

"You've been hit," he said. "Take your jacket off."

Nigel screamed as he attempted to take the garment off.

"Our physician will attend to you the moment we land."

Nigel's vision faded.

"Stay with me, kid."

Norris took something out of a white plastic box, and then shoved it into Nigel's good arm. A jolt of adrenaline shot through his system. For a moment he forgot all about the pain. Norris removed his jacket, then used the supplies in the white box to bandage the wound.

"You're lucky, the bullet went through. I've stopped the bleeding for now. But you will need medical attention."

Nigel heard the words. The combination of the adrenaline and whatever else Norris shot into him was having an effect.

It took less than an hour to get to his destination, but it felt like an eternity.

I'll be with you soon, Jet . . . I hope!

Later that evening

Nigel awoke in a hospital bed, but he wasn't in a hospital.

"Good, you're awake," a man said.

Nigel couldn't see the man clearly due to the overhead positioning of the lights, as well as the smoke emanating from the man.

"Who are you?" Nigel asked.

"I'm Damien Wilde, but my friends call me Dragon."

Nigel looked around the room. He could hear several people but couldn't make out any of the words. He could also hear the engines of vehicles and aircraft.

"You're safe for the time being, but we will need to move out soon. If Chen hasn't sent for you soon, then you will come with us."

"Where?"

"I'm not going to divulge that information just yet—not all the Angels are accounted for."

"Sally—she was captured. I tried to get to her, but the men . . ." Nigel trailed off.

"I know, son. It's not your fault. She knew the risks. She's a good soldier; she will not give us up."

"Thank you for attending to my injuries."

"It's the least we could do, but we should be thanking you."

"For what?"

"You took a bullet for the Angels, and we don't forget our friends. If you ever need us, we will be there."

The man gave Nigel something on a gold chain. Nigel noticed the man was in his mid-forties and had an eye patch. His sleeveless black shirt revealed a tattoo of an enormous snake fighting with a dragon.

Nigel held up the gold chain; attached to it was a pendant that resembled an angel made of obsidian.

"If you ever find yourself in need, just show that emblem to any Dark Angel and they will die for you. You are one of us now," Damien said as he left.

Moments later, Norris and several engineers came to check on Nigel.

"How you holding up, kid?" Norris asked.

"Better, but my arm and shoulder feel like they got run through a meat grinder," Nigel answered.

"I know that feeling well, but it will pass. I just wanted to let you know someone from Chen's organization will pick you up soon."

"Are we going after Sally?"

Norris gave Nigel a pained look. It was the most emotion he'd seen from the man.

"As much as it pains Damien to leave his little girl in the custody of the Feds, we cannot go after her. Too much is at stake."

"Sally is his daughter?"

"Yeah, she's had a rough go of it. She will need to endure captivity—for the time being, anyway."

Nigel repressed a pang of guilt.

I'll help you, Sally, but Jet also needs my help.

"It was a pleasure working with you, sir," an engineer who looked like he was fifteen said.

"What's your name?" Nigel asked.

"Where are my manners? This is Chip, he is my son," Norris said.

Nigel was speechless. He had no idea that Norris took his family on missions. Chip was the engineer that Norris had given the gun to.

Brave kid—but it probably goes with the territory of having a commando for a father.

The other engineers introduced themselves, and Nigel took mental notes of their names: Phillip, Jack, and Blaine.

Nigel heard some commotion some distance away; he couldn't tell what was going on, but several men were shouting, and he heard the clicking sounds of weapons.

"Stand down," Damien said.

"I think your ride is here. It was a pleasure working with you, son," Norris said.

Nigel gave Norris a nod.

Moments later, Blanka was escorted in by Damien. Nigel tried to get out of bed and almost fell. The engineers helped him stand.

"Bring him to the car," Blanka said.

Nigel and Blanka were driving through a darkened forest, heading back to the city.

"Where are we?" Nigel asked.

"Southern Connecticut," she replied. "The Dark Angels have several bases among the islands just off the coast."

"Thanks for picking me up. Are you taking me to see Jet?"

Blanka didn't say anything for a long time.

"No, Nigel, I'm sorry, but you're needed at the Bromwick."

CHAPTER 24

JET AWOKE to the sound of machinery. Her entire field of vision consisted of the floor. She tried moving her head, but something prevented it. She tried again with more force, and while she was able to move it slightly, a wave of pain shot through her neck and shoulders.

"Hello? Is there anyone there?" Jet yelled.

She didn't expect anyone to answer, but to her surprise someone did.

"My dear, you better not fret, the doctor will be here soon," a woman's voice said.

"Who are you?"

My name is Gretta, and you were brought to the doctor after your . . . accident."

"When will the doctor be back? This is uncomfortable, and—"

"The doctor will be back soon, dear. You cannot move your head without further injuring yourself, but I do have some VR goggles I can put on your head."

"Do you have access to the Colossal Machine?"

"The *what*?"

"It's a game. Maybe if you could download it, I could play."

"Of course, dear. Give me a moment and I'll see about getting it installed."

About an hour later, Jet was controlling her avatar. She used the retinal recognition through the VR interface to get in.

I'm glad I had the biometrics setup, otherwise this woman would know my password, Jet thought. She was in her microcosm, a private area in the Colossal Machine where she could build anything she wanted.

I wonder if I can get back to the dungeon master.

Jet didn't waste any time finding out. She stepped outside her microcosm and was instantly transported to a circular-shaped room with rows of seats that wrapped around her. She was seated in an oversized chair that resembled a throne. She was the only one in the room. She wondered if anyone else was going to show up, or if there was a specific time this council met. She was about to give up when she glimpsed the old man standing nearby.

"Hail, JetaGirl," he said, "are you ready to begin the trials?"

"I am."

"Very well. Once you start you will need to complete all the trials. If you quit early, then you will need to wait a fortnight before resuming. Do you understand?"

"Yes, but I have a question."

"Very well."

"Can you tell me about the trials?"

"It is the ultimate test of your chosen path. Since you are already a Magi, you have a chance to become the highest rank in that path. You will be granted powers befitting the rank, but you will not be all powerful—balance still needs to be maintained."

"How many Grand Magi are there?"

"If you pass the trials, then you will be the first."

"Very well, I'm ready to get started."

The dungeon master waved a gnarled staff, and orbs of light appeared throughout the room. Moments later, nine people and the dungeon master sat nearby.

A beautiful red-haired woman in a formal dress appeared. Her long flowing hair shifted position as she moved toward Jet.

"JetaGirl, I am Countess Negas of the Kingdom of Nigh. Since I hold the position of first chair, I will be moderating the proceedings. Are you ready to be judged?"

"I am ready," Jet said.

"You will be asked a series of questions from each council member. If you answer satisfactorily, you will be granted the title of Grand Magi. This title is permanent and takes precedence over all other titles. Do you understand?"

"I understand."

An old woman with long silvery hair wearing a full-length blue dress stood at the podium positioned about ten feet away.

"I am the Baroness of the High Terrace," the woman said. "You are entrusted with the royal purse of the kingdom. But first you must answer this question." The woman paused, looking steadily at Jet. "You come across a starving man who has not eaten in weeks. He asks you for a silver piece. You only have the money entrusted to you. Do you give him the silver piece, or do you let him starve?"

"I would give him the silver piece so he could buy food. Then, when I get back to court, I would beg the King's forgiveness, then offer to reimburse the royal treasury," Jet said.

The old woman left and was replaced by an older fighter who bore many scars.

"I am Sir Gladdus of Strombach, and please answer true," he said.

"I will, Sir Knight," Jet replied.

"You are assigned to guard a gate that has not seen battle for many moons. You are asked to join in a battle to slay a dragon that has plagued the kingdom for ages. The commander asks for you to join. If you do, the party has more than a good chance at victory. Do you join in the battle knowing you can deny your involvement if the battle doesn't go as planned, or will you uphold your oath and guard the post?"

Jet thought about it for a moment before answering.

"I would obey my orders and maintain the post I was assigned."

The man gave Jet a look of surprise, but she thought she saw an approving look on the man's face.

Many more questions were asked, Jet answered honestly. The last council member took Jet by surprise: Queen Amerdelle, the Mad Queen, stood before her.

"It is good to meet your acquaintance again," Queen Amerdelle said.

"Thank you, Your Majesty," Jet said.

The Mad Queen smiled.

"You are married to the most handsome man in all the land," she began. "He has taken ill and has only days to live. You can extend his life by feeding him the heart of a virgin. You calculate your village has more than fifty across the lands. Will you kill the virgins to save your beloved, or will you watch him die in your arms?"

What kind of question is this? This must be a trick.

"I will not harm others for personal benefit," Jet said.

The Mad Queen looked disappointed, then left without another word.

The countess took the podium.

"We shall discuss your answers. Enjoy our hospitality while you are here," the countess said.

Jet watched the council members leave the chamber and enter a side room. She didn't know how long they would be gone, but she intended to not go far. She left the council chamber from a different exit than the one she had entered the last time she'd been here. She found herself atop a large parapet. She gazed over an enormous chasm. Waterfalls, streams, and mountains could be seen from her vantage point. A small child, about five, was perched atop the railing.

"Hello, are you the Magi?" the boy asked. "Are you ready to become the first Grand Magi of the realm?"

Jet didn't answer for a long moment. The boy looked at her.

"I'm not sure," she replied. "It would depend on the requirements, I suppose."

"Why is that important?"

"Because, my priority is my beloved, and if he needs help, then he would come first."

"Good answer," the boy said.

Then the boy aged almost a hundred years in a few moments. It was the dungeon master.

"You have passed the ultimate test," he said. "You are fit to be Grand Magi. We shall announce you to the kingdom in one fortnight. Until then, you have all the powers and privileges of a Grand Magi. Your first assignment is to investigate disturbances of power in the circle of Nexus."

"Is this another test?" Jet asked.

The dungeon master laughed.

"Not in an official capacity, but you will need to learn how to defend against dark powers. The person causing a disruption has been elevated to power that is beyond the capabilities of a Grand Magi. If you put an end to the disturbance, you shall be heralded throughout the lands as the Avatar, the champion of the realm."

"Sure, I will heed the challenge."

What do I have to lose?

Jet was pulled out of the Colossal Machine.

She pulled off her VR goggles and blinked. Moments later

an older man who looked at least eighty appeared. His white hair and chiseled facial features reminded her of her grandfather.

"Hello, Josephine, I'm Dr. Gruber, and I need to perform another surgery on your lower back. Are you ready to proceed?"

"Where am I?"

"We have stopped the bleeding, but we need to get to work quickly if we are to save your legs."

The stark reality came crashing upon her.

Rick Watson awoke in his hotel room with a massive headache. He had not slept very well since that cyborg mistress had put him up to all of those . . . activities.

I never thought a whip could bring so much pleasure—and pain.

He got up and was about to use the restroom when a rapping noise interrupted his hangover. He opened the door to find Dr. Ash with a worried look.

"I hate to bother you at such an early hour, but could I have a moment of your time?" Dr. Ash said.

"Sure, come in," Rick said.

"Nozomi has gone missing for more than twenty hours. She's never out of touch for that long."

"From what I've seen, she can take care of herself."

"Indeed, but I have a bad feeling about her situation. I account for all of her nutrition cartridges. That means she doesn't have a spare. She could be injured, or worse . . ." Dr. Ash trailed off.

"What's worse than being injured?"

"Being captured!"

"I don't think that happened. Who would want to capture Nozomi?"

"Someone that wishes to study her—wait, I think I know where she is."

"Where?"

"She's with a Dr. Sylvester, otherwise known as Doc Chop."

"Who the hell is that?"

"Someone that Nozomi was brokering a deal with. We were supposed to be trading cyborg technology secrets, but he has double-crossed Nozomi," Dr. Ash explained. "I'm needed here, but could you check on Nozomi?"

"Consider it done, but where should I look?"

"His last known location is near the abandoned train station. Near Sakura Park, he has a lab nearby and out of sight."

"Sure thing."

Dr. Ash thanked Rick, then left him to his thoughts.

Blanka assisted Nigel with gathering ice and applying it to his shoulder. The ordeal at the windowless tower and the trauma of getting shot had taken a lot out of Nigel. He took one of the pills the medic provided.

Only a few left. I'll need to get more if I want to keep the pain at bay.

Nigel was snapped out of these thoughts by an incessant knocking on the door. When Nigel didn't get up, the knocking turned into banging.

"Just wait, I'll be right there," Nigel scoffed.

"No, rest, I'll get rid of them," Blanka said.

"Is Nigel here?"

Nigel recognized the voice of his father.

"I think you should leave and let Nigel rest," Blanka replied.

"Rest? From what? Too much sex?" Rick said as he barged in.

Rick paused when he noticed his son.

"What do you want?" Nigel asked.

"You're hurt!"

"Yeah, that happens when you get shot."

The blood drained from his father's face. He started pacing; Nigel knew from experience he only did that when he was worried about something. He remembered how much his father had paced when Ralphie had been born.

"I'll come back—"

"What is it now, Rick?" Nigel said.

"I . . . need your help, Nige. Something bad has happened."

"Bad? Like getting shot?"

"She's gone!"

A pang of fear gripped Nigel. "Who is?"

"Nozomi. Dr. Ash thinks she's been captured."

I thought he was talking about Jet for a moment.

"I need your help to locate her," Rick said in an urgent tone.

"She hurt Jet, why should I help her?" Nigel asked.

Rick paused for a moment.

"She's the only one who knows where Jet is."

He's probably lying, but maybe if I help him, he will help me get Jet back.

"I'll do it on one condition. You take me to see Jet."

"That isn't true," Blanka said as she applied ice to Nigel's shoulder.

Rick looked unsure of himself. "Yeah," he said, "but we need to get Nozomi back first."

"Where is Jet?" Nigel demanded.

"Jet is at a safe location—only Madam knows," Blanka said.

"And when were you going to tell me that?"

"Tonight," Blanka replied. "It all happened fast—I was going to tell you, I promise."

Rick looked like a wild animal about to chew off his arm.

"She is well taken care of. She is being treated very well by a doctor and his wife," Blanka said.

"I'm sorry for deceiving you, son, but I was afraid you wouldn't help . . ." Rick trailed off.

No one said anything for a long, tense moment.

"Can you give me any clues to her last known location?" Nigel said.

Rick looked relieved. "According to Dr. Ash, she was going to meet someone near Sakura Park a couple of days ago," he said.

Nigel motioned for his laptop, and Rick handed it to him. Moments later, he pulled up a map of Sakura Park. "This area is huge," he said. "Did you get any other clues?"

Rick seemed to be straining to remember something.

"Oh—she did say something about a lab being close to an abandoned train station—near 91st street."

"Those areas are several blocks apart. Let me see what I can find."

"Okay, I'm going back to New York tonight."

"What? Why? Does the cyborg mean that much to you?"

"I gave Dr. Ash my word," Rick said.

Yeah, you care more about a murderous cyborg than your real family, Nigel thought bitterly.

"Well, how do I contact you? The cell phone Blanka gave me doesn't have a SIM chip."

"Can't you message me?"

"No, this phone is locked down. It only contains the authenticator apps I need to get into certain hacking sites. I can't use any conferencing apps anyway, since Mr. Chen has all of those ports blocked."

"Wait, I'll be right back," Rick said as he left.

Nigel busied himself by doing a little research about the abandoned train station. In 1959, the station had been closed because there were two other stations five blocks on either side of the station.

I guess people didn't want to walk as far for the train back then.

Nigel found all sorts of other interesting information about the abandoned station. Other than the graffiti, the station appeared to be in good shape. Nigel found some videos online of the station; they showed much of the same information he'd found from pictures online, with one notable difference. Whoever had taken the video had run down the tracks as he filmed. He noticed a maintenance entrance. The tracks were well lit, but the side tunnels appeared to be pitch-black.

I wonder what surveillance footage is available.

"I'm going to get you some more ice," Blanka said as she left him to work.

Nigel checked the street cams around the park and the surface area of the abandoned station and saw nothing of interest. He researched for another fifteen minutes. He was fascinated with the hidden crevices he was finding. He didn't even have to hack anything. The information was readily available online.

The door opened, and Nigel watched Blanka enter with a bag of ice, and something else.

"Your father asked me to give you this. He said it's only to be used in an emergency," Blanka said as she handed Nigel a new cell phone.

"Thank you," Nigel said.

Instead of answering, Blanka gave him a kiss. "I hope you

find her. You are a good person, Nigel, and she's lucky to have you."

Nigel was speechless. Both said nothing for a long moment.

"I've got to go," Blanka said.

Nigel stood there for a long time.

I'm going to find you, Jet, I promise.

Nigel put the cell phone behind the laptop where he could retrieve it easily, then continued his reconnaissance. He performed a search of wireless cameras in the immediate area of Sakura Park using an online scanning tool called Show-ALLD. He was able to log in to many of these cameras using the default credentials he got from another surface web information site.

It never ceases to amaze me how many people keep their devices unsecured. They buy them, connect them to Wi-Fi, then stop any attempts at security.

He viewed the live camera footage with views into Sakura Park. He pulled up an online map and made several correlations. He scribbled on some notecards he found in the desk drawer.

Time to get some archival footage.

He couldn't find any archival footage cache attached to any of the cameras, since they were consumer-based models. He accessed the metadata on a few random cameras and, after following the directions on the manufacturers' websites, he was able to log in to the archived video footage using the serial number on the cameras and a password supplied by the owner. After a few more web searches Nigel discovered that when someone bought one of these cameras and created a login, the archived video footage could be accessed from that login—or the camera's serial number—using the same password.

I don't have the time to crack any passwords. I bet I could guess these, though. I'll try a few before using my cracking program.

Nigel tried a few passwords based on Broadway plays and sports teams. At first he was unsuccessful, but he found a camera that faced an area where kids played baseball and tried a few sports passwords. He was in on the third attempt.

Who uses a password of metswon2015, *anyway?*

Nigel was mildly curious if the sports team had a major win that year, but decided he didn't care enough about it, and accessed the footage. He found that the camera had an excellent zoomed-in view of the park. The angle covered the main play area of the park, he could clearly see anyone walking by. He scrubbed the video footage until he found someone resembling Nozomi's appearance. She had been walking and looking at one person. He couldn't see who it was, but he was able to see which direction she went. He used a similar process to access other web cameras in the area. He caught additional glimpses of the person that looked like Nozomi. The best shot came from a camera placed in front of a parrot's cage with a view of the street.

I guess someone wanted to look at their bird while they were at work!

Nigel scrubbed the video footage until he got to the approximate time when Nozomi had taken her stroll. He stopped the footage when he made an identification. Nigel continued this process for what seemed like hours until he had an approximate map of where Nozomi seemed to go. He hit a snag when Nozomi appeared to walk into an alleyway. He pulled an aerial satellite view of the neighborhood and could determine the alley was a dead end.

Two hours later

Nigel awoke to a buzzing noise.

Did I fall asleep at the computer? The buzzing is coming from the direction of the computer.

His shoulder was on fire. He tried to get a pill out of the bottle, but the remaining ones spilled on the floor. Nigel finally swallowed a pill. The buzzing noise resumed.

Nigel retrieved the phone that rested on the computer and answered.

"Nige," Rick said, "I'm at Sakura Park. Can you lead me to the area where Nozomi might be?"

Nigel rubbed the sleep from his eyes.

"Yeah, give me a sec. What time is it, anyway?"

"It's 4:38 a.m."

Nigel examined his hand-drawn maps and led his father to the dead-end alleyway.

"Are you sure this is where she went?" Rick asked.

"I'm positive. She must have entered a door or something."

"I'm not finding any exit from the alley—wait—it can't be?"

"What are you talking about?" Nigel asked.

"I see a utility hole cover, but that's it. I can't see how she could have opened it."

"She's a cyborg and has the strength of at least two or three men. She backhanded me and flung me into the wall, and I was out cold for a while. Opening a utility hole should be easy."

"Let me look for a crowbar. I'll get back to you once I've checked it out. It leads to the sewers or something."

"Don't let the alligators bite."

"What?" Rick asked in a confused voice.

"Nothing, it was a poor joke. I'm going back to sleep."

"Thanks, Nige. I know Nozomi isn't your favorite person, but she's important to me."

Is my dad falling for a cyborg?

Nigel shuddered at the thought.

❖

Nigel was awakened again, this time to a booming sound.

What the hell was that?

Nigel moved as quickly as his injury would let him. Upon opening the curtain, the scene unfolding before him gave him pause. Several people seemed to be rioting outside the Bank of Newport. It was difficult to make out what they were saying with the window closed, but Nigel thought he could hear the words "give" and "money" clear enough. Moments later, the house phone rang with a tone that seemed louder than necessary. Nigel picked up the phone.

"We need you downstairs for lunch in ten minutes," a woman's voice said.

Is that Dahlia? She sounds annoyed.

Nigel got dressed the best he could with his one good hand.

I wish Blanka were here to help me.

Nigel was getting accustomed to having her help him. He was missing her. Moments later, he shuffled into the conference room. All members of the Cabal were present.

"Good afternoon, Nigel, how is the arm?" Mr. Chen said.

"It hurts, and I'm almost out of meds," Nigel snapped.

Blanka and Vedrana helped him into one of the oversized chairs. Nigel noticed another teenager about his age glaring at him.

What's his problem?

"Before we have lunch, we need to go over the plan," Chen said.

"What plan?" Nigel said.

"The plan to raid the Ohio Valley Nuclear Reactor, of course!" Mr. Tage said.

"What? Why are you doing that?"

"Will someone please bring Mr. Watson up to date," Mr. Chen said.

What the hell is going on here?

Mr. Tage and Dr. Ash gave Nigel an overview of the overall plan, and why it was crucial to get the nuclear material.

"We need this material to create the new cyborgs, right? What about the existing cyborgs, like Delta or Nozomi?" Nigel asked.

"Nozomi is part of the Echo series of experiments, which are more advanced than Delta. She has an expected lifespan of sixty years."

"And the Delta series?"

"The Delta series was expected to have a similar lifespan. However, I examined a recent blood sample from Nozomi, and the breakdown of her genetic material has already begun," Dr. Ash explained.

"How long does she have?"

"I estimate she has less than a year remaining, perhaps less. I'm so sorry," Dr. Ash said.

"Now that is settled, here are the assignments. Vedrana, Eva, and Blanka will take point on the mission with Mr. Watson and Freeman providing support. Dahlia will be the commander in charge," Chen said.

"We need a hacker in the field in case there are remote connectivity issues," Dahlia said.

"I will volunteer to go with the onsite team," Freeman said.

Good, because I'm not. Ohio seems like a long way off.

"Out of the question," Dahlia said to Freeman. "We need someone with field experience. I've seen Nigel Watson in action—he will provide the onsite support."

Nigel thought he saw a slight smile on Blanka's face.

"When is this mission taking place?" Nigel asked.

"In less than ten hours," Chen said.

"What? No way I'm going until I know Jet is okay. Are you going back on our deal, Chen?" Nigel said.

The room fell silent. No one said anything for a long time.

"I will honor our arrangement, but if you could help us one last time, you will be a rich man."

"I don't want your money!"

"Nigel, this mission is necessary to help April. She is dying. Her organs are failing. The nuclear material will preserve her life. I think Jet would have wanted that."

Nigel swallowed hard. He was speechless.

"Josephine is safe and resting at the home of a dear friend of mine in a safe location. I will take you there after the mission is complete," Dahlia said.

Nigel's eyes blurred. He wiped away some tears. He hated showing any emotion in front of these vipers. He only trusted one person in this room. After a long moment of reflection, he agreed.

As if on cue, Ezekiel entered. "Lunch is now served."

Blanka and Vedrana assisted Nigel to the banquet hall.

"Vedrana, do you want to dine with me?" Freeman asked.

"No, I'm dining with my sisters and Nigel," she replied. "We need to prepare."

Freeman looked like he had been punched in the stomach. He gave Nigel a contemptuous stare. Nigel shrugged, then followed his lovely companions to their table.

Lunch was delicious. Nigel had duck and several side dishes. He couldn't remember the last time he'd eaten. The assault on the tower seemed like a long time ago. To his surprise, Melissa entered the dining hall. She was alone and sat well away from everyone in the room.

"Melissa!" Nigel yelled, waving his good arm.

The sudden movement caused the pain to resurface. She ran over to him.

"You're hurt," she said.

"I was shot yesterday. It hurts like hell, but it's not the first time someone has taken potshots at me."

Vedrana and Blanka gave each other a look.

"Join us," Blanka said as she made room for Melissa.

"What are you doing here?" Nigel asked.

Melissa gave Nigel a sad look.

"I just sold my stake in the island to Mr. Chen's company."

I'll make Chen pay for this.

Nigel and his female companions shared their experiences from the past several days. A strong bond was forming with the unlikely group. He didn't know Vedrana and Eva as well, but he thought he could trust them.

"Dahlia is going to take us to see Jet once this nightmare is over. You should come," Nigel said.

"I would like that," Melissa said.

A ringing sound emanated from the back of the room. Nigel looked over to see Chen standing and tapping on an expensive-looking glass with a butter knife.

"Your attention, please. Mr. Chen would like to say a few words," Ezekiel said.

"The mission you are about to embark on is not only important to our bottom line, but will allow us to save dear friends and loved ones from extinction," Mr. Chen said. "As Dr. Ash has already informed us, the cyborg known as Delta requires an isotope from the nuclear reactor to survive. Join me in wishing the onsite and remote teams luck."

Melissa looked alarmed.

"Is it true?" she asked Nigel.

"I just found out, Mel—this mission is the only thing keeping me away from Jet," Nigel said.

"Nigel, are you ready?" Dahlia asked.

"We are leaving now?"

"Yes. Get everything you need for the mission and meet in the hotel lobby in thirty minutes. We will travel by train."

Two hours later, Nigel was riding in a luxury coach, heading west toward the Ohio Valley. The train's Wi-Fi was better than he expected. Nigel pulled up the specifications for the reactor. Dr. Ash had provided him with a control module for the cyborgs, and he was to use it only if the cyborgs couldn't function. He checked the signal of the cellular access point that would provide him internet access in the field. The plan was for Freeman to monitor the mission and provide help if Nigel lost signal or couldn't maintain a stable connection to the reactor.

The door to his private sleeper room opened. It was Blanka.

"You look worried," she said. "Are you ready for the mission?"

"I think we have all the contingencies in place, but I'm a little concerned."

"You got this, Nigel."

"It's Freeman. He is my age, but he seems a little immature. He acts like a child sometimes. I'm not sure if he's ready."

Blanka considered this for a moment.

"Do you have the ability to take control of the cyborgs?"

"Yes, I can take ownership if I need to, but it's a last resort, and I may not be able to give control back. It's a risk because mobile connections are unreliable."

"Madam Dahlia will make the right choice. If she senses incompetence or any hesitation of Freeman's part, she will take over. We have you for backup, if nothing else."

"I suppose you're right. I'm so tired."

"Get some rest, Nigel. I'll be in the room next to this one if you need me. Remember, we have the entire carriage, and Vedrana and Eva are watching in shifts. So you can rest easy."

Nigel gave Blanka a smile and watched her leave.

He checked the code one last time before closing his laptop.

CHAPTER 25

TWELVE HOURS later

Freeman and several members of the Cabal crowded into the conference room. Video feeds from body cams on each cyborg were sectioned into squares and displayed on the gigantic screen that took one long wall of the conference room.

"I have modified the code we got off of ProgHub," Freeman said. "All you need to do is tap this button, and the reactor's cooling system will shut down. It should create enough of a diversion to get the materials we need and get out of there."

"Perfect, we will be ready," Dahlia said.

"You won't have much time before the reactor goes into meltdown. We have less than thirty minutes before the rods will overheat. It is crucial the cooling system gets put back online before that happens," Dr. Ash said.

"I'll take that into consideration. It is crucial we get this material," Dahlia said.

"Our agents are in place," Dr. Ash said.

"You're early! Remain on standby, I will call you just before we go in," Dahlia said.

"Nigel, are you ready?"

"Yes, we are in an open field with a direct line of sight to the reactor. I'm prepared to engage manual control if needed," Nigel replied.

"Do that only if necessary. The cyborgs have access to the computational power of my AI. They will lose access if you take control," Dr. Ash said.

"Acknowledged," Nigel said.

"I hope your bots are ready for action, because the guards are on the move," Dahlia said.

"Not to worry, I have everything under control. The agents know what to get from the reactor," Dr. Ash said.

Dahlia examined the camera feed, the cyborgs appeared without any special gear or any other protection from the radiation. "Why don't the cyborgs have protection?"

"My agents—my hunters—are resistant to radiation. I designed the latest generation of the Echo project to thrive in hostile environments. Nuclear energy is not hostile to the hunters—they will use the excess energy as fuel," Dr. Ash said.

"Won't their skin melt off?" Dahlia asked.

"They do not need skin. My hunters will survive. They are in position, shall we proceed?" Dr. Ash said.

"Yes," Dahlia replied as she tapped the red "STOP" button.

A timer superimposed the tablet interface and started counting down from ten minutes.

"Your hunters have less than ten minutes, tell them to move —now."

"Plenty of time, dear," Dr. Ash said in a patient tone.

Dahlia watched as the cyborgs ran toward the guards. They moved so fast that the camera only picked up a blur. Dahlia switched to another camera from the perspective of the closest entrance. She switched just in time to see a cyborg yank a man's arm out of its socket. The man grasped at his damaged arm and attempted to flee, but the cyborg moved in to finish the job. Dahlia couldn't hear anything, but it looked like he was screaming. The cyborg took the guard's gun then shot several times at the elbow, yanked again, and the arm was ripped off. Similar visions of carnage could be seen from different camera angles.

"Look," the Sultan said, pointing to a monitor.

Several armed guards were taking positions outside one of the reactor's side entrances. An object about the size of a tennis ball was thrown into view from off camera. The men tried to scatter—and then the monitor turned to static.

"Why are the cyborgs attacking? We have little time!" Dahlia yelled into the radio.

"I can hear you, dear, you don't have to shout," Dr. Ash, said as if she were talking to a child.

Dahlia switched camera angles. She could see a small group of men huddled around a workstation. They appeared to be trying to figure out what happened. She was about to turn away when a female cyborg with black hair strode into the control room with a samurai sword. She began hacking away at the engineers. Blood sprayed on the walls, and body parts flew like confetti in the wind.

"This carnage is unnecessary and barbaric," Kurtzen said.

"Dr. Ash, the bots are killing everyone in their path, and we need these men to get the reactor back online," Dahlia said.

"My children are at play," Dr. Ash said, smiling.

"I wanted to keep this on the down low," Dahlia said.

"Remember that Ukrainian nuclear meltdown a week ago? History is repeating itself in the Ohio Valley."

"Why are you doing this?"

"I'd thought the answer would be obvious. We have replicated the hack, and once the IT geeks piece everything together, the Red Falcon hacking group will be in jail, and we will be long gone with enough power to bring hundreds of cyborgs online, ushering in the Gamma phase. Not only will the cyborgs be resistant to most environments, they will also live hundreds of years," Dr. Ash said.

"I hear explosions coming from the plant. What the hell is going on?" Nigel asked.

Dahlia tried pressing the green "RESTART" button to get the reactor back online, but it wouldn't respond.

"Freeman, are you there?" she asked.

"I'm here, D," he answered.

"I cannot control the reactor."

"I know!"

"Can you override it and bring it back online?"

"I can, but the cyborgs have not finished their mission."

"They have the material, I saw them take it," Dahlia said.

"That is only part of the mission. The rest of the plan involves melting down the Ohio Valley Nuclear Reactor."

"What? I'm putting a stop to this," Nigel said.

"A meltdown will kill thousands of people," Dahlia said, turning to Dr. Ash.

"Hundreds of thousands, once you calculate the prevailing winds," Dr. Ash interjected.

"It doesn't make sense to attract so much attention, not with the big attacks that Chen has planned," Dahlia said.

"I tried to take manual control, but a skinless cyborg just destroyed my laptop," Nigel said.

"The order to cause a nuclear accident came directly from Mr. Chen. I want my big payday, so that's what we are doing," Freeman said.

"I didn't think the infamous Black Heart would mind killing a few people," Dr. Ash said.

"No, I will not let this happen. I'm going in. I have my tablet, I just need to get close enough to the reactor's network to stop the meltdown," Nigel said.

"I wouldn't advise that, Nigel. Radiation levels at the

reactor are already at 4000 mSv, most die within months of exposure," Dr. Ash said.

"There's no need to kill innocents."

"The revolution has begun. The cyber hunters have set us free," Dr. Ash said.

Several members of the Cabal applauded.

"Well done, team," Mr. Tage said.

Dahlia shot up and appeared to be scanning the room.

"Where's Chen?" she asked.

Nigel watched as several emergency vehicles were dispatched to the Ohio Valley Nuclear Reactor. Although his position in the field was almost a mile away, he wondered when the radiation would come. The cyborgs were returning from their missions. Most of the skin had melted off of their metal frames; it was an eerie sight to behold, with the burning reactor in the background. One of the mechanical monstrosities charged, then stopped short of Nigel. It reached out and placed a metal cylinder in Nigel's hand. To Nigel's surprise, the metal was cool to the touch.

"Decontamination necessary—don't want to damage humans," the cyborg with half a face said.

The remaining cyborgs began to search the immediate area.

What are they looking for?

Just as Nigel finished the thought, the cyborgs began clawing at the soft ground. It looked like they were trying to tunnel their way out.

"Found the decontamination supplies," another cyborg said as it unearthed something. "Step back, human,"

Nigel watched in fascination as a cyborg hoisted heavy-looking canisters out of the ground and hosed off its cyborg comrades.

About five minutes later, an enormous van, large enough to seat ten, stopped less than fifty feet away. Its side door opened.

"We need to leave," Blanka said.

The cyborgs made an attempt at burying the decontamination equipment but gave up on the effort.

"Come with me, human," a cyborg said.

Nigel followed and climbed in the van. He sat in the front with Blanka. Vedrana and Eva sat just behind.

Soon the van was heading east toward Newport.

"I detect you are driving too fast, human. I suggest you slow down so we do not attract any unwanted attention," a cyborg told Blanka.

"You'd better listen to our robot overlords," Nigel told her.

"It will take about ten hours to drive to the Bromwick, so get some sleep," Blanka said. "I'm good to drive for a few hours."

A sudden wave of exhaustion hit Nigel. He hoped he would dream of Jet as he slept.

CHAPTER 26

FREEMAN WAS RECOMPILING the code for Kracken 2.0, the latest version of the malware delivery system. He had tested the code no less than five times.

Are you ready to change the world, Freeman? he asked himself. *Time to show Nigel who the boss is.*

His red phone chirped. He checked the text message from Dahlia. It read:

Your attendance is required in the main conference room immediately.

After countless hours, the moment of truth had come. It was time to execute the malware. Moments after Freeman received the "compile complete" message, he packed his things and made his way to the conference room. When he got there, he opened the door and acknowledged every principal member of the Cabal and their respective lieutenants. There were a few missing, but Freeman didn't care. His mood changed when he realized Nigel Watson was absent. Of all the people in the Bromwick, he hated Nigel most of all.

"Freeman, glad you could join us. Are you ready to launch the delivery system for the malware?" Mr. Chen said.

"I am, I just need access to the latest version of the malware," Freeman replied.

Dahlia produced a red metal flash drive. "Nigel fixed the detection problem," she said. "Please deploy this version."

Freeman grimaced at the sound of Nigel's name. He inventoried the contents of the flash drive, then packed the malware: a process that made it nearly impossible to figure out the true intent of the malicious package. Once he verified the code, he launched his delivery system for the identity-exposing malware.

"It's done. The malware that I call the Kraken has been unleashed," Freeman said.

"The breach of the windowless tower has already caused quite the stir among the law enforcement community. They have dispatched their best cyber defenders to mitigate against the attack," Kurtzen said.

"If that's the case, then won't it be more difficult to expose everyone?" Dahlia asked.

"No, Madam, we got the information we were after," Seymour said.

"What's happening to the map? The colors seem to be changing," Mr. Chen said.

"Those red and orange dots all seem to be concentrated on the United States. So far I don't see a worldwide impact," Dahlia said.

"What's that orange dot? It looks like it is near us, and it is getting larger," the Sultan said.

"It's one of the malware distribution hubs. It's where the malware calls home for instruction," Freeman said.

"I hope it cannot be traced back here," Mr. Chen said.

Freeman pulled up a window with a black background and green text and began typing.

"That's not right—those packets are being routed back.

302 / D. B. GOODIN

There's something wrong with the routing table," Freeman muttered.

"What does that mean?" Mr. Tage said.

"No!" Freeman said.

"What's the matter?" Dahlia asked.

"The malware is using the source IP as the beaconing target, not the hub IP," Freeman said.

"Freeman's routing problem is not the only thing broken. Anyone else have phone service?" Kurtzen said.

The room filled with discontented murmurs as each member of the Cabal checked their cell phones.

"It appears our young hacker friend has broken the internet," the Sultan said.

"I think we need to bring in someone with actual hacking skill. This amateur is not making the cut," Gratzano interjected.

"I think you should get Nigel Watson to untangle this mess," Mr. Tage said.

"I'm afraid Mr. Watson hasn't reported back in yet," Chen said.

"I will find him," Dahlia said as she picked up her phone.

I can't believe this is happening, I must have missed something, but what? What am I going to do now? Freeman thought.

Freeman watched while the traffic was getting rerouted to the Bromwick.

"Look, the orange dot is getting larger, and it appears to be growing over the Bromwick. You better fix your mess, kid, otherwise it's going to get ugly," Gratzano said as he leaned into Freeman's personal space.

Nigel was holding on to the door handle of the van for dear life, as the rain wasn't the only hazard on the road; no sooner had they left the interstate than all the traffic signals began malfunctioning. Blanka narrowly avoided several vehicles that appeared to not bother to stop at any of the red lights. Nigel witnessed a multitude of accidents.

"I've been trying to call the Bromwick since we left the interstate, and no one is picking up," Nigel said.

"I suggest you slow your vehicle to a safe speed to avoid getting into an accident," a skinless cyborg told Blanka.

Blanka slowed the van, but it was no use; cars appeared to be coming from every intersection. Some stopped and allowed others to go, but most of the drivers simply accelerated through the intersections with red lights.

"How far away are we from the Bromwick?" Blanka asked.

"My phone has lost signal, but I think we are about a half mile from the hotel," Nigel said.

"It's too dangerous to drive any further—we need to go on foot," Blanka said.

"With the cyborgs?" Nigel said, surprised.

"We have to risk it. We need to get back to the Bromwick before Freeman launches the attack," Blanka said.

"I think that has already happened."

Blanka stopped the van in the middle of an intersection. All remaining intersections were blocked with accidents or traffic. Nigel grabbed his laptop bag and the metal cylinder the cyborg had given him earlier. The outside casing was cool to the touch.

I expected it to be red hot—what's going on? Nigel wondered.

He got out of the van started jogging through the streets of downtown Newport with his motley crew of cyborgs and teenage assassins.

What a sight we must be—but I'm sure it looks badass.

Nigel ran like the wind as rain continued to come down in rivulets; he had to slow his pace to avoid slamming into people. The passersby saw the skinless cyborgs and jumped aside, giving them plenty of room.

"Great costume, dude," some guy said as they passed by a group of young hipsters.

"There," Blanka said, pointing to the hotel.

"Let's cut through the park," Vedrana said.

"I don't think that park looks safe."

The park was at least a couple of city blocks wide and was the only obstacle left in their path. Nigel picked up the pace and started running toward the Bromwick as fast as his legs would take him. He looked back for a brief moment; Dahlia's young assassins and the cyborgs were just behind him. Then the world went black. Nigel couldn't remember what happened next. It was a blur, but something hit him. His vision blurred, but he was able to see a shape of someone trying to hit him with something heavy.

Am I being attacked? Nigel thought as his vision faded into unconsciousness.

Sometime later, Nigel awoke as splotches of rain soaked his body.

"What happened?" Nigel said, trying to get up.

The pain of getting hit with the baseball bat and landing on his bad arm incapacitated him. But after a brief rest, the pain subsided.

"You got hit with a baseball bat," Blanka said, helping him up. "The man apologized, then ran away. He looked like a homeless person. Are you okay?"

"We will protect you from all future attacks, sir," the skinless cyborg said.

"I'm okay, let's just get to the Bromwick," Nigel said.

The team shuffled toward the hotel at a slower pace. Nigel

couldn't believe the chaos he was witnessing around him. People were smashing windows and looting local stores. Some looters wore face masks to avoid detection, but others didn't bother. Flames engulfed buildings, and vehicles were scattered about like discarded toys. Traffic lights were flashing, and roving groups of people pulled others out of cars and started beating them. Billows of smoke rose from every direction. The Bromwick was the only building that remained unharmed; the massive gathering of armed guards at the front entrance discouraged violence.

This is nuts! What has Freeman done?

Nigel entered the crowded conference room with his group of unlikely companions. Gratzano seemed to be grilling Freeman about something, and the kid looked like he was headed for a nervous breakdown. Everyone—including the giant Ezekiel—gave Nigel and his companions a wide birth.

"There he is, the man of the hour," Mr. Tage said.

"Do you have the material?" Dr. Ash said.

Nigel opened his bag and produced a medium-sized metal cylinder. Solomon grabbed it out of his hands.

"Is this what you need to get started?" Mr. Chen said.

"Yes," Nigel replied. "I'll start my work as soon as I get back to the lab."

Freeman's mouth was wide open, and he glared at Nigel. He looked both frightened and surprised at the same time.

"Show me how everything is constructed. I need to know everything if I'm going to help you," Nigel said to Freeman.

"About a week ago, a series of phishing emails went out to the victims that would act as my zombies. The malware was successfully installed on those computers, and I confirmed I had control over them. Everything looked perfect until we launched the Kraken code," Freeman explained.

Nigel grabbed Freeman's computer as he was typing.

"It will be faster if I just look at what you've done here," Nigel said.

Freeman attempted the take his computer back, but Dahlia grabbed Freeman's hand.

"Let him work," Dahlia said.

Nigel compared the code on Freeman's computer against similar code he had written himself. About fifteen minutes later, Nigel looked up at one of the screens.

"The traffic is getting rerouted away from our location and back to the intended eastbound hub. There was an error in the code you acquired from ProgHub. It created an internet black hole."

"Our cell phones don't work," the Sultan said.

"What Freeman did overwrote some internet service providers' routes to the internet, which caused all local traffic to be routed to an invalid location. This caused a denial-of-service attacks on all local networks," Nigel explained.

"Have we been compromised?" Mr. Chen asked.

"It's too early to tell, but my gut tells me someone has been tracking you. I need to dig into the logs a bit more to know for sure."

"Good job, Nigel," Dahlia said.

"You just hold up your end of the bargain," he replied. "I want to see Jet tonight!"

"It will be done. Blanka and Vedrana will accompany you," Dahlia said.

"We should have hired Nigel from the beginning—Freeman almost cost us everything. See, Chen? I told you Nigel is the best hacker I've seen," Mr. Tage said.

Freeman flushed with anger.

"Is your girlfriend JetaGirl, by chance?" Freeman taunted.

Nigel just stared at Freeman.

"Your friend Dahlia put a contract on her. But I think the true culprit is Tony Gratzano," Freeman said.

"Is this true?" Nigel said to Dahlia.

"You better watch yourself, kid," Gratzano said. "If I want someone dead, they don't stay alive for long. And besides," he turned to the rest of the room, "why would I want Nigel's girlfriend dead?"

"Maybe it's because she killed your father? I think she was escaping captivity from him," Freeman spat as he pointed to the Sultan.

"How do you know this?" Nigel asked.

"I'm not the only one who does his homework," Freeman said.

Moments later, Gratzano grabbed Freeman by the throat then shoved a gun in his mouth, pulling back the hammer. "Choke on this, you insolent little roach."

"Stop this!" Mr. Chen demanded.

The room went silent. Moments later, Gratzano withdrew his weapon then pistol-whipped Freeman, who screamed and cowered from Nico's assault.

"The board has changed," Vedrana said.

"They have restored cell phone service," Kurtzen said.

The bot net traffic was normalizing, and the network beaconing traffic was no longer being routed through the black hole.

"Is that it?" Mr. Tage asked, trying to change the subject.

"No," Nigel said, "there are plenty of other things we need to check before we can call it. But before I help, I want your word that Jet will be safe. She's already been stabbed by that crazy cyborg."

Later that evening

Nigel verified the remaining code for the Cabal's botnet. With a heavy heart, he looked at Freeman's world map he had used to track the progress of the bot. After some fixes and adjustments, the code was more efficient than ever. A wave of anxiety overcame Nigel as hundreds of thousands of bots rampaged over the internet. He monitored network traffic websites for signs of compromise. With Nigel's code adjustments, more than one hundred and ten thousand confirmed infections were reported in a few short hours.

Mr. Tage and Chen looked like kids on Christmas day, with their eyes lighting up as news headlines came in from across the world; "Three hundred dead after the Ohio Valley Nuclear Reactor burns," "Millions exposed in massive data breach," and "Hundreds of critical surgeries interrupted as massive cyberattack crippled hospital systems" were just a few examples. Each headline was accompanied by a slew of horrific images. It seemed like the media was going out of its way to show the most gruesome and desperate-looking photos imaginable.

Every time a sensational headline appeared, cheers reverberated throughout the room. Nigel tried not to think about the mayhem he had at least partially caused. Tears filled his eyes when he dwelled on it.

"Businesses are not the only targets of this cyberattack. At least two people died after a piece of hospital equipment failed," Kurtzen said as he checked his phone.

Nigel's phone vibrated incessantly. He glanced at the hundreds of alerts he was getting. One headline was particularly disturbing: "Humble man's secret exposed by the massive data breach. Kills family of eight before taking his own life."

"Travel is also affected. Air traffic control systems are down across the eastern seaboard. Planes are being diverted. Some have dangerously low fuel levels," Freeman said.

"I just got three multi-million-dollar contracts to clean up nuclear waste in the Ohio Valley. Yesterday that business was bankrupt, and today it is saved," Mr. Chen said. "And after showing the Ohio Valley cyborg takedown video to my Chinese and Russian contacts, I got thousands of orders for cyber hunters. Do you think you can fill those orders, Dr. Ash?"

"I'll need a proper lab, but yes, I can do that," Dr. Ash replied.

"Splendid," Chen said. "I'll start construction on a new cyborg factory on the island at once."

"So money was your motive? You've killed thousands of innocents for profit? You people make me sick," Nigel said.

Blanka gave Nigel a look of regret. Even Freeman seemed appeared to be in a melancholic mood.

"Before you throw stones at others, I think you need to look at your own actions. You demonstrated you would do anything to save the people you love. So in a way, you also profited from the misery of others," the Sultan said.

"Money wasn't our prime motivation," Chen said. "It may not look like that to you, but we formed the Cabal on the foundation of the Quintessence Society—a group formed to protect humanity from itself. We had the opportunity to expose people who have committed unspeakable acts, and they are paying for it."

"At what cost? Innocents are suffering directly from these actions. Some are paying the ultimate price," Nigel said.

"And that is regrettable. But think about the countless others who will be spared," Mr. Tage said.

"It all makes sense—people will put an end to the worst offenders themselves. I don't think the world will cry over a few dead pedophiles or murderers. I can't think of a better way to reset," Freeman said.

"You all make me sick!" Nigel yelled. "I did my part. I want to go to Jet—*now*."

"I'll take you," Dahlia said. "I need my girls to come with us,"

"Wait a second. You don't all need to go with him," Gratzano said.

"I'm out of the Cabal Nico. I can no longer be part of this," Dahlia said.

"Are you serious?" Gratzano asked.

"You people applauded when hospitals got attacked by the virus you unleashed. It is causing all sorts of damage. Doctors cannot treat patients, pharmaceutical companies cannot create life-saving vaccines, public transit is offline, even shipping companies are affected. You have done it, Chen. You have stopped the world and are now king of the scrap heap. There is no honor in that," Dahlia said.

"D is right. Copycats have launched their own attacks with ransom demands," the Sultan said. "The victims pay, and the crooks take their money and laugh when they don't provide a solution. It's like you have a franchise on this crazy behavior."

"That's not the half of it, some countries have been hit so hard they are disconnecting themselves from the internet," Freeman interjected.

"Is that possible?" the Sultan asked in disbelief.

"Which countries?" Mr. Tage asked.

"Ukraine did it after several of its power plants went dark. A cyberattack against another nuclear plant has also begun. I guess the country has had enough of these attacks," Nigel said.

"Russia is also in the process of disconnecting. I've never seen anything like it," Kurtzen said.

"Countries like Russia have performed isolation tests, and

siloed their people from the rest of the world's infrastructure. I fear this is only the beginning. Service providers will charge more for their services, and the internet will never be the same. You have put the internet bridge trolls back in business. This single event has effectively wiped out net neutrality," Nigel said.

Nigel headed for the door. Ezekiel pushed Nigel, throwing him back into the conference table.

"You go nowhere without the boss's approval," Ezekiel said.

Nigel was no match for the six-foot five-inch Samoan. He put his good hand up, hoping to not antagonize the giant any more than he had to.

"You say I'm not a prisoner, but you sure as hell are not treating me like a guest. I did what you asked, and is this my payment?" Nigel said in a contemptuous tone of voice.

Nigel made another attempt for the door. This time he anticipated the Samoan's moves. Ezekiel was bigger, but Nigel was faster. Nigel opened the door and was on his way out when he heard something that terrified him: the distinctive sound of a pistol being cocked. Nigel froze, then slowly turned to find a large gun pointed at him. Nigel did not know what kind of gun it was, but it had a long barrel, and that was good enough for him to stand down.

"Are you serious, Chen? I demand your man stand down at once!" Mr. Tage said.

"Nigel, I'm afraid you are not going anywhere. I invite you to enjoy my hospitality here," Mr. Chen said.

"How long will that be, exactly?" Nigel asked.

"Until I deem you will no longer be a threat. I like you and would rather not have to shoot, but everyone in this room really does have a vested interest in staying here and watching the start of the end of the world with me. It will be fun! Now, what do you say?" Mr. Chen said.

*Maybe it's the lack of sleep or the throbbing pain in my
shoulder, but has he gone crazy?*

All eyes were on Nigel and Mr. Chen. No one spoke.
Besides the blaring of the news broadcasts, you could have
heard a feather drop in the room. Ezekiel emphasized the point
by jamming the barrel of the gun against Nigel's neck.

"Whoa, alright, I'm staying. Aren't we all friends here?"
Nigel said.

The next moments were a blur. First Blanka threw something at Ezekiel; Nigel couldn't tell what it was. Ezekiel started
making gurgling sounds. Then Vedrana unsheathed her short-
bladed katana and chopped off Ezekiel's gun hand at the wrist
before he could pull the trigger. The giant made a bloodcur-
dling shrieking sound; Nigel cringed. Eva plunged two knives
into Ezekiel's back for good measure. Dahlia had a knife
pressed to Chen's throat. He was bleeding.

"It's your move, Chen. How do you feel about Nigel
leaving now?" Dahlia said in a low, menacing tone.

"I think the lady has a point, Chen. I suggest we listen to
her," Gratzano said as he slowly put his weapon on the table.

The Sultan surrendered his weapon as well.

Chen raised his hands. "Nigel can go, but I'm keeping
Freeman."

"He should let all of us go," Nigel demanded.

Dahlia removed her blade. "I can live with that."

Freeman grabbed Vedrana by the wrist. "I thought you
liked me, and yet you protect this cur?" he snarled.

"Get your hands off me," Vedrana demanded.

Freeman ignored her and, in a bold move, pulled her close.
To Nigel's astonishment, she didn't resist. Emboldened, he
tested the waters and ran a hand through her hair.

"You are so beautiful. We should be together," Freeman
said in a low voice.

"Never!" Vedrana said as she spun around and hit Freeman's chest.

Moments later he was rolling on the floor, crying.

"I think we are done here," Dahlia said.

Eva, Vedrana, and Blanka hurried Nigel out of the room. Dahlia backed out of the room with a gun in one hand and a knife in the other.

"Vedrana," Freeman said.

She didn't even look in Freeman's direction as she helped rush Nigel out of the room.

CHAPTER 27

NIGEL WAS MOSTLY silent on the drive to visit Jet. It had been at least an hour since they'd left the Bromwick in Newport. Nigel tried turning on the radio, but all he heard was news about the hack he'd helped bring into reality. He sat in the back seat with Blanka and Vedrana. Both were resting their heads on Nigel's shoulders. Rick's phone chirped in Nigel's pocket.

Leave it to Dad to screw up a pleasant moment! Has he found Nozomi? Nigel wondered.

Nigel fished out the phone and unlocked the screen. It was a video message. Nigel played it. Rick, his father, was tied up in a chair. He was bound and gagged; a female hand removed the gag.

"Son," Rick gasped, "I hope you receive this soon. I'm being held against my will by some crazy surgeon. He has ripped Nozomi apart looking for who knows what. He's going to experiment on me soon. Send help, but don't endanger your-self. I love you, son," Rick said as tears rolled down his face.

Nigel was speechless. Dahlia pulled the car over and faced Nigel.

"What just happened?" Dahlia demanded.

"My father is being held captive by some crazy doctor," he answered. "That's all I know."

Nigel's mouth went dry. He thought he hated his father, but all the feelings he'd ever had for the man—good and bad—bubbled up to the surface.

"Do you know where he is being held?"

"He's in New York, near Sakura Park. Before he left, I used webcams to triangulate a potential entry point. He found a manhole in the area I directed him to. I think he's somewhere in the underground."

"Let me see the video," Dahlia said.

Nigel handed the phone to her. She was silent as she watched the video.

"We will help you, but you have a decision to make. From our position we are about an hour's drive from Jet, and about a four-hour drive to New York in the opposite direction. We can't fly because of the hacks, and traveling to the city will be utter chaos. We will support your decision no matter what."

Nigel considered this for a long moment. He wanted to see the woman he loved more than anything, but Rick was blood, and as much as he hated the man, he didn't want to leave Ralphie without a father. But he didn't think he could live without Jet. Nigel couldn't believe Dahlia had helped him escape, let alone prepare to go into battle on his behalf.

"Let's head to the city," Nigel said.

Blanka gave him a pained look.

"All of you have helped me so much," he continued. "I don't know how I can repay you."

"One day I will ask for your help, but today we are at your side," Dahlia said. She put a comforting hand over his. Vedrana and Eva did the same. He looked into their eyes, smiled, and took comfort in their steely resolve to help him.

CHAPTER 28

Two Months Later

Josephine Smith awoke in a sparsely furnished bedroom with a view of the mountains. Fresh snow fell. It was so quiet.

Where am I? This is not Milford, or anything like it!

An IV was feeding medicine into her left arm. Numbness and pain were all she had known since waking. Everything was a blur—getting stabbed, waking in an animal hospital while an unskilled surgeon closed her wounds.

I can see all of their deaths! The look on that doctor's face will haunt me for the rest of my life. I tried to stop her from killing them but couldn't. Is this a dream?

An older man with white curly hair and round glasses entered the room.

"You're awake—good. You will need your strength for the trials to come," the old man said in a thick European accent.

"Wait, where am I? And who are you?"

"I'm Dr. Gruber, and you're my patient."

The old man looked sad and tired. It was like he carried the weight of the world on his shoulders.

"What do you mean, doctor? What trials?" Jet said in a confused tone.

Dr. Gruber looked at Jet and said nothing for a long moment.

"The world as you knew it has changed," he said. "It's been twenty-three days since you were brought to my estate. You are safe here. My men have secured the perimeter, and we have enough food for at least a year—more if we relocate to the bunker below the house. I think we have food that will sustain five people for ten years, perhaps more if we ration."

"What are you talking about?"

"She doesn't know, dear," an older woman said as she entered. "You get so wrapped up in the moment that you can't see what is in front of you."

The old woman had long white hair pulled back and tied up. She looked like an old woman from a fairy-tale.

"Who are you people?" Jet demanded.

"Shhh, you will wake the little one," the old woman admonished.

Jet followed the older woman's gaze. April was resting on a bed across the room.

"Hans didn't know how to operate on the machine girl, so we left her. I'm Gretta, and this is my husband, Hans. He saved your life."

"How did I get here?"

"An ally of Nigel Watson," Gretta said.

"Nigel? Where is he? Here?"

"No, dear, he is with the Black Heart. They went into the city to rescue his father—"

"That's when it happened," Dr. Gruber said.

"What happened?" Jet asked. She gave the older couple an impatient glance.

"It started with a massive cyberattack that crippled most of world's critical infrastructure," Dr. Gruber began. "As soon as new computers were brought online, they would get infected.

According to the news channels, the best defenders and hackers couldn't stop the multiple waves of attacks. An expert said something about an unprecedented amount of zero-days were unleashed on the world, which infected hospital equipment, crashed financial systems, and virtually stopped all commerce."

"How did this happen?"

"First, a secret government building was attacked. Commandos and hackers invaded and infected the facility. Every machine burned. The virus was launched there. Days later, a nuclear facility in the Ohio Valley melted down to its core. By the time cleanup crews were dispatched, it was too late. An area of at least thirty miles will be uninhabitable for hundreds of years. Teams are still trying to clean up the mess."

"Didn't anyone try to stop this madness?"

"Teams of people are still trying, but a war broke out on American soil, if you can believe it. Large cities have turned into battlegrounds. The national guard has been deployed, and the riots have slowed. It got scary for a long time. You're lucky you missed most of that."

Jet tried sitting upright; she ached everywhere, but her lower back hurt the most. It was like someone had taken a club to her back and pounded.

"I . . . can't feel my legs," Jet said.

The older woman gave her a pained look and placed a hand on her shoulder.

"I'm sorry—I did the best I could," Dr. Gruber said as he rubbed his eyes.

Jet flung the covers off of her. She was thrashing about, trying to make her legs obey her commands. Her eyes filled with tears.

"Tell me this is temporary?" she cried.

"I don't have the equipment to confirm, but I believe you have permanent spinal damage resulting from a knife wound," Dr. Gruber explained sadly. The blade was serrated, which causes additional tissue damage. I wish I could take you to the hospital, but it is not safe."

"Why isn't it safe? What are you not telling me?"

"I used to work at the local hospital—I have friends there. When my many calls for an ambulance failed, I called one of them. The computer virus infected all the local hospital's computers. Machines like the MRI scanners—which are needed to properly diagnose your condition—work, but the computers required to operate them have been infected."

The light in the room went out, and her IV machine started beeping.

"That dammed generator," Doctor Gruber said as he walked toward the door.

"Don't go out there. Have one of the men check the gasoline levels," Gretta said.

Hans waved a hand over his head as he walked out of the room.

"I'm good with computers. I bet I could fix that hospital's computer," Jet said.

"I bet you could, dear, but you are in no condition to do that."

"Can you contact Nigel for me?"

"Cell phone communications have been spotty these past few days. The emergency instructions on the radio said we shouldn't use it. The phone company has set up portable cell towers for families to reach loved ones. We can only use them once a day, but now is not the time."

"Jet?" April asked in a sleepy voice.

"April, come here!" Jet yelled.

The young cyborg ran past the old woman and gave Jet a hug.

"What have you been doing since I've been resting here?" Jet said.

"I've been so tired since I woke up. I don't remember much," April said.

Suddenly, gunshots rang throughout the estate.

"Nooo! They are trying again," Gretta said.

"Trying what?" Jet asked with panic.

"Get down, and don't move."

April froze. "No—she's coming, Jet, I'm scared."

"There's no reason to be—"

Before Jet could finish her sentence, a robot crouched its head as it ducked under the archway leading into the bedroom. The bedroom had low ceilings, and the robot barely fit. Light from the fading light of the late afternoon reflected off its shiny metal frame.

"Hello, Jet," the robot said.

The old woman was crouched on the floor with her hands over her head. Jet noticed April did the same.

"Gretta, how many times have I told you? I mean you no harm. Especially since you have looked after my friends these past weeks," the robot said.

This is too creepy—why does the robot think it knows me? But there's something about this robot that is familiar.

"Who are you—err, who programmed you?" Jet said.

I feel dumb questioning a robot.

Jet couldn't tell for sure, since it didn't have a human face, but the robot seemed to be gloating.

"I'm hurt you don't know who I am. Do you really not know me after all we have been through?"

Jet shook her head.

"I'm the one who put you in that bed. I'm Nozomi, and all

bots will obey me. At least until I get my body back. Oh, I so miss my body, and all its . . . desires."

Holy shit, what really happened? What don't I know?

"Why are you in this metal body?" Jet asked.

"It's me, or rather a backup of my consciousness. Dr. Ash restored me into this construct. Apparently she was uploading my experiences to her mainframe without me knowing anything about it. So in a way, there are two of me out there."

"This is crazy, I did not know this was possible. Why did you come back here?"

"I don't know, but I needed to find Delta-51."

April grabbed Jet's hand. "Don't let her hurt me again, Gretta," April cried.

"What did you do to her?" Jet demanded.

"Dr. Ash gave this construct new abilities. In short, I was able to upload the AI contained within the Delta-51 construct and merge its programming with mine. Now we are one," the robot said.

Jet was stunned. She didn't say anything for a long moment.

"I'm sure you're wondering what has happened to Delta and her sister," robot Nozomi said.

"You were absorbed? Is April with you now?"

"No, her bond to you was too strong—and besides, I don't need to merge with any immature code. Now that I've merged with the most powerful AI in history, I can move on. I still would like to find my human body, but that is not the priority."

"What's the priority?"

"I need to take control while there's still time."

"Control of what?"

"For someone so smart, you seem to ask a lot of dumb questions. The backbone of the internet is still mostly intact. I can control what remains once I get to a central hub, but I had to merge with Delta first. Don't you see? I have unleashed hell on all the bad actors. These people are being hunted in the streets. I've distracted the meddlers and others that intended to stop me, but I've done all I can from here. I need to get to central processing, or the windowless building, where everything was set into motion."

CHAPTER 29

MARCH EQUINOX

Rick Watson awoke alone in a darkened room. A dripping sound echoed throughout the chamber. To his surprise, he was not restrained in any way. A wave of nausea overcame him as he tried sitting up. His heart pounded; he was drained like he'd just finished running a marathon. He took a few deep breaths to try to calm himself, but it was no use.

Did the doctor experiment on me? Has my appearance changed?

Rick tried to stand. He held on to the bed to steady himself. He glanced around the room; it was a circular chamber about thirty feet across. A bloodstained surgical chair was in the center of the room. A dirty and cracked mirror was on the wall across the room. He looked at his hands, and in addition to the grime, he glimpsed something else: a slight reflection, like a ring catching the light. When he examined his hands more closely, he noticed metal rods with dried blood through open skin patches. As he moved each finger, he thought he heard the faint sound of a servomotor. He touched his face; it was different.

I've got to see what I've become.

Rick stumbled and nearly fell over, but with much effort he

made it over to the mirror. He didn't look much different at first. A metal plate reflected light near the hairline. The light in the chamber was poor, so it was difficult to see clearly. He pulled back his hair and gasped at what he saw. Most of the scalp on the left side of his face was missing, replaced by rubbery-looking skin. The rush of blood filled the fleshy side of his face, and he couldn't feel anything on his left side. It was like someone had ripped half his face off and replaced it with metal skin.

I'm going to kill that doctor, not only for what he's done to me, but for Nozomi. I have failed you, my love.

His skin seared like it was on fire; he was burning up all over and needed relief. He took off his shirt and realized the true extent of the damage. More than half of his torso had been replaced with the metal skin. In fact, his entire left side had been replaced. Repulsed, he punched the mirror; without warning, a flame shot from his fist and crawled up the wall, looking for something to singe.

What the . . .

He looked at both of his hands. One minute they looked normal, and the next they were aflame.

Why doesn't this hurt?

"Remarkable, isn't it?" a man's voice said.

Rick turned to see Dr. Sylvester. "What's wrong with me?"

"Nothing. I've enhanced you. You will no longer feel pain, but you can inflict it on others. In fact, I will require you to do so very soon."

"I'm not hurting anyone!"

"What about the bad people who ruin the lives of innocents? Don't they deserve to be punished?"

"I won't let you."

Rick grabbed a piece of broken glass and flung it at the doctor. It seemed to change shape and catch on fire as it sailed toward its intended target. Dr. Sylvester tapped something on his arm as the glass projectile bounced off an invisible shield.

"Good," the doctor said with a smile, "let's get that aggression out of your system."

Rick flung both of his arms toward Sylvester.

Let's see if I can fry his ass.

Two white beams with flames jutting out of them shot toward the doctor. He pressed another button on his wrist and the beams expanded, then shot into the tiled chamber; moments later, flaming fragments of the ceiling rained down. They burned Rick's skin as they landed. Dr. Sylvester pressed another button on his wristband, and then made a flinging motion to Rick. He was immediately protected against the flaming tiles that dropped from the ceiling.

"You have only begun to explore the gifts I've given you," Sylvester told him. "Together we will do great things. When we have enough of us we shall rule this city. You have just the right blend of moral gray I was looking for. You don't care about people—not *really*. That's what I found out during our weeks of testing."

"Weeks? How long have I been here?"

"Six months or so, but I wasn't counting on such a chaotic mess the city has become since you arrived."

"Where is Nozomi?"

"She's been undergoing some enhancements. Don't worry, you will be with her soon. I'm looking forward to a long-lasting relationship that will benefit all humankind. The powers I've given you are just the beginning."

Rick looked down at his flaming hands. For many years he had fantasized of having absolute power over people; now his only wish was to see his family again. Rick buried his face in his burning hands. To his surprise, the flames didn't affect his skin.

He wept for all the people he had hurt, and he wished he could take it all back and set things right.

"What's the matter, lover?" a voice cooed.

Rick looked up, his face wet with sorrow.

"Nozomi?" he asked.

"No, lover, she is dead. I'm the catalyst of pain."

CONTINUE THE ADVENTURE

I hope you enjoyed reading **Reckoning of Delta Prime.** I invite you to continue Nigel's adventure with **Crisis at Worlds End**. The exciting sequel to Reckoning of Delta Prime.

I invite you to join my reader group to learn more about more books in the Cyber Teen Project. To sign up visit: https://reckoningofdeltaprime.com

A FAVOR

Thank you for reading my book.

Reviews are very important for an author. When I get more reviews on my books, it allows them to stay more visible. If you want to help me put out books more quickly, then please review this one.

Thank you.

D. B. Goodin

ACKNOWLEDGMENTS

Special thanks to my launch team and beta readers: The early feedback helped considerably. This book is better for it.

Cover design by Andrew Dobell (Creative Edge)
Developmental Editing by Matt Machin
Copy Editing by Hayley Evans
Proofreading by Beth Doward

D. B. Goodin has had a passion for writing since grade school. After publishing several nonfiction books, Mr. Goodin ventured into the craft of fiction to teach Cybersecurity concepts in a less-intimidating fashion. Mr. Goodin works as a Principal Cybersecurity Analyst for a major software company based in Silicon Valley and holds a Master's in Digital Forensic Science from Champlain College.

Blast Off
Cassidy's Fleet (Fall 2021)

www.ingramcontent.com/pod-product-compliance
Lightning Source LLC
Chambersburg PA
CBHW051606100726
47898CB00001B/243